STAGECOACH WOMAN

Dorothy Dowdell

FAWCETT GOLD MEDAL • NEW YORK

A Fawcett Gold Medal Book
Published by Ballantine Books
Copyright © 1991 by Dorothy Dowdell

Library of Congress Catalog Card Number: 91-91824

ISBN 0-449-14658-8

Manufactured in the United States of America

First Edition: June 1991

To Jill, James, and Stephanie Walsh

With gratitude for my Sacramento writing friends, especially Ethel Bangert, Irene Donelson, Virginia McCall, and Jean Giovannoni.

Chapter 1

Her father was trying to get up his courage to tell her something, Jessie realized with a feeling of dread. He always acted this way when he was about to reveal some information that he knew she wouldn't like.

He laughed too easily and kept twisting in his chair to gaze at the other diners in the luxurious restaurant. Anything to avoid looking her straight in the eye.

What was it this time? Had he gambled away his only possession—his small stagecoach line? His beautiful red Concord coaches with his teams of horses that he drove between St. Louis, Missouri, where they lived, and Springfield, Illinois? They were his pride and joy, besides being a means of earning a modest living. But nothing was sacred to Carl Henderson's obsessive gambling.

With mixed emotions, she looked at him across the table, which was set with starched linen and polished silver. He twirled his crystal wineglass, reflecting the soft candlelight. Since her mother had died three months before, she cherished her relationship with her father even more. In fact, she was completely devoted to him. But sometimes he was so impulsive—acting without thinking things through—he nearly drove her out of her mind.

He ran his fingers through his graying brown hair and laughed nervously. "I'm expecting a guest, Jessie. Someone I'm anxious for you to meet."

"You are?" So something *was* in the wind, just as

she'd suspected. That explained why they had come to one of the finest restaurants in St. Louis for dinner—why he had asked her to wear her pink velvet dinner dress with its big skirt that flared around her chair now. "Who is this person?"

"A young man named Antonio Maguire. He's from California, but his family all live in Chicago. He and his cousin have a stagecoach line out of Sacramento. I met him at the livery stable."

A wave of annoyance swept over her. "Papa, you're not trying your hand at matchmaking again, are you? I told you before—"

"No, no. Nothing like that. I swear it. I know Henry Baker's courting you, and I wouldn't interfere for the world. He'd make a fine husband for you. He can support you with his hardware store a lot better than I ever have."

Jessie started to tell her father that she had no intentions of marrying stodgy Henry Baker, in spite of his prosperous hardware store, when Carl looked across the room and said, "Here's Antonio Maguire now." He pushed his chair back, rose, and put out his hand.

The man approaching was even taller than her father, with broader shoulders. Not only his name revealed his Italian-Irish heritage, his black curly hair and startling blue eyes did so as well. She guessed his age to be about twenty-four or so.

"My daughter Jessie. Antonio Maguire," Carl Henderson said, introducing them.

"How do you do, Mr. Maguire."

When he held out his hand, she shook it—and felt the callouses caused by handling the reins of a team of horses. Somehow they made her too intimately aware of him. There was something so masculine and dynamic about the man, it took her breath away.

"Everyone calls me Tonio." While he held on to her hand, he looked her over with such unabashed appreciation, her cheeks flushed. "I'm mighty pleased to meet you, Miss Henderson." Finally he released her hand, grinned, and sat down in a chair next to her. He glanced at her again with a mischievous glint in his eyes and repeated, "Mighty pleased."

Feeling completely flustered, she groped for something to say. She'd never met a man like him before, one with such an impact. "Papa says you're from California."

"That's right. That's the place to be when you're in the stagecoach business."

A waiter came to their table with menus, and she gratefully opened hers, pretending to be completely absorbed. With her father acting as if he were up to something—*and* this astonishing stranger sitting close to her—she needed to compose herself.

After they gave their orders, her father said to the waiter, "Bring us a bottle of your best champagne."

When it came and their glasses were filled, he proposed a toast. "Here's to us—and the beginning of a rewarding association."

They touched glasses. As she sipped her champagne, she stared at her father. What did he mean by "rewarding association"? Why was he making such a fuss over this Tonio Maguire? He really couldn't afford this expensive dinner and champagne. She kept the books for his stagecoach line and knew only too well how business was falling off. So why this splurge? Something was in the air, and every instinct told her it was not to her liking.

While they ate their dinner, the conversation was kept on neutral subjects such as the weather and the newly inaugurated pony express, which carried mail on horseback from Sacramento to St. Louis. But all the time, Jessie felt her apprehension growing.

After they had eaten their dessert and were drinking another cup of coffee, Carl said, "Tonio, explain to my daughter just what you have in mind."

"All right." As Tonio turned to her, she was aware again of his complete self-confidence. There was no hesitancy or self-doubt about him. He seemed to know exactly who he was and what he stood for.

"As you know, the tremendous growth of the railroads

here in the Midwest has taken a terrible toll on the stage lines. They're rapidly becoming obsolete."

"Oh, I wouldn't say that," Jessie protested.

"I'm sorry, Miss Henderson, but I'm afraid it's true. Anyone wanting to stay in the coaching business should move to California. That's where the opportunities are. I've suggested to your father that he return to California with me and go into business with my cousin and myself."

Openmouthed, Jessie stared at him. She was too astonished to think. Finally she burst out, "Go to California? That's absurd!"

Tonio leaned toward her. "Why? What's wrong with going to California, may I ask?"

Her eyes snapped in annoyance as she answered, "My father's an established businessman right here in St. Louis, where he was born and raised. Why should he leave a charming, civilized city like this to go out to the Wild West?"

"But, Jessie," Carl interrupted, "I agree that the stagecoach business is doomed here. You've been keeping my books, so you know how slow things are. It's just a matter of time before the railroads'll get all the passengers."

"Papa, when that time comes, why can't you trade one of your coaches for a hack and drive passengers around the city? Or take visitors sight-seeing?"

Her father gaped at her in astonishment. "Me, a respected coachman with my own stage line, be a cabby? That's unthinkable. I'm surprised that you'd suggest such a thing."

"Then do something else. You don't have to leave St. Louis and go so far away."

Tonio spoke up, his expression full of amusement. "I take it you're not very venturesome, Miss Henderson."

Venturesome, indeed. The nerve of this brash man! Anger flared in her. But she fought for control and answered, "Let's just say that I know my father should stay here."

If Papa left for California, he'd lose everything at a

gambling table on the way, she told herself. It was her mother's influence, and now hers, that kept some control over his obsession with cards.

Besides, how could she live without him? He was all the family she had—except for an old maid aunt in Kansas City whom she couldn't stand! In spite of his faults, she loved him. How could she bear saying good-bye to him, perhaps never to see him again? Just thinking about it made a leaden ball in her stomach.

Tonio finished his coffee. "I can understand how you'd miss him. I've been mighty homesick for my family in Chicago. Fortunately I have a cousin in Sacramento, which helps."

Why doesn't this man mind his own business? Jessie asked herself. She glared at him. This was a discussion between herself and Papa—and this Tonio Maguire didn't need to butt in! It was too bad that he'd come to St. Louis in the first place and put these crazy ideas in her father's head.

"Papa, I'm sure you've been fascinated by Mr. Maguire's talk about California, *and* his experiences. Right now you're all excited and may want to go, but once you think it over, you'll realize this is where you should stay."

Her father shook his head. "I've longed to go to California ever since they discovered gold out there twelve years ago. I ached to be part of the gold rush. When I was driving my stagecoach, I'd dream about picking up nuggets or panning for gold on the riverbanks." He closed his eyes and his voice trembled. "God, how I wanted to be part of it all."

Jessie stared at her father. "Papa, I had no idea. . . ." It struck her how little we know about the people closest to us—about the dreams and aspirations they have inside of them. "It's too bad you weren't able to go."

"It was out of the question, Jess. You were just a little eight-year-old tyke, and your mother wasn't well even then. Her heart had already started acting up. I couldn't go off and leave you."

"But what about now? How can you go off and leave

me now, as if I didn't matter?'' A stab of hurt thrust through her.

"Of course you matter. But aren't you fixing to marry Henry? He's been courting you long enough. Besides, you're twenty years old. High time you got a husband and started a family.''

Tonio leaned forward, his eyes full of devilment. "There's plenty of time for a wedding. No problem at all.''

Jessie glared at him. "Really, Mr. Maguire—''

"I'm leaving on the train for Chicago tomorrow morning—to visit my family and take care of some business,'' he went on. "It'll be about a month before I get back. This is the first of May; I thought Carl and I could start out for California around the first of June. He can wind up his affairs . . . and get you married off.''

Her temper flared. "This is no concern of yours, Mr. Maguire! Not that it's any of your business, but I have no intention of getting married. And I'm sure my father will come to his senses by the time you get back from Chicago.''

Carl put his hand on her arm. "Just calm down, gal. No use flying off the handle. But you might as well know that I've made up my mind. I am going to California.''

"Oh, Papa, how can you?'' She blinked back tears.

"If you're not going to get married right now, we'll make some other arrangements for you. You can always go and stay with your Aunt Bertha in Kansas City and help her run her boardinghouse,'' her father said.

"That sounds like a good idea to me,'' Tonio put in.

Jessie glared at him again and started to say something—when she realized he was trying to get her goat. What an impossible, mischievous buttinsky this Tonio Maguire was! How could Papa possibly consider going into business with him?

Apparently Carl felt it was time to change the subject. "Now tell me about California, Tonio.''

"From what I hear, it's settled down a lot from the first madness of the gold rush. But San Francisco is still a busy port, with the bay filled with sailing ships. There's lots of permanent buildings made of wood now. Some even of stone and brick. In '48 and '49 it was just a tent city sprawled over the sand dunes. Now some of the streets are paved with cobblestones. Of course, a lot of 'em are still dirt. In the winter they're just mud holes.''

''But Papa said you lived in Sacramento.''

''That's right,'' Tonio went on. ''Sacramento is up-river, in the big central valley. About eighty miles north-east of San Francisco. It's located right where two rivers come together—the Sacramento and the American. They've overflowed their banks for centuries, and I tell you that valley soil is about the richest in the country. It's a thriving place. The state capital. Must have a population of about twenty-five thousand now.''

Carl shook his head. ''It sounds wonderful.''

''Oh, it is. Excellent climate. Beautiful scenery. Unlimited opportunities to make a fortune. You'll be crazy about it, Carl.''

Her father turned to her. ''Surely you can understand why I want to go.'' He put his hand on her arm. ''Even so, it about breaks my heart to leave you, Jess. Now that your mother's gone, you're all I have left.''

As she looked at him, a lump gathered in her throat. Her voice was husky as she pleaded, ''If you must go, Papa, take me with you.''

''Unfortunately, it's out of the question,'' Tonio put in.

''Why?'' Jessie asked.

''Because you're a woman.''

Anger flared in Jessie. ''Don't be ridiculous, Mr. Maguire. Women have been crossing the plains in wagon trains for the last fifteen years.''

''That's right. In wagon trains—where they have some protection. But we'll be alone most of the time, traveling light and fast. It'd be too dangerous for a female.''

''If you were a son, I'd be mighty glad to have you along,'' her father added.

''But I'm not your son. I'm your daughter, and I don't want to be left here by myself, Papa.''

"I'm sorry, Jess. We'll have to work something out for you."

Tonio's blue eyes sparkled with amusement. "It seems to me you only have two choices—Henry or Aunt Bertha."

Jessie whirled around to face him. "I'll thank you to keep out of this, Mr. Maguire! It's none of your business."

"I beg to differ, Miss Henderson. It's very much my concern. If you were along, it would be up to me to protect you." He pretended to be aiming a rifle.

Glaring at him, she put her hands on her hips. "Protect me from what?"

Trying to suppress a smile, Tonio looked her up and down. "I can think of all kinds of things. A buffalo on a rampage. An Indian chief looking for a new squaw. A smitten desperado along the Emigrant Trail." He held his hand to his brow. "My very life could be at stake. So I'm making a rule—no ladies allowed."

Carl motioned for a waiter and asked for his check. He turned to Tonio. "I know you have an early train to catch in the morning, so we'd better leave."

Outside they found a hack and took Tonio to his hotel. After he had thanked Carl, he turned to Jessie. "Do send my congratulations to Henry. Some men have all the luck." He took her hand and kissed it before he climbed out of the cab.

As they rode away, Jessie sputtered, "He's impossible!"

"He's full of the devil, I'll admit that," her father answered, with a chuckle. "And I imagine he's quite a Don Juan with the ladies."

"How can you possibly consider going to California with him—let alone into business?"

"Jess, underneath that fun-loving exterior he's a capable businessman."

"How do you know that?"

"Because he offered me cash for one of my Concord coaches and six of my horses. That's a pretty piece of change, I can tell you."

Jessie hoped that her father didn't have the money yet. If so, it would be gambled away long before the month was up.

"Tonio's business is expanding," Carl went on. "I've lived long enough to size up men, and I just know that he is a man of honor and courage."

"For your sake, I hope so."

Her father took her hand in his. "I meant it when I said I'd take you with me if you were a man. It's going to be mighty hard to leave you, my dear."

Unable to sleep, Jessie lay in bed thinking about her father going off to California. How could he manage without her to look out for him? He wouldn't eat right. He'd gamble too much. He'd grieve over her mother. Although Rose Henderson'd had poor health for some time, her actual death from heart failure was sudden, a terrible shock to them both.

Jessie pounded her pillow in exasperation. If she were only a man, she could go with him. Suddenly she sat up in bed. Why not go as a man? Why not, indeed? Her heart pounding with excitement, she climbed out of bed and lit the gas lamp by the full-length framed mirror.

After she pulled her cotton nightgown tight, she stared at her figure. For the first time, she was grateful that she'd inherited her father's tall, slender, wide-shouldered frame instead of her mother's shorter, more curvaceous one.

Her breasts? Although they were small, they did stick out against her nightgown.

"I'll fix that!" she muttered aloud. She went to her closet, got out an old sheet, and tore a long strip from it. She pulled the nightgown over her head, wound the cloth around her breasts, and pinned it with two safety pins from her lace pincushion.

Turning this way and that, she took inventory of her naked body. Could she masquerade as a man? Shoulders would do all right. Bosoms flattened by the strip would get by. Not too much difference between her waist and hips.

Yes, she guessed she could pull it off. Of course, when she was dressed in men's clothes she'd be more convincing, she told herself. She rubbed her hand on her cheek. No facial hair. But what if she pretended to be a boy—about fifteen or sixteen? That would work. She could even keep her own name, just spell it differently. Jesse instead of Jessie. No one would need to know that it was really Jessica.

But her hair . . . Now it hung in heavy braids for the night, one on each side of her head. Wistfully she lifted one of the braids and let it fall. It would have to be cut off. It hurt just to think about it. Her thick hair, the color of burnished mahogany, was her only vanity.

Usually she wore it parted in the middle and let it fall into its natural waves as she brought it to a bun at the back of her head. Everyone complimented her on her lovely hair. It, along with her huge dark brown eyes, were her only claim to beauty. Without them she'd be quite plain, she told herself. Too tall, too slender, with long hands and feet, she hardly fit the mold of the dainty, shapely belle so in vogue in 1860.

The next morning, when her father kissed her good-bye before he left on his stage route to Springfield, Illinois, he said, "While I'm gone, you'd better start packing. Be thinking about what pieces of furniture you want to keep, and we'll have to put them in storage. You'd better notify the Smithsons that we're vacating this flat the first of June. According to our lease, we have to give them a month's notice."

"Yes, Papa. I'll start sorting through things."

"We have a lot of stuff around here that we don't need. For example, that extra wardrobe in my bedroom is full of old clothes I don't wear anymore. You might as well bundle them up and give them to the church for the missionaries."

Jessie nodded, but she told herself that she might have another use for them. In fact, as soon as he left, she ran to the wardrobe and yanked a pair of brown wool pants off a coat hanger. She was out of her gingham housedress and petticoat in no time. She stepped into the trousers and pulled them on.

They were big in the waist and too long, but she could fix them. She picked out more pants and shirts she could wear. She even found a heavy lumberman's jacket and a coat sweater that were still wearable. For the next few days, she washed, ironed, and altered her father's old clothes.

While she worked, she kept asking herself, What will Papa say when I tell him I'm going? Even more worrisome was that horrible Tonio Maguire. What would he say? What would he do? Every instinct told her that a rocky time lay ahead.

When her father returned from his stagecoach run, she hid the clothes under her bed. She wasn't ready to tell him her plans quite yet.

One morning, after he'd left again, she took the streetcar downtown and bought a wide-brimmed man's hat, a sturdy pair of boots, and some leather gloves. As she walked down the street, she saw a sign in a second-story shop that read WIGS AND HAIRPIECES MADE.

With a sinking heart, she climbed up the stairs to the shop. She wouldn't mind wearing men's clothes, but to have her hair cut off was awful. Would she even feel like a woman with it gone?

A bell jingled as she entered the shop. A glass counter filled with stands holding wigs divided the customer area from the workroom. She could see two women working on hairpieces in the back.

An older woman rose, walked to the counter, and asked, "May I help you?"

Jessie's face flamed with embarrassment. As she took off her hat, she tried to find the words to explain what she wanted. "My father is planning to go to California by stagecoach, and I want to go with him. But as his son instead of his daughter. It will be safer that way."

The woman nodded. "Yes, it would be. You couldn't pay me to go to that wild country."

"He's all the family I've got, and I don't want to be

left here all alone.'' Her voice shook. ''I'll have to look
like a boy so I can go with him.''

''I suppose so. I take it you want to have your hair cut
off. It's a shame, because you have beautiful hair. So
thick and wavy.''

Jessie swallowed the lump in her throat. ''I hate to
have it cut. But once we get settled in California, I can
let it grow out again. Could you take the hair you cut off
and make a hairpiece that I can pin on when I want to
dress like a woman?''

''I think so, miss. Come into the dressing room and
take your hair down and we'll see what we can do.''

After Jessie unpinned her hair and let it fall down to
her waist, she almost changed her mind. How could she
bear to have it sheared off and look like a man? It seemed
to her that she would lose her very identity, her sense of
self.

The saleslady pulled a strand up from the side of her
face. ''It should be cut off about this length, so you can
pin it up on top of your head and wear the hairpiece over
it when you want to dress like a woman. We'll have to
make the hairpiece into a long French knot to cover all
the ends.''

Jessie nodded. ''Go ahead and cut it before I get cold
feet.'' She closed her eyes so she couldn't watch.

But she could hear. *Snip*. *Snip*. *Snip*. Her heart sank
lower and lower with each sound of the shears. She
cringed inside. The snipping went on and on. Finally she
heard, ''That about does it, miss.''

As she opened her eyes and stared into the mirror, she
felt she as if she was looking at a stranger. She didn't
look familiar at all.

The saleslady gathered up the long strands of shorn
hair. ''It will take us about an hour to make the hairpiece. In the meantime, you can try combing your hair
like a man's. It might need more cutting.''

Jessie tried combing her shoulder-length hair various
ways while she fought back tears. Straight back over her
ears looked the most masculine. But trying to pass her-

self off as a man was going to be harder than she thought. . . .

As she greeted her father that evening, she wondered if he would notice her different hairstyle. But he paid little attention to her appearance, quizzing her about her progress with the packing while they ate dinner.

"Have you arranged for storage for our furniture?"

"Yes, Papa."

"Have you written to your Aunt Bertha?"

"Yes." She had written her aunt, but had not mentioned anything about coming to live with her.

Later, when he went into in the living room with the evening paper, Jessie cleared the dining room table. While she washed the dishes, she decided that this was the time to tell him that she was going to California with him. What would he say? Would he get angry and refuse her?

When her chores were finished, she went into her bedroom and bound her breasts, then dressed in her father's old clothes. She pulled on her new boots. Finally she took the hairpiece off her head, combed her short hair back over her ears, and put on her man's wide-brimmed felt hat.

When she stood in front of the mirror, the reflection of a fifteen-year-old boy stared back at her. A slender youth about ready to grow taller and put on weight to become a man. The generous mouth, determined chin, and high cheekbones could easily be those of a boy. Only her large brown eyes framed by long lashes looked at all feminine. But there were men with eyes like hers, she reasoned.

Her father was stretched out in his comfortable chair with his back to her as she stepped into the living room. She stood behind him and put her arms around his shoulders.

"Papa, please take me to California with you. It'll about break my heart to have you go without me."

He kept his eyes on his newspaper. "You know I'd take you in a minute if you were a boy." His voice sounded low and sad.

She kissed him on the top of the head and murmured, "Do you mean that, Papa?"

When he murmured, "Yes," she walked around in front of him, took off her hat with a flourish, and bowed low.

"Father, behold your son!" She stood with her feet far apart and her hands on her hips. "I'm fifteen years old going on sixteen, and my name is Jesse. J-E-S-S-E."

Carl Henderson gaped at her in astonishment. His mouth fell open. His eyes widened. The color drained from his face. "Daughter, what have you done to yourself?"

"Turned into a boy so I can go with you." She knelt beside him.

He ran his hand over her head. "But your hair? It was long a few minutes ago. Did you just cut it?"

"I had it cut earlier and had a hairpiece made. I'll get it and show you."

Jessie scrambled to her feet and dashed into her room. When she returned with the hairpiece, she placed it on top of her head. "When I want to dress like a woman, I put this on." She took the hairpiece off, placed it on a table, and knelt beside him again. "You'll have to admit that I look like a boy, don't I? A lot like you, as a matter of fact."

"I guess you do."

"Then take me with you, Papa. Please, I beg you to." Tears glistened in her eyes. "I don't want to be left behind."

"But what about Henry Baker?"

"He proposed, but I turned him down. I don't care for him at all. I want to be with you. You'll take me, won't you, Papa?" A tear trickled down her cheek. Impatiently she brushed it away.

"No, I won't. It's too hard a trip for you, and much too dangerous. Besides, Tonio wouldn't stand for it." He put his hand over hers. "The best I can do is take you as far as Kansas City and leave you with Bertha."

Jessie bit her tongue to keep quiet. Long ago her mother had warned, "Don't argue with your father. He can be very stubborn, and once he makes up his mind it's hard to get him to change it. So if you bring up something he objects to, just let him think it over awhile. Later, when he's in a good mood, talk about it again." Her gentle, tactful mother knew how to handle him.

So Jessie kissed him and said, "All right, Papa." But she made up her mind she was going to California.

Chapter 2

The sunlight glistened off the bright red Concord coach that her father had parked in the backyard of the building where they lived. It was large enough to hold twelve passengers. Jessie looked up from the cooking utensils piled around her and took a moment to admire it.

Gold scrollwork decorated the curved panels resting on the thick leather thoroughbraces that stretched from the front axle to the back. More gold swirls and curlicues framed a painting of the Mississippi River on the door. Just under the luggage rack on the top were the words HENDERSON STAGE CO. Shiny black leather containers called boots hung from below the driver's seat and also down the back of the vehicle. Vivid yellow wheels and running gear completed the picture.

It's a gloriously beautiful stagecoach, Jessie told herself. No wonder Papa is so proud of it.

She had been preparing the coach for the journey for the past week. First she and her father had lined the leather interior with canvas to protect it. She had made her bed on the rear seat. The space between it and the middle seat was to be her dressing area. Her father had shown her how to lower the leather curtains on each side to give herself privacy. They stored his small tent and folding cot on the middle seat.

"I don't know what Tonio is going to think about your

16

coming along to Kansas City," her father had said more than once.

"It's none of his business. I don't have to get his permission," she'd retort. But she wondered just what he *would* do. He could arrive any day now. Drat him, anyway!

Now she concentrated on her packing. Carefully she checked off her list as she placed the cooking utensils in the grub box between the front and middle seats: Dutch oven, camp kettle, frying pan, coffeepot, rolling pin, bread pan, tin plates, tin cups, knives, forks.

As she worked, she thought about all of her activities since her father had given permission for her to go partway. There had been shopping for the journey, loading the coach, and packing articles that were going into storage, as the movers would be coming in a few days. Someday, when they were settled in California, they would have their belongings shipped out to them by boat.

Saying good-bye to her friends had been the hardest. The girls in her stitchery club had given her a farewell luncheon. Her young ladies' church group had honored her at a tea party. A neighbor had had her and her father for dinner. It would be a wrench to leave all of these familiar people, perhaps never to see them again.

Just as Jessie placed some tin spoons in one corner of the box, she heard a noise behind her.

"Hi!"

As she backed out of the stagecoach, her hairpiece caught on a coat hook, was yanked off her head, and fell on the seat. Hairpins flew in all directions. Her short hair fell down over her face.

She straightened up, gazed through the wavy strands at Tonio Maguire, and exclaimed, "You!"

Flushing with embarrassment, she reached behind her for her French knot, then tried to pin her hair back in place. "Good morning. You startled me."

He was even bigger than she remembered him. His eyes, now filled with amusement, were even bluer, the impact of his magnetic personality even stronger. How awful to have him show up just now and see her like this!

"You seem to be falling apart." He grinned and leaned over to pick up some more of the hairpins. "What did you do to your hair?"

"If you must know, I had it cut." Her face scarlet, she snatched the hairpins out of his hand and jabbed them into the hairpiece. Drat this Tonio, anyway.

"You're all mixed up. Here, I'll help you." Without waiting for her consent, Tonio unpinned the French knot and handed it to her. "Hold this." He draped the shorter strands back, pinned them, and placed the hairpiece the way it should be. "Why did you cut your hair? It was great the way it was."

"I don't wish to discuss it, Mr. Maguire."

How adorable she is, Tonio thought to himself, with her face flushed, her chin in the air, and her eyes sparking with annoyance.

Out of politeness, she forced herself to say, "I hope you had a pleasant time in Chicago, Mr. Maguire." Still flustered, she leaned against the stagecoach. Why did this man have such an effect on her?

"Sure did."

"Then if you'll excuse me, I'll get on with my packing." Oh, if he would only go away, she told herself. Off to one side was a small chamber pot. While he stared at it, Jessie thought she'd die of mortification. She wished the earth would open up so she could drop in.

He turned back to her. "I'll help you. If there's one thing I know something about, it's loading a stage-coach." He walked around to the back boot, unhooked it, looked in, and let out a low whistle. "Your father's taking a hell of a lot of gear. How come?"

"You'll have to ask him." Of course, sooner or later this annoying man would have to know that she was going along. Should she tell him now and get it over with? What if he said she couldn't go? She had planned on her father breaking the news.

Tonio pulled a hatbox out of the boot. "What's this doing in here?"

"Mr. Maguire, put that back. It's no concern of yours

what I'm loading." Her voice rose in fury. "I'd appreciate it if you'd just go about your own business."

But Tonio ignored her and stuck his head further in the boot. He began reading the labels on the suitboxes aloud: "Pink velvet dinner dress. Brown gabardine daytime dress." He whirled around and grabbed her shoulders. "So you think you're going with us, after all."

Jessie shrank away from the blazing anger in his eyes. "Yes, I am. But—"

"I thought I made myself perfectly clear that we were not taking any females!" He gave her a little shake.

"If you'll just listen—"

"What happened to Henry? Didn't he propose after all?"

"Of course he proposed, but I turned him down. I don't love him, and I refuse to marry him just for your convenience!"

"And Aunt Bertha?"

"Papa agreed to take me to her in Kansas City. But I want to go clear to California with you." She twisted out of his grasp and rubbed her shoulder while she glared at him.

"Where's your father? I'm going to tell him our deal is off."

"At his office cleaning it out. But you can't just back out of your arrangement. He's planning on it." Her heart rose in panic. Papa would be furious if the trip fell through because of her.

"Well, he's the one who broke the terms of our agreement. I made it perfectly clear that you were not to go along. No women. Not even as far as Kansas City." He turned to leave.

Jessie grabbed his arm. "Just a minute. Listen to me. I'm going as his son."

He looked her up and down, particularly at her protruding breasts, and started to laugh.

Her cheeks flushed. "You are the most insufferable man I've ever met! I know I can get by with it."

His lip curled. "I know you can't, young lady."

"Come upstairs with me. I'll prove it to you."

She stamped up the back stairs to their flat, getting madder with every step. Drat this Tonio Maguire.

Tonio followed her, his eyes gazing at her shapely ankles, which showed below her flapping skirt.

After Jessie disappeared into her bedroom, Tonio settled himself in a wicker armchair and placed his hat on his knee. This was a big waste of time. Of course she couldn't masquerade as a man. She was too feminine to fool anyone. However he had to admire her spunk.

But they couldn't take her along. Especially to California. It was too dangerous. Besides, there were all the rigors of the weather—rain, heat, and even snow in the mountains. Her father would be able to stand the fatigue of traveling over the rough trails for long hours, but he doubted if a woman could.

The main reason he couldn't take her was Iris Cunningham, the girl waiting for him in Sacramento. Just thinking of her beautiful face, her petite, feminine body, and her enchanting personality made him weak inside. He was determined to claim her as his bride. Every instinct told him that Iris wouldn't like it one little bit if he traveled across the country with another woman. She might not accept his proposal if he did. No, it was out of the question. They couldn't take Jessie with them.

He looked around the sunny, cheerful room. In spite of the fact that all the pictures were down and that packing boxes lined the walls, it was a comfortable, attractive home. How would a girl used to this stand the primitive conditions on the trail? Even when they arrived in Sacramento, it would be hard to find a flat like this in the new, crowded city.

No, she couldn't go with them, and that was that. He'd made it very clear to Carl Henderson. Perhaps later on they could arrange for her to come around the Horn by ship and meet her in San Francisco.

When she returned to the living room, wearing men's clothes and the wide-brimmed, floppy hat, he gasped in astonishment.

"I'm fifteen, going on sixteen, and my name is Jess. I'm Carl Henderson's son." She pulled off the hat, exposing her slicked-back hair. With her hand on her hip and her feet wide apart, she challenged him. "I'm going, dammit, whether you like it or not."

A mixture of emotions stirred through him as he stepped toward her. Anger, dread, admiration, desire.

"I'll admit you look convincing. A lot more like a boy than I ever expected. But it's a tiring, bone-breaking trip. You have no idea how hard it is. You won't be able to take it."

"Oh, yes, I will."

"Nonetheless, you can't go."

Her head flew back. Her chin jutted out. She stared right at him. "I am going."

His temper snapped. "I say you're not. You'd be too much of a burden."

"I won't be a burden. Papa can teach me to drive the stagecoach.

"That's preposterous."

"Of course I can learn."

His temper flared again. He spread his feet wide apart and put his hands on his hips. "All right, come with us as far as Kansas City. But, by God, you'll carry your weight like a man every foot of the way. You'll help take care of the horses. You'll drive the teams and take your turn as a whip. You'll learn to shoot so you can stand guard. Don't you dare weasel out because you're a weak little woman."

"I swear, I'll do my part."

"I'm warning you, Jessie Henderson, you've bitten off more than you can chew."

As Tonio shoveled dirt on their breakfast campfire to put it out, he said, "You'd better ride with me this morning and have your first lesson in driving a team."

Jessie wanted to tell him that her father was capable of teaching her anything she needed to know, but she held her tongue. It was their second day on the trail, and if she riled Tonio too much, he'd insist on leaving her in Kansas City with Aunt Bertha. So she had to be careful.

"Put your gear away while I harness the team," he ordered.

Walking away, he told himself that he'd show her what it meant to drive a six-horse hitch. She'd soon realize how difficult it was and would be glad to stay with her aunt in Kansas City.

While she rinsed out the coffeepot, she told herself that he had to be the bossiest, most provoking man she'd ever been around. She hated the way he always put her on edge, ready to protest everything she said or did. He was deliberately trying to get her goat. She could hardly define her reaction to him. But she felt like a banty hen, clucking and scurrying around with her feathers all ruffled.

Quickly she washed and wiped the dishes, utensils, and frying pan and stored them back in the grub box.

When her father approached with the team, she said, "I'm going to ride with Tonio this morning. He's going to teach me how to drive a coach."

"I don't know whether I approve of that, Jessie. It's mighty tiring when you're not used to it. Besides, we'll be in Kansas City in a few days. Not much point in your learning."

"But I want to try, Papa."

She gave him a quick kiss and hurried to Tonio's coach, which was already hitched to a six-horse team. Perhaps her father didn't want her to learn because she was a mere woman and it would detract from his importance if she did.

While the men rounded up the extra horses they'd brought along, Jessie climbed up on the coach. She still felt awkward and clumsy doing it. The seat was seven feet above the ground, and there were only three step plates leading up to it. The lowest was at the height of the front-wheel hub, the next at the top of the thorough-brace standard, and the third at the base of the box that contained the driver's seat.

Her father and Tonio slung themselves up with such grace, but it was all she could do to get there—in spite of being so tall and slender! If she were wearing her voluminous skirts and petticoats, she could never make it without help.

The morning sun, low in the horizon, cast a pink-gold glow over the prairie and the slowly moving water of the Missouri River. The tall grass undulated in long waves with the breeze. A meadowlark sang a pure, sweet note. Why would anyone want to leave such beautiful country, so level and familiar? A pang of regret ran through her. Tonio spoke so often of the rugged mountains, harsh desert, and pounding Pacific Ocean. They all sounded so alien. Would she ever get used to them?

The coach lurched sideways when Tonio climbed into the driver's seat. He glanced at her, smiled, and pulled on his gauntlet gloves with long cuffs. "Welcome aboard, Jess Henderson. As soon as the team gets limbered up, we'll start training you to be a whip."

"That's fine with me."

"Good thing you've turned into a boy. I can't imagine a woman being able to handle a six-horse hitch."

"I'll learn to do it." Her jaw was set with determination.

"You'll have to." Tonio suppressed a smile. He had to admit she was plucky. But before he was through with the lessons, she'd be glad to stay with her aunt. "First you should learn the positions of a six-horse hitch. The first two are leaders. You want to pick your smartest, most alert ones to lead. Ones with experience, if possible. They don't have to be the strongest, but they should have git up and go. Real heart."

"I see." It had never occurred to her that she would have to pick the horses for the various positions on the team.

"The middle two are swingers. They need to have strength, as they take a lot of the weight of the load. Remember that when you harness your team."

Harness them? She suppressed a gasp. Her stomach

tightened at the thought. She had assumed that the men would take care of the animals. But apparently Tonio expected her to do her share. Down deep she'd been terribly afraid of horses—ever since that one she'd been riding had thrown her when she was twelve. Would she be able to conquer that fear?

"These horses just in front of us," Tonio went on, "the ones next to the coach, are the wheelers. Put your biggest, strongest horses here because they pull the most weight."

As Tonio paused to let that sink in, he glanced at her out of the corner of his eye. He sensed that she was already having second thoughts about being a male. He smiled to himself. In spite of her men's clothes, she looked adorable with her sunburned cheeks and the few freckles across the ridge of her nose. She'd complicate the journey, he had no doubt. And for his future with Iris, he sure had to dump her in Kansas City.

"Now to go on with our lesson. There is a separate rein for each horse." He held up his right hand. "These are the off reins, for the horses on the right side. The ones in my left hand are the near ones, for the horses on the left side."

"I'll try to remember that."

"Notice that the reins for the leaders go between the fore and middle fingers, those for the swing team between the middle and third fingers, and the wheelers between the third and little fingers. An experienced coachman like your father is able to manipulate all six reins simultaneously, each one independent of all the others."

As she stared at him, her mouth fell open. "Can you do that?"

"Of course."

"Surely you don't expect me to?"

"No, it takes years of practice. My father started training my brothers and me when we were little kids. He put a set of reins up in the woodshed in our backyard in Chicago, and we spent hours learning to use them."

"Did he have a stage line?"

"No. He's a teamster and does hauling and moving. My cousin Gianni and I worked for him for a while, but we struck out for California and started our stage line. But having experience with horses—and learning to be a teamster—was sure helpful."

The road stretched flat and easy ahead of them, following the banks of the Missouri River. Her father's coach moved rapidly along in front of them, with a string of six extra horses tied to the back. A plume of dust from their hoofs hung in the air.

Tonio glanced at her. "Now let's change places. I'm going to turn the reins over to you so you can give it a try."

Her heart pounded. Could she do it? "The horses won't run away or anything?"

"No. They'll just follow your father's coach. Put up your right hand." Tonio put the off reins between her fingers and let the ends hang down together over the palm of her hand. "Now you grasp the whip between your thumb and forefinger, with the butt held securely by the heel of your thumb."

Soon the near reins were intertwined in her left hand, with the ends looped over her thumb and allowed to hang.

Taking a deep breath, with her heart pounding, she held her arms rigid. Soon they began to tremble. How could a coachman stand this position very long? she wondered.

Tonio let her suffer awhile, then spoke up. "A real whip rests his hands on his knees and lets the reins hang a little slack."

With a sigh of relief, she plopped her hands down and relaxed her shoulders. "But how do you control the horses?"

"You learn to climb the rein you want by drawing the finger on each side of it one at a time. That gathers it in and makes the rein tighter. Try doing it a little for your leader on your off side. His name is Bozo."

Awkwardly she moved her fore and middle fingers back and forth until the rein became taut.

Tonio nodded in approval. "Now separate the fingers just enough to let the rein slip out a little. Try practicing that. Climb it in. Let it out."

Jessie maneuvered her fingers on the rein for a while, then glanced up at him. "Bozo's not doing a thing. Look at him. He just trots along and pays no attention to me at all."

"He's not getting a real command. When a whip means business, he'll reach his right foot out to rest it on the pedal of the brake shaft. He'll press down lightly, and, instantly, the ears of every horse'll spring to attention."

"Why will they do that?"

"Because they know that reining always follows the sound of the sliding brake beam. The brake slows the coach enough to take the slack out of the traces. The reins, too, will be taut enough for the leaders to feel the bit in the corner of their mouths. If they're to turn left, that side will feel more pressure. The same if it's a right turn. But we'll go into that another time."

It was going to be harder than she thought to learn to be a coachman, she told herself. Finally she said, "I imagine it takes real skill to make a turn."

"You bet it does. You can flip a coach over real easy if you make too short a turn with a six-horse hitch. You have to command each span of horses just right. The leaders, the swingers, and the wheelers all turn just a little different. You have to know how to brake, too. Reining and braking go together. But today we'll concentrate on going straight ahead. Now try climbing your reins for your swing span. Use your middle and third fingers."

Jessie drove the rest of the morning. Her fingers ached from climbing the reins. Her back hurt from sitting rigid so she wouldn't slide across the seat. The dust blew in her face, but she was determined not to complain.

Tonio suppressed a smile. She was going to succeed if it killed her. He'd bet a dollar she was aching all over. He wanted to tell her that she hadn't seen anything yet. They were still in the easy part.

They stopped at noon and ate the sandwiches she had prepared before they started.

She rode with her father in the afternoon. As she sat next to him, she said, "I always have the feeling I'm going to pitch right over on top of the horses."

"That's because we're not carrying a heavy load. We're tipping forward just a bit. If we had a few passengers on the rear seat, you wouldn't have that sensation. How did you get along with Tonio?"

"He's teaching me to drive a coach. When I've had a few lessons, I'll be able to spell you, Papa."

"Maybe you *should* learn. Then we'd have a spare driver. Never can tell. One of us might get sick . . . or get an arrow stuck in us by some Indian."

A shiver of foreboding ran through her. Would they run into hostile Indians? She tried to push that fear into the back of her mind while she listened to the pounding of the horses' hoofs on the road.

In the late afternoon, her father turned the coach into a meadow next to a grove of trees. "I thought this was a good place to spend the night," he yelled at Tonio when he drove up alongside them.

"Fine. Jess, as soon as you get down, you can help me unhitch the team. You might as well learn that right now."

As she climbed off the coach, she tried to forget her fear of horses. Drat this Tonio Maguire! He was a regular taskmaster. Why didn't he take care of his own animals? She had to build a fire and fix their supper. Didn't that count for something?

"Shake a leg, Jess. It'll be dark pretty soon," Tonio called to her.

As soon as she hurried toward him, he began his lesson. "You have to give each horse a pat on the head. Or scratch him between the ears." He glanced at her. "Better get that scowl off your face. You have to be pleasant and let each one know that you appreciate the good job he's done." He turned to the leaders. "Good boy, Bozo. Attaboy, Popcorn." Soon he had them unhitched and led away to graze.

The two swingers gave Jessie a baleful look. Timidly she reached out to touch the near-side one. How huge he seemed! His teeth looked big, as well. Would he bite? Her voice squeaked as she said, "Nice boy." Her heart pounded. Her throat felt dry with fear.

"Show some enthusiasm, for gosh sake. His name's Tupper," Tonio yelled as he approached.

"Good boy, Tupper." She forced herself to rub his muzzle.

"That's better. The other swinger has to be petted, too. They get jealous, just like humans."

"What's his name? It's easier when you know the names."

"George."

"Who on earth would name a horse George?"

"Your father did." He grinned to himself as he unbuckled the harness. "Now take the swingers over there to graze."

As she led them away, she hoped they wouldn't step on her feet. How big their hoofs were. Her heart thumped against her chest wall.

"Tie them to a tree so they won't wander away," Tonio yelled after her. He knew she was afraid. She'd be glad to stay with Aunt Bertha after this workout.

When he joined her with the wheelers, he said, "I'll finish up. You can get supper started."

"Thank you, Tonio Maguire. How kind of you to let me," she snapped back. She wanted to tell him that he was the bossiest man she ever had the misfortune of being around, but she held her tongue. They had to be safely away from Aunt Bertha before she could give him a piece of her mind.

Jessie hunted around for some kindling wood and dry leaves. Soon she had a fire going—and a triangular rack over it from which to hang the camp kettle. She peeled carrots and put them on to boil. She reached in the front boot, where she kept some of her food supplies, and took out a can of baked beans. They were expensive, and she had planned to save the canned goods until later in the trip, but she was so tired she tucked the can between two burning pieces of wood. She fixed a pot of coffee and put it on the fire.

While the supper cooked, she unfolded a camp table and covered it with a piece of oilcloth. While she put the tin plates and cups on the table, she could see the men leading the horses, a few at a time, to the river's edge to drink.

She unfolded three camp chairs and placed them at the table. A little later, Tonio walked over to his coach and took out a wash basin. After he washed his hands, he walked toward the fire.

"What's that in there?" he asked.

"A coffeepot."

"No, that round tin."

"A can of beans, if you must know."

"But you can't heat a can of beans that way."

Her temper flared. "Tonio Maguire, will you just mind your own business!"

"But I'm warning you. Take it out."

"You're the bossiest man I've ever known. Besides, I'm the one getting supper."

"But—"

"Oh, be still."

Just then the can of beans blew apart in a terrific explosion. Beans flew against her pants. Beans landed on Tonio's coach and ran in a brown ooze down the side. Beans dripped from the tree branches.

The horses whinnied in alarm. Carl shouted, "What the hell happened?"

"A can of beans exploded, Papa."

"I tried to warn her—" Tonio yelled, and then bent double in laughter. He slapped his leg and howled. He leaned on the table while his shoulders shook. He mimicked, " 'Tonio Maguire, will you just mind your own business? You're the bossiest man I've ever known. Besides, I'm the one getting supper.' "

"Oh, shut up!"

"Anyone with a grain of sense knows you have to punch a hole in the can to let the steam out."

Jessie's face turned scarlet. She wiped her pants with a dishrag. Drat Tonio, anyway. He was impossible. Besides, what could she serve for supper?

Chapter 3

The next morning, Jessie took special care with breakfast to make up for the disastrous meal the night before. Her biscuits were especially light, and, for once, the milk gravy made from bacon grease had no lumps.

When Tonio finished eating, he said, "Jess, I'll give you a hand in cleaning up the dishes."

She gave him a suspicious look. What was going on in back of his mind? "Thank you, but I can manage."

But he started scraping the dishes into the campfire and stacking them, anyway. "No, I'll help. Then I want you to learn to harness the team. Any whip worth his salt has to know how to do that."

They had the dishes washed and packed and the campfire put out in short order. She had to admit that he made every motion count and got the chores done with dispatch.

"Now come with me," Tonio ordered. "I've kept my horses separated from your father's." In long strides he crossed the meadow to where his twelve animals were grazing.

Just looking at so many horses together struck terror in her heart. Her knees shook. The palms of her hands were moist. But no way was she going to admit to Tonio that she was deathly afraid of them. She was determined he would never, never know.

She watched a black-and-white mare reach her muzzle

30

out toward him, then move nearer and rub her forehead against his chest. "Good girl, Peggy." Tonio stroked her muzzle while she whinnied.

He turned to Jessie. "We'll give the ones that were hitched yesterday a rest. They'll trail along behind us, but they won't have a coach to pull. Now see if you can pick a couple of leaders from the others."

She looked the horses over carefully. "I don't know about leaders, but that big gray one over there would make a good wheeler. He must be six feet tall."

Tonio grasped his forehead. "You don't measure horses by feet. You say so many hands. Roscoe is sixteen hands. And, yes, he *would* make a good wheeler. Now pick out your leaders."

"Well, how about Peggy, for one? She seems to have a lot of spirit."

"All right, and we'll match her with that chestnut."

They soon had the team chosen, and Tonio showed her how to lead the wheelers to the stagecoach. As she listened to their hoofs *clump, clump* in the soft soil of the meadow behind her, she felt a shiver of fear run down her spine. They were so huge and heavy. She glanced over her shoulder at them. Would they rear up and trample her? But she would never let on to Tonio, who followed behind with the other four horses.

When she arrived at the stagecoach, he called out, "Now back them into position. Obviously the wheelers have to be harnessed first."

In spite of her shaking knees, she whirled around to face the animals, grasped the halters tighter, and began pushing them backward so that one stood on each side of the pole in front of the coach.

Tonio glanced at her ashen face and shaking hands. She's scared spitless, he told himself. Absolutely petrified. For a moment he was tempted to comfort her, tell her that from now on he would take care of the horses. After all, she was just a girl. But he hardened his resolve. She had to conquer her fear, and the only way she could do it was to learn to handle the horses. She had to earn their respect. God knows what lay ahead of them.

"Help me get the harness out from under the stage-coach," Tonio said, pretending not to notice her discomfort.

Soon he was showing her how to put on the collar and the hame with the attached traces that fastened to the single tree. "Now check all the straps to make sure they're straight and smooth. Then pat Baldy and tell him what a good boy he is. You want him to relax before you cinch up the bellyband. Otherwise he'll take a deep breath and hold it so you can't make it tight."

What ornery critters horses are, she thought. Her voice squeaked as she patted the animal on the back of his head. "Good Baldy. Nice boy." Could she ever get courage enough to reach under him for the bellyband? Her mouth felt full of cotton. She couldn't swallow. A trickle of cold sweat broke out on her forehead and ran down the side of her face.

The horse turned his head and glanced back at her suspiciously. A quiver ran along his hide. Jessie felt it ripple under her hand. What was he getting ready to do?

"Hurry up!" Tonio yelled. He had already finished the other wheeler and was backing the swingers into place. It was all he could do to keep from coming to her rescue, but this was her battle—and she had to fight it on her own.

"Nice Baldy." She patted the horse again. "Steady, boy." She gritted her teeth. This was it. She couldn't postpone things any longer. Her arm trembled as she reached under the horse and grasped the hanging belly-band. Sweat ran into her eyes, so she shook her head.

"Be a good horse," she murmured as she cinched up the bellyband. Was he holding his breath? Would the bellyband be too loose, so Tonio would have something to complain about?

"You harness the leaders while I round up the horses that trail behind us," Tonio ordered.

Jessie wanted to yell at him to harness his own horses, but she didn't dare. He must never know how afraid she was of the darned animals.

Carefully she went through the steps in her mind as

she fished the last of the harness from under the stage-coach. The leaders were waiting in position.

"Nice Peggy," Jessie murmured. Somehow the mare didn't seem so formidable. In the first place, she was smaller than the others and there was a friendly, lively air about her. Besides, she was a female like herself, and Jessie felt some rapport with her.

Getting the collar on, the traces fastened to the single tree, and the bellyband cinched went much faster. "You're a sweetheart," Jessie whispered in her ear.

When she was finished and had all the reins gathered in her hands, she slumped against the side of the coach, out of Tonio's sight, gasping with relief. At least she'd gotten through that crisis without him guessing how she felt.

Finally she pulled herself up onto the seat. She glanced out over the horses' backs with a feeling of real accomplishment. She thought of them as fellow creatures inhabiting the earth for the first time.

Grudgingly she had to admit that the horses looked splendid, so glossy and content. Perhaps they liked to be harnessed to the stagecoach with a job to perform. Did they get bored sometimes just grazing, with nothing purposeful to do?

The early morning sun silhouetted Tonio as he led the other horses that were to follow them. His floppy-brimmed hat sat well back on his head; some of his black curls were showing. He took long, confident strides; his stomach was flat and trim and his shoulders were back. As he passed the coach, she heard him talk to the team. "Hercules, you're to trot right along with us, okay? No trying to go off on your own. Prince, I want some cooperation out of you, boy."

When the animals were securely tied, Tonio grabbed the seat railing to swing himself up onto the coach, tipping it to one side. Jessie braced herself to keep from sliding. Figuratively she also positioned all her armor to protect herself from the impact of his personality. How annoying to be so aware of him all the time, so on her guard. She hoped he wouldn't have too much to say about the exploding beans from the night before. Her cheeks burned in embarrassment just thinking about it.

He glanced at her. "I told Carl that we'd take the lead today. That way you'll learn to be a real whip instead of just following along behind. Now put your right foot on the brake pedal and release it."

Just as he had told her before, the horses' ears stood up. "Pull in the reins and release them. That's their signal to start." She did, but nothing happened, so Tonio reached across, grabbed her right hand, and gave it a quick jerk. The whip snapped above the horses' heads. "You've got to get 'em down to business. Let 'em know who's boss."

The horses started off with a brisk trot. The coach lumbered and creaked behind them. "You seldom have to hit them with the whip," Tonio went on. "Just crack it above their heads. That gets their attention, all right."

Nervously Jessie waited for him to say something about the beans or her ineptness in driving, but instead he reached under the seat for a guitar. He strummed it and began to sing, "Come Where My Love Lies Dreaming," in an achingly beautiful tenor voice.

Jessie glanced at him. "You're full of surprises. You're such a big man, I thought you'd be a baritone."

He looked at her and grinned. "With a name like Maguire? And Antonio? How could I miss being a tenor? Come on and sing with me. Do you like Stephen Foster?"

Soon they were singing "Oh, Susanna" and "Swanee River." When she began "Jeanie with the Light Brown Hair," Tonio changed it to "Jessie with the Dark Brown Hair."

What fun to be driving along singing and listening to the *clip-clop* of the horses and the rumble of the coach wheels. She could smell the fragrance of prairie grasses, the rather pleasant odor of leather and horseflesh. How good it was to be alive. Tonio noted her sparkling eyes and glowingly lovely skin and wished he could read her thoughts.

Soon he exclaimed, "Uh-oh!"

"What's the matter?"

"I can see a sharp turn to the left ahead."

She handed him the reins. "Here, you do it."

"No, you've got to learn. First, step lightly on the brake and tighten your reins. Keep going straight ahead, and, the minute Peggy and Star's tails hit the middle of the turn, climb their reins so they feel the signal in the left corner of their mouths so they'll turn left."

"I see." But her voice came out in a squeak. Could she do it right?

"Now at the same time," Tonio went on, "you have to keep the swingers going straight, so give them a bit of pressure to the right. Wait until their tails are in the center, then turn 'em left. But in the meantime, you have to keep the wheelers going straight. You have to swing around the corner. Don't cut it short or you'll upset the coach."

Her heart thrashed as she tried to keep all the reins under control. Of course the horses were walking slowly, so she managed. She marveled at all the times she'd seen her father or Tonio swing around a corner with a minimum loss of momentum.

As soon as the turn was completed, Jessie released the brake and slackened the reins. The horses picked up the spanking rhythm of their trot again, their hoofs striking the ground at the same time.

What did he think of that turn? Jessie kept glancing at him, waiting for him to say something. Finally she could stand it no longer. "How did I do?"

"Okay for the first time, I guess. But it's going to take a lot of practice for you to become a real whip."

Anger flared up in her. "Of course it's going to take practice. I'll bet you and Papa didn't do any better when you first started."

"I don't know about that. I think reining comes more natural to us men." He rubbed his hands on his knees. "I doubt if a woman could ever be as good as a man."

"Oh, is that so?" Her face flushed in annoyance. Drat him, anyway. What an impossible man he was! She'd show him.

Tonio smiled to himself as he noticed how her mouth clamped shut and her chin stuck out. He was sure going to miss her when they dropped her off in Kansas City.

She drove for the rest of the morning, but her fingers hurt from climbing the reins, and her legs ached from bracing herself on the seat. The wind blew in her face, and the sun glared in her eyes. Ahead loomed mile after mile of monotonous prairie. And this was supposed to be the easy part! Her heart sank in dread as she thought of Aunt Bertha. How was she going to talk the men into taking her?

On the day they stopped in Kansas City, Jessie put on a printed gingham dress and pinned the French knot on the back of her hair before they went to the boarding-house. It seemed so good to feel like a lady again. She sat inside the coach to keep her hat from blowing off and tried to smooth the wrinkles out of her skirt.

Finally they pulled up in front of a dreary two-story frame house. Jessie hoped that Tonio would stay with the coaches and horses tied to the elm trees on the street, but her father said, "Come with us and meet my sister," so he followed them up the stairs.

They rang the bell, and Bertha Henderson opened the door. She was tall and reed-thin like her brother, but her plain, scowling face showed no resemblance to his affable personality.

"Land sakes, I've been expecting you for the last week. Ever since I got your letter." She led them into the dark parlor with the shades pulled down to protect the flowered Brussels carpet, even though it was worn. She indicated that they were to sit down on the horsehair sofas.

"Carl Henderson," the older woman exclaimed after they were settled, "I can't believe you're going clear out to California. You must have lost your senses." Her thin lips clamped shut like a snap purse. "You stay right here with me, girl."

Jessie cringed. She waited for Tonio to butt right in and support Aunt Bertha. And what was Papa thinking?

No one spoke, and finally Jessie screwed up her courage and said, "Thank you very much, Aunt Bertha. You're very kind to suggest it, but I want to go to California with Papa."

"Jessica, I won't permit that. You need to be under the guidance of a woman. Now that you've lost your dear mother, I'm the only one left. You stay right here with me and help me run this place. I won't charge you a cent. You'd get your room and board free. Carl, you'd send her a little allowance for her other expenses, wouldn't you?"

"Of course. I planned to leave her here all along."

Jessie's heart sank. "But, Papa—"

"I won't hear of anything else," Aunt Bertha interrupted. "It's too dangerous for a female out there in the Wild West. Especially one as young and seemly as you. Don't you agree, Mr. Maguire?"

"Oh, absolutely. You can't imagine how rough and tough it is on the trail." Tonio slapped his leg in emphasis.

Jessie glared at him. Drat him, anyway. He was the most impossible man she had ever known.

"That's why she was smart to go as a man," Tonio went on.

Appalled, Aunt Bertha stared at him. "Land sakes, what in tarnation do you mean?"

"She got dressed up in her female duds today. But usually she looks like a fifteen-year-old boy."

"You mean she wears trousers?" Aunt Bertha screeched.

Tonio nodded solemnly. "That's right."

"But what about her hair?"

Tonio reached over and pulled on Jessie's hat. The hairpiece came with it. The short hair dropped down to her shoulders.

The color drained from Aunt Bertha's face. She could hardly speak. "You've cut your hair!"

Furiously Jessie grabbed her hat and plopped it on her head. She pushed her short strands under the brim. "You've got your nerve, Tonio Maguire. This is none of your business at all.'' She'd like to kill this man with her own two hands.

Fanning her face, Bertha looked at her brother. ''Carl, how could you permit such a thing? What kind of a father are you?''

''She had it cut while I was gone with my coach.''

''You mean you left her there alone? Without a chaperone?'' She stretched herself to her full height. ''This just proves how badly she needs to be under my supervision. Jessica, you're to let your hair grow out beginning right now. Go out and get your belongings and I'll show you to your room in the basement. I have some things stored in there at the moment, but we can clear it out.'' She stood up. ''Come with me.''

They all rose and followed Aunt Bertha into the dark hall and down narrow stairs to the basement. She snapped on a light switch and led them to a storeroom. It didn't even have a window in it.

Panic rose in Jessie. She felt doomed to a life with this horrible woman in this awful room. She looked at her father, but he didn't meet her eyes.

''There's a cot there in the corner. And a dresser where you can put your things, Jessie. Now if you men will just help me, we'll take the rest of this stuff out.'' She picked up a box.

Tonio stuck his head in the storeroom. He shuddered in distaste. He couldn't leave Jessie here to live in this hole. He just couldn't do it. She was much too alive and full of gumption to stand it. This old battle-ax would break her spirit. They had no choice; they'd have to take her with them to California. He looked at Carl, who also seemed appalled at this setup. He put his hand out. ''Not so fast, Miss Henderson. Not so fast. I think you're jumping the gun.''

''What do you mean, young man?''

''Your niece is twenty years old. She's still a resident of Missouri, and in that state she was of age when she was eighteen.''

''And so?''

''It means that she can decide where she wants to live

and what she wants to do." Tonio smiled in his most charming manner. "She's already stated that she's hankering to go to California with her father, so that's that. Don't you agree, Carl?"

The older man nodded. "Yes, we'd better take her with us."

Jessie blinked back tears of joy. "Oh, Papa, thank you." She threw her arms around his neck.

Aunt Bertha's face reddened in fury. She crossed her arms over her breasts. "Carl, supposing something happens to you out there with all those Indians and outlaws. What will Jessie do then? Answer me that."

"Don't worry," Tonio put in. "I promise you that I'll find a suitable husband for her. I'll make that my special obligation." He started for the stairs. "We'd better be on our way. Our rigs are taking up too much space on the curb."

"At least you can stay for doughnuts and coffee." Aunt Bertha thumped up the stairs, every movement showing how mad she was.

It wasn't until that afternoon, when Jessie was driving Tonio's coach, that she could thank him properly. "I'm much obliged to you. If you hadn't rescued me, I'd be stuck back there with Aunt Bertha in that awful, dreary place."

"We couldn't have that. I sized her up right away. She had it all figured out that she could make a slave out of you. You'd be working your tail off for nothing." He tried not to think of what Iris would say—or of all the complications of having Jessie with them on the journey. But he looked at her and smiled. She sure added zest and interest to the trip.

"Anyway, thank you, Tonio. She's a horrid, stingy, mean-spirited person. I can't stand her. And Papa sure changed his mind when he saw that storeroom."

For the rest of the day, she took special care with her reining so Tonio would be pleased. But something told her that sooner or later she would pay a price for his cooperation that morning.

As each day passed, Jessie felt a little more at ease with the horses. Tonio pointed out little differences in their personalities. "Always harness Bunty on the near or left side. He's got a tendency to move to the right, so if he's on the far side he'll pull the team too much that way." "Take Jupiter. He's a jealous devil. Be sure you give him plenty of attention. Pat his muzzle first. If you don't, he'll nip the horse that you've been talking to."

She learned the names of all twenty-four horses and their various idiosyncrasies. The better she became acquainted with them, the less she feared them. But, still, it took all the courage she could muster to harness them or lead them to pasture. The sound of their hoofs behind her still made shivers of fear along her spine.

It always impressed her how much both her father and Tonio loved horses and treated them with such kindness. She often wondered if she would ever share their devotion.

One balmy evening as they sat around the campfire and she was marking their progress on a map of the United States, she asked, "We seem to be heading northwest. Are you sure you know where we're going?"

Tonio gave her a disgusted glance. "Of course I know where we're going. We're following the Central Overland Stage Route. It goes along the North Platte, through the Territory of Nebraska. We're just about in the Territory of Wyoming. There we'll cross the Rockies, over the lowest pass, then head for Salt Lake City. There's another route that goes over a high grade to Denver and then on to Salt Lake, but I decided this was better."

"I suppose the stage companies have found the best way."

"You can be sure of that. Besides, there'll be some stations along the way where we can buy supplies—especially feed for the horses. We won't always have this lush prairie grass for grazing. We'll have lots of deserts through Utah and Nevada before we hit the Sierra and go into California."

Jessie took out her calendar and marked a cross through the day. "Do you want to know what day it is?"

"Not particularly." Tonio stretched out his long legs as he leaned against the side of his coach. The firelight cast a pink glow over his face.

"Well, it's Saturday, June seventeenth. I always like to know what day it is. How many miles do you think we traveled today?"

"About fifty-five."

Jessie wet the point of her pencil and wrote that down. She added a column of figures. "We've gone approximately nine hundred and seven miles."

"Well, it's nine hundred and seven of the easiest miles, I can tell you," Tonio said. He pushed his hat farther back on his head. "I never knew anyone that kept track of things the way you do."

Carl leaned back in his camp chair. "She's always been like that. She learned to tell time when she was just a little tyke. I bought her a watch that she wore on a chain around her neck."

"I still do, Papa. Here it is." Jessie held out her watch. "I wind it every night before I go to sleep."

"And look at it a hundred times a day," Tonio put in. "If you watched the sun, you could tell the time close enough. What difference does it make? Doesn't matter as long as you pitch camp before dark."

"Well, I think it's very important." Her voice rose in annoyance.

"It's a lot of foolishness," Tonio said, deliberately trying to get her goat.

"What about your stage route? Or don't you care when your stages depart and arrive?"

"Nobody's complained so far."

As Jessie carefully folded her map and slipped it inside her journal, along with her calendar, she told herself that a body had to keep track of things. Tonio was the most exasperating man she'd ever known. She'd be glad when they arrived in California and she wouldn't have to be around him so much.

The next afternoon they passed a crudely lettered sign that said WELCOME TO WYOMING TERRITORY. A line slashed through WYOMING, and the red-painted word

SIOUX appeared above it. Little rivulets of dry paint looked like blood. Shivers of fear ran through her as she looked at it.

They made camp early, and Tonio said, "I think you'd better have some lessons in how to look and act like a man."

Jessie glanced at him. From the expression on his face, she could tell he was perfectly serious. "And I ought to learn how to shoot a rifle."

"That's right. Let's begin with acting more manlike. In the first place, a man spits." He demonstrated. "See what you can do."

"Honestly, Tonio—"

"Come on."

"That's better," he finally declared, then added, "a man's apt to stand with his thumbs hooked in his pants pockets or over his belt. Practice that for me."

She did until he was satisfied.

"I would avoid crossing your arms over your chest. That looks more feminine. And when you walk, try not to swing your hips. Instead stride straight ahead like this, with long steps." He showed her how.

Then he picked up a rifle. "Here, you hold it, and I'll show you how to aim."

Jessie felt his arms around her. For a moment, she closed her eyes and relished the sense of being safe and secure with him. She thought of the sign that looked like dripping blood. What lay ahead here in Sioux country?

Chapter 4

The next morning, the horses plunged into their collars as soon as they were harnessed, as if they were anxious to get started. Jessie gathered up the reins and mounted the coach on the driver's side. While she waited for Tonio to climb aboard, she placed the ribbons between her fingers in proper order.

She winced as she flexed her wrists, as they were still tender and sore from driving. Perhaps Tonio was right in saying that women didn't have strong enough wrists to be skilled drivers. But she was going to prove him wrong. She'd develop hers until she could handle a six-horse hitch as well as he could. What a provoking man. She'd best him yet, she determined.

While she shivered in the cool morning air, she watched him shovel dirt on the campfire. She had to admit how efficient and competent he was in everything he did. Soon he replaced the shovel in the back boot and swung himself up on the seat.

"Try to keep the team bunched together," he instructed. "You have a tendency to let them get too spread apart."

Her cheeks flushed with resentment, but she hastened to do as she was told. After she climbed the reins for Dawn, one of the leaders, to make her move over, she turned her attention to Trusty, a big roan in the wheel position, and got him closer to the pole.

"Okay now?" She glanced at Tonio.

"Yes, I guess so."

His Highness was not in a very good mood this morning, she told herself. Apparently there was no pleasing him. But she settled herself down and listened to the hum of the wheels and the jingle of chains as they followed the trail across the prairie. Occasionally a horse would snort and shake his head, but on the whole the team trotted along in perfect rhythm.

Later in the morning, threatening clouds began to cover the sky. Jessie was just thinking that she'd better get out her rain gear at the next stop, when Tonio let out a low whistle. "What's the matter?" she asked.

"Look over to the right. There's a huge buffalo herd."

She glanced in that direction and saw a dark mass at the foot of a low range of hills.

"If we don't bother them, aren't they likely to leave us alone?" Jessie asked.

"It's not the buffalo I'm thinking about. You get that big a herd and you're bound to have Indians nearby. They pretty well follow the animals."

A flicker of alarm ran along her spine. "Is Papa right behind? We ought to stay close together, shouldn't we?"

"Yes." Tonio stood up in the box and looked around. "I don't see any sign of Indians. But they could be up in those hills ahead watching us. Of course, it's our horses they'd want."

Fear tightened the pit of her stomach, but she was determined not to show it. If she said anything, Tonio would remind her that it wasn't his idea that she was along. She kept her mind on her driving to make sure that the team stayed bunched together.

Out of the corner of her eye, she could see Tonio grope for the rifle that he always kept by his feet. He lifted it and placed it across his knees.

The sky filled with dark clouds, and the muggy air felt oppressive. All morning little streaks of lightning zigzagged above them, followed by rumbles of thunder. After they stopped for lunch, she dug out her raincoat and sou'wester oilskin hat.

When they were ready to start, Jessie asked Tonio, "Do you want me to drive? Then you'd be free to keep an eye out for the savages."

He nodded, so she walked over to her father, who was preparing to leave, and told him that she wouldn't ride with him as she usually did in the afternoon.

"Don't you think you'd be a lot safer if you rode inside our coach, Jessie?"

"No, Papa. We haven't even seen a sign of an Indian yet. I can get in later if necessary. I told Tonio I'd drive so he could keep a lookout."

Jessie climbed into the driver's seat and adjusted the sou'wester's broad brim in the back to protect her neck in case it started to rain. Tonio put a rubber poncho over his shoulders and pulled the hood up on his head before he sat on the seat beside her. When he was settled, he placed his rifle on his lap and covered it with his rain gear.

A streak of lightning brightened the sky, a loud clap of thunder followed, and the rain began to fall. The horses tossed their heads and neighed restlessly. She released the brake and signaled with the reins to go.

As they sped through the falling rain to the pounding of hoofs and jingling of the trace rings and chains, she inhaled the fresh-washed air and smelled the damp earth, the wet leather harnesses and the horses. In spite of her nagging fear of the Indians who might be lurking in the hills, it was exciting to be hurtling along the trail, not knowing what lay ahead. How different and adventure-filled her life was now. Would she ever be able to settle down to doing housework after this?

When she glanced at Tonio, she realized that he had been watching her. He smiled and said, "You'll be a knight of the road yet, Jessie. A regular jehu. You've surprised me."

"Well, I've learned to like driving."

"But you feel safer up here in the box—with the horses below you—than when you have to harness them."

Her cheeks flamed. Drat him, anyway. So he had

known how afraid she was of the animals. "You're a brute to make me handle them."

"It's the only way for you to get over that foolishness."

The rain came down in a torrent for a few minutes, then stopped. The sun peeked out of the clouds.

Tonio spoke up again. "Look over to your right. To the top of that hill in the distance."

Silhouetted against the sky, with the sun at their backs, five Indians on horseback rode over the crest of the hill and came down toward the herd of buffalo below them. Their rifle barrels glistened in the light.

Instinctively she cracked the whip to make the team go faster.

"You don't have to panic," Tonio said. "They're probably a hunting party."

A cloud covered the sun, and the thunderstorm began again. Lightning pierced the dark sky, followed by a clap of sound and a sudden downpour.

In the distance, she could hear shots and the pounding of hoofs as the buffalo herd began to move.

Suddenly a great bolt of lightning streaked through the sky in a blinding flash and struck the earth in the midst of the buffalo. Thunder crashed around them. Vibrations yanked the coach from side to side, almost tipping it over.

The horses reared up on their hind legs, neighing and screaming with fear. Their mouths gaped open and foam trickled out. Their eyes rolled back in their sockets.

The rain came down in a torrent, striking her on the head, drumming on the top of the coach, and pounding the backs of the horses.

From off in the distance came an ominous roar of buffalo on the run—a thousand hoofs striking the earth.

"They're stampeding!" Tonio shouted, and jumped off the box. "Turn the coach so they won't hit it broadside!" He ran to the leaders and yanked at their halters. "Calm down, Baldy. Attaboy, Roscoe."

Somehow he got them under control while Jessie tightened the reins on the left and got the coach turned.

"There's no way we can outrun the buffalo, so we'll just have to wait here until they pass," Tonio shouted. "Keep a tight grip on the horses so they won't spook! I'm going to bring the others alongside."

Soon the horses that had been trailing behind were lined up against the left side of the coach and tied securely. Their eyes rolled in fear and sweat broke out on their flanks, only to be washed away by the rain.

Jessie looked down at them and, in a frantic, shaky voice called out, "We're going to be all right. Now calm down, Tupper. Nice girl, Beauty."

The horses hitched to the coach strained at their collars and kicked up clods of mud, as if they wanted to bolt. Jessie braced her feet against the floorboard and gripped the reins with all her might to keep them under control. Her wrists ached. The muscles in her arms quivered, but she hung on.

Lightning flashed above the nearby hills, followed by the thunder claps, then the rain.

Tonio guided Carl's team so that the coaches formed a V angle at the back, toward the oncoming buffalo. The extra horses packed the space in between them, so they were protected as much as possible. He jumped back on his own coach and took the reins from Jessie.

Carl called out, "Get inside the coach, Jess!" But the buffalo surrounded them before she had a chance.

The mammoth animals, six feet tall at the shoulders and weighing about a ton each, black and shiny with the rain splashing off their backs, thundered past. Their fronts were covered with long, shaggy hair.

Jessie stared at them in horror, her blood freezing with fear. Each one had a huge hump in back of his head. Thick horns curved from their foreheads above their red, rheumy eyes. A tuft of hair hung down from their throats.

The buffalo bumped against the coach as they scrambled for room in their haste to get past. Jessie bit her lip to keep from screaming. The coach swayed back and forth with the force of the herd pounding by. Would she and Tonio get knocked off their seat high in the box?

Desperately she gripped the wet, slippery railing beside
her with both hands.

She could smell their soaked hides, hear them gasping
for breath as they rushed by in the curtain of rain. Their
red eyes glared ahead. Their hoofs splashed the mud high
in the air. On and on they came in their wild stampede,
banging against one another, snorting and snarling in
their fear.

Even through the rain, flashes of lightning illuminated
the sea of stampeding animals. Hundreds of buffalo
passed them. The noise of their hoofs hammering the
ground almost drowned out the thunder that followed the
lightning. It was a scene from hell.

Tonio braced himself and kept the reins as tight as
possible. He could see his horses shuddering with terror.
Foam dripped from their lips as they tossed their heads.
The coach swayed back and forth as the frantic buffalo
brushed against it in their rush to get past. If the coach
got overturned, they'd be trampled to death.

He glanced at Jessie's rigid body and ashen face as she
gripped the railing beside her. If she was afraid of horses,
what must she be feeling now that she was in the middle
of this stampeding buffalo herd? She must be beyond fear,
into a state of terror she had never known before. Yet
there was a stoical calm about her. God, how he admired
her courage.

When a huge bull slammed into Roscoe, the horse
reared and neighed with pain and fright. It was all Tonio
could do to keep him down. All the horses shivered and
stamped their hoofs. Their eyes rolled back, and foam
dripped from their mouths.

Even though the herd stretched in long parallel lines
across the flat land, it took two hours for all the buffalo
to pass by them. Finally they were gone; the sound faded
away. By now the rain had stopped and the westerly sun
peeked through the clouds.

Tonio put down the reins. "They're gone now. You can
let go of the railing."

But she kept her grip as if she were frozen.

"It's all over, Jess. Take it easy."

She nodded but couldn't speak.

Tonio stared at her for a long moment. Finally he leaned across her and pried her fingers loose from the railing. Gently he rubbed her hands, which were still curved and rigid as two claws. As she began to relax a little, he pulled off her sou'wester and put his arm around her. A rush of tenderness came over him, so he laid his cheek against her short, damp curls and held her close. He felt so sorry that she'd gone through this ordeal . . . and vowed to protect her from any danger in the future.

"Jessie, the buffalo are a long ways away now. You haven't anything to fear." But although the air was warm, he could feel her shivering against him, heard her teeth chattering. Her breath came in quick, little gasps.

As he held her closer, he tried to think of something to distract her. "Did you know that the name buffalo is a misnomer? It should be bison. That's their real name—American bison. They flourish here in the prairies, west of the Mississippi. They're found clear down to New Mexico."

Just then Carl stepped over to them, asked, "Is Jessie okay?"

Tonio answered. "Sure. She got the bejesus scared out of her, but she'll be all right in a minute."

"Then I'll see to the horses."

Jessie snuggled even closer to Tonio. How comforting his arms were, but her heart still thrashed against her chest wall and her blood pounded through her veins. Finally tears of relief ran down her cheeks and sobs shuddered through her.

Tonio murmured in her ear, "Go ahead and cry. Get it all out of your system."

After he pulled a bandanna out of his pocket, he gently wiped the tears from her cheeks. He handed it to her so she could blow her nose.

She managed a little smile. "I didn't know you could be so nice."

He caressed the line of her jaw while he looked into her huge, dark eyes. He could still see the remnants of her terror there. She'd probably be haunted by this experience for years to come.

"I'm all right now, Tonio," she said at last. They exchanged a long look—and both knew that their relationship had altered somehow.

Although they had passed several wagon trains on their way, they had never camped near one because the surrounding area could be overgrazed with so many animals around.

But late that afternoon, they came to the top of a rise and looked down at a circle of wagons tucked in the bend of the river. People were building campfires, and children played close to their rigs. Tonio pulled to a halt and pointed.

Carl yelled, "Yes," then turned to his daughter, who was sitting beside him. "I think it's just as well we cozy up to other folks for the night. It's a lot safer with so many Sioux around."

Jessie nodded, but she also thought that the buffalo would be likely to leave them alone as well if they camped with a train. She shuddered again as she thought of them.

Slowly they drove down the rise toward the circle. People stopped their chores to watch their approach. Finally a tall, bearded man walked out to meet them.

Carl called out, "Howdy. We'd be much obliged if you'd let us camp with you for the night."

"I reckon you can. Able-bodied men are always welcome in case there's trouble." He put out his hand. "I'm Jeb Rossito, wagon master."

The men shook hands, and the wagon master showed them where they could pull their coaches into the circle.

While the men led the horses out to pasture and tethered them, Jessie got a fire started and put some cooked beans on to heat along with a pot of coffee. She whipped up some biscuits and placed them in a portable oven next to the fire to bake. With plum preserves, which she'd brought along, they'd have a tasty supper.

Later, after they ate, the twilight deepened. Throughout the campground, kerosene lanterns were lit. Tonio got his rifle and said, "I'll stand guard over our horses the first watch."

As soon as he left, her father stood up and stretched. "Guess I'll walk around a little."

Jessie watched him go, knowing that he'd try to find a card game someplace.

As she cleaned up their supper dishes, she could hear children shouting as they played, dogs barking, and people talking and laughing throughout the campground. From not too far away came the lowing of oxen and neighing of horses. In the covered wagon next to her a baby fussed and cried.

As soon as the dishes were done, she had to put beans to soak and bake the loaves of bread that had been rising all day in the coach while they traveled. Then there was the oatmeal mush to start; it could cook over the coals during the night.

In the center of the circle of wagons a big bonfire sent flames into the air. A man played his fiddle while people square danced. Jessie decided that she'd go join the others as soon as her bread was ready. She could smell its fragrance as it baked in the portable oven by the fire.

However, before she left, a small woman about her own age, with wisps of light hair coming out of her bun, climbed out of the covered wagon next door and walked over to her. "Hello, I'm Sarah Edwards. Where you from?"

"St. Louis. I'm Jess Henderson. Care to sit down? I think there's a little coffee left in the pot."

Soon they were seated at the folding table and drinking coffee in the lantern light.

They could hear the fiddler start another tune. "I should think you'd be over there dancing, Jess."

"I'm going later. I've got to wait for the bread to bake."

"My husband's there. He loves to dance," Sarah said.

"So do I, but I don't dare leave the baby. He's been fussing most of the day."

"What's wrong with him?"

"I don't know." The young mother's chin trembled;

tears flooded her eyes. "If I was back home I could ask my mother. My folks have a farm right next to the one we had. In fact, our houses were right across the road from each other. I could run over and get Ma to help me anytime I needed her." She turned away and wiped her eyes. "I shouldn't be bothering a young boy like you with all this. But I had to talk to someone. I'm so homesick I could die."

A wave of homesickness and grief for her mother washed over Jessie as well. She could sympathize with Sarah. "It's too bad you left home."

"It wasn't my idea. It was the last thing on earth I wanted to do." She thumped her fist on the table.

"Then why?"

"It was all my husband's doing." The girl's voice trembled with bitterness and anger. "When we got married two years ago, my pa bought the farm next door and gave it to us for a wedding present. All free and clear."

"How marvelous. That was mighty generous of your pa."

Sarah went on, eager to talk. "I thought Elias was just as content as I was. But it seems he wasn't at all."

"He wasn't? When you had your own farm?"

"He wanted to go to California and seek his fortune. He thinks he can pick gold nuggets up right off the street. But I don't believe that at all."

"Then why did you agree to come?"

"I didn't agree. I wasn't asked. He just up and sold the farm and bought this wagon and outfitted it."

Jessie stared at her, too appalled to believe it. "But how could he? Isn't that against the law?"

"No." Sarah's voice trembled. "You're a boy. You wouldn't understand how it is."

"No, I don't understand. Are you sure that he had that right? Did you ask someone?"

"Yes. When Elias told me, Ma took me right into town to see a lawyer. I'll never forget what he said. 'When a man and a woman get married, they become a single legal person, which is the husband. Married women are no longer responsible citizens but dependents, like children and idiots, relying for protection on the legal status of their husband-guardian.' Those were his very words. I'll remember them as long as I live.''

"But that's not fair.''

"Of course it ain't fair. But he opened one of his big law books and showed me. Married women have no rights. They can't vote. They can't serve on a jury. And they can't hold a public office.''

"But your farm? It was given to you by your father.''

"I know. But legally it was Elias's. He gained outright ownership to it—could sell it if he wanted to—which he did.''

"But couldn't you sue him?''

"Oh, I wanted to. Believe me, I did. I talked to the lawyer about that. But he showed me in the big Blackstone book that since wives have no legal identity, they can neither sue nor be sued.''

"It's as if a woman ceases to exist legally once she gets married.''

"That's right. He showed me all kinds of things in that law book.''

"Such as?''

"If a woman works—like being a maid in a hotel or something—she owes her wages to her husband. He can beat her as long as the stick isn't bigger than a man's thumb. He can make her stay right in her home and refuse to let her have visitors. If she tries to get a divorce, he gets custody of the children. You see, the men made all the laws, so they get the best of it.''

"It's hard to believe.''

"You can be thankful that you're a man.'' She wiped her eyes with the back of her hand. "I shouldn't be telling you all these things. I might be putting ideas in your head.''

Jessie smiled. "Don't worry about that. . . . So your husband had your wagon built and outfitted and you joined this train.''

"That's right. But there was nothing else I could do. When I objected, he threatened to take the baby and come without me.''

"And, of course, you couldn't let that happen."

"No. At least I have my child. Elias says I'll get over missing my folks so much. But I reckon I never will." She wiped her eyes with the bottom of her apron.

Jessie took the bread out of the oven and turned it upside down on a rack on the table to cool. She waited for Sarah to leave, but the girl seemed anxious to talk some more.

She began again. "I've hated every bit of this trip. We trudge along day after day in the heat and dust, then we have to cook victuals over a campfire instead of at a decent cookstove."

Jessie nodded. "I've found out how hard that is."

"The guide has us stop overnight in these campgrounds, where all the other wagon trains have stopped. They're cesspools, that's what they are, from all the human waste and animal droppings. Ugh, it's so awful. You have to be so careful where you step."

For the first time, Jessie noticed the unpleasant odors. "Why does the guide bring you to these places?"

"Oh, there's a good reason, all right. They're usually safer. Like this one. The bend in the river makes it harder to attack the train. He says we'd hear the Indians coming when they splashed across the river. And I expect we would."

They listened to the lively music and laughter. "It sounds as if some of the women are enjoying themselves," Jessie said.

"Oh, they like the dancing and the fun part, all right, but most of them hate it as much as I do. Most of them had no idea they'd be starting West in a covered wagon until their men told them they were going."

The baby started to cry in earnest, so Sarah returned to her wagon.

For a long time, Jessie stared into the fire . . . trying to deal with what Sarah had told her. Finally she threw her shoulders back and struck her fist in the palm of her other hand. I'm not going to be like that, she vowed to herself. I won't be at the complete mercy of some man! I'm going to be my own person!

Somehow she'd establish her own identity, build her own security. Never, never, never would she be just chattel!

Chapter 5

It rained for the next three days. All along the way, they could see herds of buffalo through the mist and knew they were still in Sioux country.

When they stopped at the end of the day, the men placed the stagecoaches side by side. Tonio stretched a canvas tarp from the top of one coach to the top of the other so they could still cook and eat outdoors in spite of the rain. He taught her how to make a low-burning campfire that wouldn't scorch their coaches or send off sparks to catch the tarp on fire.

By now they were approaching the Rocky Mountains. They could see its forest-covered slopes off in the distance. It was the first time she had ever seen real mountains. The range loomed up ahead, magnificent, awe-inspiring, with peaks still white with snow. But it was so different from Missouri.

Before they headed for the pass that bisected the range, they camped for the night on the shores of a little lake. The next morning, they woke up to a clear, sunny day. Everywhere the grass was jeweled with dew. Spiderwebs, shimmering and perfect, festooned every bush. Great patches of buttercups and lupin glowed with color.

"What a glorious day!" Jessie exclaimed as she watched the early morning sun reflect off the lake's mirror surface. How good it was to be alive!

While they ate their oatmeal mush sweetened with molasses, Tonio said, "Once we get over the Continental Divide, we might not be near this much water for a while. I think we ought to spend the day here and wash our clothes and get cleaned up."

"Good!" Jessie cried. "Everything I own is dirty." Including myself, she thought. She'd take a real bath in the lake and shampoo her hair.

Carl finished his coffee. "I'd sure like to wash the mud off the coach. The wheels, especially."

Tonio stood up and stretched. "I'll get out my washtub. If you'll give me a hand, Carl, we'll fill it up and put it on the fire to heat."

They worked all morning, washing their clothes and spreading them on the grass to dry. They hung their sleeping bags and other bedding in the sunshine. Jessie brushed the dirt out of the coaches, while the men rinsed the mud off the wheels and bodies. With the campfire going all day, it gave Jessie a chance to bake bread and cook dried apples and prunes.

In the middle of the afternoon, Carl announced that he was going fishing, so he took off. Jessie picked a clean, dry towel off a bush and told Tonio that she was going to find a private spot along the lakeshore and take a bath.

She walked for nearly a mile until she found a sheltered cove. Aspen and birch trees grew along the shore. A completely private spot for a bath, she thought, as she pulled off her clothes and waded into the water.

At first she shivered with cold, but soon she grew accustomed to the water's temperature. How good it felt on her bare skin. So much better than the sponge baths she had to take in the coach. She rubbed her lavender soap all over, scrubbed her hair, and finally splashed water on herself. Just after she tossed the bar of soap up on the sand, she heard a sound. A rustle of leaves. What was it? A tremor of uneasiness rippled along her spine. She waited, but nothing happened. It must have been a deer finding its way through the woods, she decided, and waded out to where it was deeper to swim and rinse her hair.

But it wasn't a deer. All the time Jessie bathed, two

young Indian braves, hidden by the trees, watched and waited. Their faces, painted tan and green, blended in with the foliage. Their eyes glistened with lust.

Finally she came out of the water and stood on the beach. She raised her arms high above her head, glorying in the warm sunlight. After the long days of driving the coach through the rain, feeling the horses slipping in the mud, and bracing herself to stay on her perch, it felt so good to stretch and soak in the sun's rays.

Their breaths came in little gasps as the braves observed every move she made. She was as graceful as a doe when she wiped herself with her towel. She patted her face and neck, rubbed her white, satiny arms, then the back and front of her body, finally her feet, her calves, and her thighs. Beads of sweat broke out on their brows as they watched.

But why was she binding her breasts with a cloth? Why was she putting on a man's shirt and pants? Where was her full skirt? Why was she wearing boots?

They waited until she picked up her towel and rubbed her hair again. Soon she flung it over her shoulder and started back the way she came.

As silent as a leaf falling, they followed her. When they were close enough, one clapped a hand over her mouth, and the other grabbed her arms and twisted them behind her.

Frantically Jessie turned her head this way and that and saw their painted faces. Terror flooded through her, bringing strength to every part of her. She twisted, turned, and tried to pull away. She kicked one on the shin with her boot and heard him grunt. She raised her knee and caught one in the groin with a wicked thrust. He cried out, but tightened his grip. They scuffled in the dirt.

She could smell their body odors and hear them pant for breath as she fought. She yanked and twisted, first one way and then the other. But the one holding her arms behind her back yanked them higher, until she screamed in pain.

Jessie saw the lust in their eyes as they turned her around and headed toward their village.

Tonio looked at the sun uneasily. It was getting late. Why was Jessie taking so long? Carl had long since returned from fishing; he'd caught four trout. They had both bathed in the lake. They'd gathered up the dry clothes and linen that had been washed.

As they folded and sorted them, Carl said, "I wonder why Jessie doesn't return? She's no hand to wander off by herself. I think I'll start out and look for her."

Tonio reached for his rifle. "I'll search, too. She might have sprained her ankle or something. I didn't notice which way she went, so you go one way and I'll go the other."

As he hurried along, worry gnawed at him. Every instinct told him that she was in trouble, that something had happened.

While he followed the shoreline, he felt disgusted with himself for letting her go off alone. He should have gone along and protected her. She must have gone too far, which was a mistake. They should have all stayed together for protection. Frantically he searched for signs of her along the way. Had she fallen and injured herself?

When he came to the little cove, he looked around. With the screen of trees affording some privacy, this place would have suited her fine to take a bath. But had she? Finally he spotted a bar of soap in the sand. He picked it up and brushed it off. He smelled the lavender, her own fragrance. Yes, this must have been where she'd bathed.

But obviously she'd have started home when she was finished. Where was she now? He'd find her no matter what!

The braves stopped on their way, and, while one held her, the other took her towel and tore it lengthwise. They bound one part around her face, gagging her mouth, and one of them tied her hands together behind her back. On they went through the woods. The branches caught on her red-and-white plaid shirt and tore off a piece.

Almost paralyzed with fear, she glanced down at the strong brown fingers gripping her arm. Her knees nearly buckled under her, making her stumble. One of the braves snarled at her. She could see the naked lust in the other's eyes. The fear of rape shuddered through her. Surely this wasn't real. She must be having a nightmare. But she could hear them breathe and feel the pain in her wrists where they were bound together. She tried to scream, but only a gurgling sound came through the towel jammed in her mouth.

As they waded through a creek winding its way to the lake, they startled a deer, whose head was lowered to drink. The water seeped through her boots, making her socks feel cold and clammy.

It seemed to Jessie that they had been climbing up a rise for a long time when they finally stopped at the edge of a cliff and looked down at an Indian village in a meadow by the lake.

Buffalo-skin teepees dotted the grass. Smoke rising from campfires in front of each one trailed up into the sky. Boys and girls chased each other while their mothers cooked their dinners. The men sat in groups talking or playing a gambling game with stones.

The braves guided Jessie down the winding path on the face of the cliff. All the while a leaden lump of dread gathered in her stomach. Her blood froze in her veins. Tears of fear ran down her cheeks. What was going to happen to her? Would she be tortured? Would she be killed? Tonio and her father would probably never find her.

Her legs barely functioned as she stumbled along the narrow path with a brave in front of her and one behind. She was tempted to throw herself over the face of the cliff. It would be better to be dead than at the mercy of these Indians, who hated the white men who were taking over their lands. But as if he were reading her mind, the brave behind her grabbed the knotted towel at the back of her neck. There was no way she could escape.

Finally they were in the meadow approaching the village. Jessie could smell the stench of their garbage and excrement. A mangy dog came sniffing at her ankles. One brave kicked it away.

As they approached the village, the squaws stopped what they were doing to look at them. The children stood and stared, their big dark eyes round with astonishment. The men rose to their feet and moved toward them.

A big man, his dark face and chest painted more than the others, came forward. Two long black braids interwoven with beads hung on each side of his stern face. There was a dignified, commanding air about him. Obviously he was the chief, Jessie told herself, as a shudder of terror ran through her.

With many gestures, one of the captors explained what had happened in rapid, guttural sounds that she couldn't understand. The other pointed out her good features as if she were a horse for sale.

The expression on the chief's face didn't change as he listened. He put up his hand for silence, then turned to her. First he touched her hair. He lifted her short curls and let them snap back into place. Apparently they fascinated him, because he pulled them out and let them go, over and over again.

He issued a command and pointed to the gag on her mouth. One of the captors jumped to untie the knot at the back of her neck. As soon as it was loose, she screamed. With that, the chief scowled and slapped her across the mouth. From now on she'd better keep quiet, she thought, as tears sprang to her eyes.

The chief peered at her face and touched her cheek. He grabbed her chin, yanked her mouth open, and counted her teeth. Jessie shuddered as he felt her shoulder bones and down her spine.

He gave a command, and the towel around her wrists was untied. Then he flexed his arm; he pointed to her to do the same. She obeyed, and he encircled her bicep with fingers that felt like steel bands. She winced with pain. The other arm had to be examined as well. He studied

her hands, carefully feeling the callouses on her palms
that had come from driving the team.

He unbuttoned her shirt and yanked the cloth down so
he could see her breasts. He carefully felt each one while
she shuddered in horror. Was he going to strip her? she
wondered. Apparently not. He knelt and ran his hands
down her legs.

At last he was through. He issued a command, and the
two braves led her into the largest teepee. They gagged
her again, pulled her arms behind her, and tied her to a
supporting post. Wave after wave of terror washed over
her. What was going to happen?

As he shoved Jessie's soap into his pocket, Tonio tried
to decide what to do. Surely she didn't drown in the lake.
There were no clothes around, so she must have come
out and dressed. Had she wandered back into the woods
and gotten lost? But why would she do that? Then he
noticed the scuffled place in the dirt. Had some Indian
captured her? His blood ran cold at the very thought.

He had to do something. He decided to continue
around the lake and look for an Indian village. He followed the shoreline, as the natives would most likely live
close to water. He crossed a stream and eventually came
to a hill that protruded into a point in the lake.

It would be shorter to climb the hill, as there was no
way of getting around the point without a boat. But had
Jessie come this way? Maybe he was wasting precious
time. He fought his way through the thick woods, looking all around for some sign of her. Finally he spotted
the torn piece of red-and-white plaid cloth. He grabbed
it off the branch and examined it. It was from her shirt,
all right. He remembered seeing it on her many times.
At least he was on the right track. He tried not to think
about the savages who had her.

At last he reached the top, dropping down to crawl to
the edge so he wouldn't be seen below. When he looked
down and saw all the teepees, he felt certain he'd find
Jessie there.

He saw the path zigzagging down the face of the cliff,

but he'd be completely exposed to the Indians below. Someone was clever when he decided on the site for this village. The inhabitants were able to see a stranger approaching from the lake, the cliff, and the meadow. His only chance was to take the long way around, to the base of the cliff, and keep to cover as much as possible.

He hurried through the trees as fast as he could. Next time she took a bath in a lake, he'd sit with a gun and guard her. Dammit, anyway, he knew all along there'd be trouble if she came on the journey.

At long last he came to the meadow. Now to reach the village without getting an arrow in his back. He bent low and moved from one bush to the next until he was near. He took the safety off his rifle so it would be ready to fire if necessary.

Sweat broke out on his brow. Could he convince the Indians that this was a friendly visit? Or would he be captured himself? What chance would he have against all the men in the village?

Finally he stepped out, holding his rifle over his shoulder and raising his other arm above his head with his palm forward, hoping the Indians would interpret it as a friendly gesture.

The children stopped their playing and stared. The women huddled together and watched him suspiciously. The men approached with the chief in the lead.

The chief turned, motioned to a young boy about twelve to come forward, then stood with his arms folded across his chest.

"I'm White Cloud. I lived with a missionary for a while, so I speak English," the boy said. "I tell Chief Running Deer what you say."

"Tell him I don't intend to hurt anyone." While fear gnawed at his guts, he looked from one painted face to the other.

The chief spoke to the boy, who interpreted, "Put gun on the ground."

Even though he felt completely helpless without a firearm, Tonio placed the gun on the ground. He had no other choice.

The chief spoke again, and the boy asked, "What do you want?"

"I'm looking for a young woman. She's dressed like a man, but she's a woman. Is she here?"

After he had been told what had been said, the chief stood without answering for a long time. Behind him the young braves muttered among themselves. Finally they came forward and talked to the chief. One in particular argued his case. Now Tonio was convinced that they had Jessie.

Finally the chief barked an order, the men fell silent, and he talked to the boy.

"Maybe he give back the woman," White Cloud said at last. "What do you give him?"

Tonio put his foot on the rifle. "Bring the woman here so I know she's the right one."

Two of the braves ran to get Jessie, and, finally, she emerged out of the teepee, gagged again, with her hands tied behind her back. Her ashen, tear-streaked face, her torn shirt gaping open, made the anger boil through Tonio. But he must be careful, he warned himself. The negotiations were still delicate. The men led her forward until she stood by the chief. Some of the braves pleaded again, but the chief didn't answer.

"What are they saying?" Tonio asked White Cloud.

"They think the chief should keep her. Then when he's through with her, they can have her for themselves."

By the expression of horror in her eyes, Tonio knew that Jessie could hear the boy. He clenched his fists. It was all he could do to control himself.

The chief talked rapidly, then patted his chest. He pointed at Jessie.

Alarm raced through Tonio. "What's the chief talking about now?"

"He says the white woman's too tall and skinny. Too ugly. Hair too short. No bear grease in it." The boy patted his chest. "Too small up here. No good as a squaw."

The chief reached out and gripped Jessie's bicep. She winced in pain.

"The woman too weak," the boy went on. "The chief wants to know why you picked her."

"Because she can drive a team of horses."

As the boy interpreted, Tonio held his breath. Was the chief going to pass her over to the braves? What was going to happen?

For a long moment, no one spoke.

Finally the chief crossed his arms over his chest again and said something to the boy.

White Cloud turned to Tonio. "Chief Running Deer don't want her. Would rather have rifle."

Tonio fought down his laughter as he bent over, picked up the rifle, and held it out. "Tell the chief I give him rifle. He give me woman."

The boy said, "He wants the bullets, too."

Tonio emptied his pockets and handed the ammunition over.

One of the braves led Jessie to him. The chief spoke again, and the boy said, "Chief says he has a squaw he'll give you. Better than the one you've got."

Tonio shook his head. "Tell him that one woman is enough trouble."

The chief nodded in understanding.

When they were safely away from the Indians, Tonio stopped and roared with laughter. " 'Too ugly. Hair too short.' " He patted his chest. " 'Too small up here. No good as a squaw.' "

Jessie didn't know whether to laugh or cry. Finally she had to smile.

Tonio slapped his leg. "The old boy would rather have a rifle than you. If they had captured Iris, I'd have had to give them my coach and horses to get her back."

"Oh, shut up!"

Tears of laughter ran down his cheeks. "Even the Indians don't want you. And *I'm* stuck with you."

"Just stop it and let's go. Papa will be worried sick."

They hurried through the woods, Tonio still shaking his head and laughing.

It was almost dark by the time they reached their camp.

Carl came running and grabbed her in his arms when they arrived.

"I've been frantic. Just beside myself. I hunted everyplace for you. Tell me what happened."

"Let's talk while we eat supper," Tonio said. "I'm starved."

Carl had cleaned the trout, put potatoes in to bake, and wild parsnips on to boil already. It didn't take long to cook the fish, so they were soon eating.

Of course, Tonio told about the experience in great detail. "Chief Running Deer didn't want your daughter." His eyes sparkled with amusement. "Traded her for a rifle. I only paid five seventy-five for it." He slapped his leg and laughed some more. " 'Too tall and skinny. Too ugly. No good as a squaw.' "

"Oh, shut up!" she snapped.

"Even the Indians won't have her."

Drat Tonio. He'd never let her live this down.

After they passed through the Great Divide Basin, Jessie marked her map and announced, "We're almost two-thirds of the way."

By now it was the end of June. Just knowing that the waters flowed toward the Pacific Ocean instead of the Atlantic made her realize how far it was from St. Louis— and everything she held near and dear.

Sometimes she ached with homesickness. How she would love to see her friends again and visit her mother's grave. The Fourth would come and go with no celebration. Just their two coaches following the trail through the lonely wilderness. She tried not to think of the parade and the fun they would have back home.

"Do you ever get homesick?" she asked Tonio one night as they drove along. Because of the extreme heat, they were traveling after dark and resting in the daytime. It was easier on the horses and saved water.

"If you mean for my family in Chicago, of course I do. But I've lived in Sacramento for three years—and have so many plans—that I've gotten weaned away."

"You've talked about expanding. Tell me more about

it in detail." There was something intimate about the soft darkness that inspired confidences.

"Well, I want to concentrate on the West Coast north of Sacramento. So many of the stage lines go to the mines to the east that there isn't much room left for a Johnny-come-lately like me. But there's lots more to California than just mining. All that northern area is opening up for cattle ranching, wheat, and fruit. Those people need transportation, too. I'd like to establish routes clear to Portland, Oregon. Carl has a real future with our staging company. He'll do well."

He told her just where he'd locate his stations, how many horses he hoped to have, and the kind of drivers he wanted. As he talked, he thought how easy it was to confide in Jessie about his dreams for the future. She acted so interested.

Iris, on the other hand, always changed the subject. She'd say, "Don't talk about it. You're gone from Sacramento too much as it is." Then pout prettily. "I want you right here—so you can escort me to all the parties."

Before he realized it, he said aloud, "Iris doesn't cotton to all my ideas."

"If you're serious about her, that's going to be a problem." A queer resentful sensation ran through Jessie. If she didn't know better, she'd think she was a little jealous of Tonio's ladylove. Of course that's ridiculous, she scolded herself. What difference did it make to her whom he married?

"I'm serious about her, all right. But I've got to make sure I can support her before I court her. As I've told you, her father is mighty well-heeled. Owns half a producing gold mine. They own a great big house not far from where they're building the new capitol. Even has a ballroom. Out in the back there are stables with different carriages and six matched bays. I guess I've told you before that Andrew Cunningham is one of the bigwigs in the state legislature."

Yes, she heard many times about how important Andrew Cunningham was. And about the elegant house and the Chinese servants that kept it all running.

"Iris is used to a lot. Whether she could settle down to being a stagecoach driver's wife, I don't know. If she weren't so bewitching, I'd forget all about her. But I guess she's got me under her spell."

Jessie lowered her arms, held the reins loose, and relaxed. Once again she was expected to listen to Tonio sing Iris's praises. Maybe the big moon casting a silver sheen over the countryside made him feel romantic.

"Iris is the exact opposite of you, Jess. She's small and dainty, but has a real feminine figure. You know, an hourglass form with a tiny waist. I can put my two hands around it." Jessie glanced at him as he made a circle with his fingers.

"Boy, is she a beauty," Tonio went on. "Her hair is the color of gold. I swear, if you held a nugget up to her hair it would be the same. Her eyes aren't as big as yours, but they're a beautiful blue. She has long dark lashes, though. I'd say her feet are about half the size of yours. Her hands, too."

"Thanks a lot."

"Well, she could no more drive a six-horse hitch than fly to the moon. She couldn't make the trip across the country like you have. She'd have to come by ship. Doesn't have your stamina."

Jessie never felt so overgrown and hefty in her life. "I guess you have to be dainty and feminine to catch a husband. That lets me out. Not that I'm the least bit interested in getting married."

"Don't worry. You won't end up an old maid like your Aunt Bertha. Women are mighty scarce in California. Any female could get married. Even you." He grinned to himself. He knew he was getting her goat again. But his face fell. Somehow he didn't like the idea of her being someone's else's wife. What if some guy mistreated her? God, he'd kill a man with his own two fists if he didn't treat her right.

"What are you going to do when we get to Sacramento?" he asked at last.

"The first thing I must do is find a place for us to live. I want to make a comfortable home for Papa."

"It won't be easy. Sacramento's such a new place, there isn't much available."

"In any case, I want to do something to earn a living."

"You won't have to, Jess. Carl will do real well with us. He'll be able to support you. And I'll get Iris to introduce you to all her friends so you can go to all the tea parties."

Somehow the idea of spending her days going to tea parties with Iris didn't appeal to her at all. She wanted to accomplish something in her own right, to be independent. It had been wonderfully satisfying to learn to drive a stagecoach. Even Tonio would have to admit she was good at it. And she had conquered most of her fear of horses, which was something.

Once this journey was over and they were settled in Sacramento, what lay ahead for her?

Chapter 6

When they arrived at Salt Lake City, in the desert of Utah Territory, Jessie suggested, "Let's stay at a hotel and have a real bath and a good meal." She was travel-worn and anxious for a change.

But when they found a hotel and went in to register, the desk clerk looked at them suspiciously and asked, "Are you Mormons or gentiles?"

"Gentiles?" Tonio asked. "What do you mean?"

"Are you non-Mormon?"

"That's right." He pulled out his wallet. "What difference does it make?"

"We don't rent to gentiles."

"You don't?" Tonio's face flushed in anger. "Then we'll go someplace else."

"You won't find anyplace in this town that'll take you." The clerk snapped his register shut. "We don't want non-Mormons here. Immigrants or travelers. We don't want you passing through our territory."

They camped at the edge of the desert town, puzzled by the hostility they found everywhere.

Even the next morning, when they stopped at a feed store to buy supplies, the owner said, "We don't sell to gentiles here. If you want something, go on to Fort Wallace and get it from the U.S. Army."

It took all morning, traveling through the desert, to come to Fort Wallace. The low, sprawling fort was con-

structed with adobe bricks baked in the hot desert sun.
When they approached the guard at the entrance, he told
them to halt while he reported to his sergeant, who finally came to greet them.

"You can pull your rigs inside our barricade at the
back, so you can feed and water your horses."

When Carl told the sergeant about their experience in
Salt Lake City, the soldier nodded. "There's lots of hos-
tility against immigrants. In a way you can't blame the
Mormons. They've been terribly persecuted."

Jessie spoke up. "Why take it out on us, though?"

"We get it all the time. One thing they resent is that
the territory has applied for statehood more than once,
and Congress keeps turning them down."

"But that has nothing to do with us," Carl said.

"The main trouble goes back to something that happened three years ago. It seems that a band of Mormons
and Indians attacked a wagon train. The immigrants sur-
rendered, but the attackers killed them all—except for
seventeen children. President Buchanan sent the troops
out here. We rounded up the Mormon who was the leader,
and he was executed. Then this fort was built to guard
the immigrants coming West. All this caused a lot of bad
feeling among the people living in Salt Lake City."

When the horses had been put in stables and fed, and
they had refreshed themselves, they went into the main
building of the fort to pay their respects to the commanding officer, Captain Blackston, a man in his forties
with long sideburns that were wide at the bottom, covering his jaw.

He shook hands and said, "We're about to have lunch.
Won't you join me?" He led them into the officers' mess
which was decorated with handsome handwoven Indian
rugs and colorful pottery.

Jessie had just settled herself at a table when she looked
up at the most handsome man she had ever seen. The
captain introduced him as Lieutenant Underwood. Tall,
erect, with his brown hair combed just so, he looked
every inch the West Point graduate. A shiver of appreciation ran through her as she gazed into his gray-green

eyes. Never before had she felt such instant attraction to a man. A long sigh escaped her. Now she knew how her friends felt when they giggled and raved over a new man they had met.

As their lunch progressed, the captain questioned them about where they were going.

Tonio answered, "We're going to Sacramento, sir. I'm in the coaching business there—with my cousin. Would it be possible to buy feed for our horses this afternoon? We'd like to start across the desert at sundown."

"Yes, we can sell you feed. We'll go to my office when we're finished and I'll write an order."

Later, when they went into his office, the captain asked the lieutenant to come in with them and shut the door.

When the order had been written, the captain leaned back in his officer's chair. "Gentlemen, would it be possible for you to take Lieutenant Underwood with you? He has some urgent business for the government to take care of in California. I believe you could get him there quicker than any other way. You'd be reimbursed, of course."

Jessie hardly listened to the rest of the arrangements. All she could think about was Lieutenant Underwood. This handsome man would be going with them—to add excitement to a journey that was getting to be very tiring and routine.

When it was almost time to leave, the lieutenant put his gear in Tonio's coach. "My name is Lyle, and we might as well start out on a first-name basis."

"Good. I'm Tonio, and this is Carl and Jess."

"We'd all like to make your acquaintance," Carl put in, "so why don't you take turns riding on the two coaches?"

"Great. Then I'll start out with Tonio." He pulled himself up in the box.

That arrangement suited Jessie just fine—because it meant that Lyle would be riding with her when she relieved her father around midnight. Now she curled herself up on the backseat on the coach to get a few hours' rest before she took over the reins.

When they stopped for their break at midnight, Lyle walked over to Carl's coach. The lamplight glowed on his attractive face. Jessie's knees felt a little weak just looking at him. Shivers of excitement ran through her.

"Aren't you kind of young to be driving such a big coach?" he asked.

Without thinking, Carl rose to her defense. "She's one of the best whips I've ever seen. Dadgummit, but it sure surprised me the way she took to the ribbons."

"She? You mean you're a girl?" Lyle stared at her in surprise.

"That's right. You might as well know it right now. And if you'd rather not ride with me, feel free to stay with Tonio."

But Tonio detected the disappointment in her voice. Wow, she sure had taken a shine to this lieutenant right off! While he walked around his team to examine a fetlock or pastern here and there, he felt a rush of anger. Dammit, why did this Prince Charming have to join them, anyway? They were getting along just fine the way they were!

But he had to admit they could use the money the army was paying them for this soldier boy's transportation. Trying to keep the resentment out of his voice, he spoke up. "There's nothing but flat desert for the rest of the night. If you can stay on your perch, you'll be okay. So hop up there. It's time to go."

Happily Jessie watched as the lieutenant climbed up on her coach. Now to get rid of her father! "Papa, it's your turn to stretch out on the backseat."

"I'll do that. It's easier to sleep now than when it's so blasted hot."

She gathered up the reins and quickly got herself in the driver's seat. Her whip caressed Popcorn's flanks, and they were off. They went bowling along, with the leaders' heads high and the wheels humming.

"I'm impressed that a young girl—"

"I'm a twenty-year-old woman."

"Tell me about yourself. You have me quite intrigued."

She told him about living in St. Louis and losing her mother. She still couldn't talk about it without getting a lump in her throat. Then she related the adventures on their journey, including her narrow escape from Aunt Bertha. "Now it's your turn."

"I was born and raised in Philadelphia. My father is a lawyer, but my grandfather was an army officer. That's what I've always wanted to be. Fort Wallace is my first tour of duty."

They talked the rest of the night, laughing and interrupting each other. By the time the sun came up, Jessie knew she had never been so enchanted with a man. When she climbed down from the box—and Tonio saw her radiant face and her big brown eyes glowing—he gave a cactus plant a vicious kick. He had little to say as he went around gathering dried materials to start a fire.

By the end of the third night, Jessie was so smitten with Lyle, she was hardly aware that a strong wind was beginning to blow.

Soon the sand-filled wind whipped across the desert, blowing tumbleweed in its path and flipping the leather curtains on the coaches. Somehow Jessie managed to keep the debris out of the flapjacks she was cooking.

"We're in for a real sandstorm," the lieutenant said. "We can't stay here out in the open. Come on, get going. We've got to find an arroyo or a dry gully to camp inside to get some protection."

Tonio's face turned dark red. He put his hand on his hip. "Look, Lieutenant, let's get one thing straight. Just because you're an army officer doesn't give you the right to issue orders to us. You're a paying passenger, and that's all."

Lyle stuck his face close to Tonio's. "Listen, I've lived here in Utah for over two years. I know a hell of a lot more about sandstorms than you do. We'd better find some place out of the worst of this wind pretty damn fast—or every bit of the finish on your coaches will be sandblasted off! And it could kill your horses. So get a move on."

By the time they were on their way, the wind was

blowing harder. It hit the side of the coaches, swaying them from side to side.

Lyle rode with Carl, and they took the lead. At her father's insistence, Jessie stayed inside the coach. They had secured the leather curtains over the windows to keep the sand out of the coaches. She looked out the back at the poor horses trailing along behind. They whinnied and neighed and tossed their heads in the air in protest to the stinging sand.

Soon Lyle guided them off the main trail to a dry gully in a hillside. They put the horses in first and parked the coaches in the entrance. Although they still felt the wind, they no longer took the brunt of the storm.

Jessie looked around. "This is a lot better."

"It's all right if it doesn't start to rain," Tonio pointed out. He still smarted from Lyle's aggressiveness. "I reckon they have flash floods in this country. That's how this gully was made in the first place."

Carl asked, "Do these windstorms always bring on rain?"

"No," Lyle answered. "Not even those that last several days."

Tonio groaned. "Ye gods, several days?"

"That's right, Maguire. All we can do is wait it out."

"We can't waste a lot of time here," Tonio said.

"We may have to. So let's settle in the best we can."

"We'll stay here for the day, but we're starting out as soon as the sun goes down." How this pretty boy riled him! "You rest inside the coach, and I'll spread my sleeping bag out beside the wheel."

As Lyle climbed in, he looked over his shoulder at Tonio. "Be sure to keep your back to the wind."

Tonio made a fist and choked down his irritation. This was only the beginning of the fourth day, and they had nearly eight hundred miles to go. How was he going to stand this guy? Soldier Boy was much too handsome, much too know-it-all. Besides, Jessie was all too smitten, as well. He didn't like that one little bit. He'd like to tell her how silly she was acting. But instead, Tonio stretched out his bag and tucked himself in. Bone-tired, he finally fell asleep, in spite of the turbulence around him.

The wind blew all day with vicious intensity, as if some evil monster had loosened his force on the land. The sand swirled across the open desert, piling up in dunes, filling the air with sharp, biting particles.

Although the coaches were in the arroyo, they still felt the backlash of the storm. As they swayed back and forth, the stiff leather boots and curtains banged against panels. All Jessie could think about was Lyle. She wanted to look more feminine and appealing, so she took the binding off her breasts.

At the end of the day, the men walked around holding the water bucket up to each horse's mouth, letting them drink only the bare minimum to save their supply.

Jessie tried to build a fire, but the sand soon smothered the flames. Her shirt plastered against her.

Of course, Tonio noticed her changed figure right away. He grinned at her. "I take it that's not for my benefit. But even so, I'm enjoying the view."

Her face turned scarlet. Drat him, anyway. Her eyes watered with the wind, and tears ran down her cheeks, streaking the dust on her face.

He took a bandanna out of his pocket, poured a little water on it, and washed her face before she could stop him. "You look more alluring with the dirt off your face."

"Tonio Maguire, you're the most provoking man I ever knew!" Yanking the coach door open, she climbed back in.

Now what could she fix for their supper? She opened the grub box, took out a loaf of bread and a bowl of cooked beans to fix sandwiches. Since there was no way to make coffee, she opened a precious can of peaches so they could moisten their mouths.

When all four of them crowded into the coach to eat, it seemed suffocatingly hot and airless with the leather curtains down. Tonio opened the door away from the wind.

Lyle spoke up. "Close it, Maguire. Unless you want the coach filled with sand."

Tonio gritted his teeth in irritation; it was all he could do to control his temper. He'd be damned if he'd obey orders from this tin soldier. But when a gust of wind whirled around the side of the coach, the door banged shut, shaking the vehicle.

Jessie let out a little sigh of relief. As she watched the two men, she sensed the hostility between them. They were like two male bears trying to establish their dominance.

"Likely the wind'll die down when the sun sets, so we'll get going again," Tonio said.

"Maguire, you're out of your mind. We're staying right here—even if the wind dies down." Lyle sat up as erect as possible.

"I say we're moving on if the storm's over." Tonio's face reddened; his eyes sparked with anger.

Lyle's lip turned up. "It's obvious you don't know much about the desert. Don't you realize that the trail has been covered with sand? Completely obliterated. How are you going to find your way in the dark? You could go around and around in circles."

Tonio couldn't answer. Pretty Boy had made him look like a fool.

"What you must do," Lyle went on, "is to wait for daylight. Whether it's hot or not, you have to travel by using a compass until you pick up the trail again." He shrugged. "The sandstorm won't be over, anyway. It'll blow all night."

Tonio had to get away from Pretty Boy or he'd explode, he told himself. He turned to Carl. "How about coming over to my coach and playing cards? It'll be light quite awhile yet."

That suited Jessie just fine. She and Lyle wiped the dishes off with a damp cloth and stacked them back in the grub box. In spite of the blowing sand, it seemed so snug and cozy in the coach. For a long time they sat opposite each other and talked. While the coach swayed back and forth, Lyle told her about his life in the army.

Finally he moved over to her side and took her hands

in his. "I'm afraid Tonio's getting provoked with me. He acts as if he's jealous. Because of you, I mean."

"Jealous because of me?" Jessie threw her head back and laughed. "Of course he isn't! He's got a girl in Sacramento. Her name's Iris."

"Oh, then I had things sized up wrong. I'd of sworn he was in love with you. And you with him."

What a ridiculous idea, she told herself. Just the same, she felt a strange jolt at the suggestion. "Well, you're mistaken. As a matter of fact, I'll be glad when we get to California so I won't have to see him all the time."

He put his arm across the back of the seat. "In that case, I'm not moving in on his territory."

The blood raced through her veins. As she looked up at him, she thought she'd melt inside. What a handsome man he was. She felt she was at a feast as she gazed at his chiseled features, his flawless, light skin, his intelligent eyes under thick brows. His light brown hair always looked so neat—in spite of the wind—in contrast to Tonio's tousled curls. He seemed so suave and sophisticated.

He reached over, tipped her chin up, and kissed her lightly. "You're a charming, lovely girl. I'm so amazed at all the things you can do." They heard the door of the other coach slam shut. "Your father's coming, so I'd better go." With that Lyle opened the door and slipped out.

As she slept that night, she dreamed that Lyle proposed to her. She awoke at dawn and lay curled up in her bed thinking about him, imagining what it would be like married to him.

Her daydream was shattered when Tonio pounded on the door and shouted, "The wind's died down, so we'd better get going as soon as possible. We can stop for breakfast later, when it gets too hot to travel."

When they were harnessing the horses, Lyle walked around studying the horizon and looking at a compass he held in his hand. He came back and said, "I think I know where to go to avoid the deep sand and to pick up the trail. So you drive, Jessie, and I'll ride with you. We'll lead the way."

Tonio's face turned dark red; his eyes sparked dangerously. He started to protest, but Carl put his hand on his
arm. "Take it easy. I'll go with you. It's better this way."

Everywhere there were new sand dunes blown up
against the gray-green ironwood trees, yucca, and oco-
tillo. Long, undulating waves in the sand reflected the
rays from the rising sun, some orange, some gold. Off in
the distance, the barren hills changed from dove gray to
pink. It was breathtakingly beautiful, as if a new desert
had been born by rearranging the old.

In contrast to the raging tumult of the day before, everything seemed especially quiet and sparkling. The
horses plunged forward, the muscles on their flanks and
loins rippling, snorting and gulping in the clear air. Jessie could feel the swaying of the coach beneath her and
hear the jingle of the trace rings and the steady rumble
of hoofs. How good it was to be alive, especially with
Lyle next to her. A shiver of exultation ran through her.

Her huge brown eyes sparkled as she turned to him. "It's
wonderful how you're keeping us on hard ground. Tell me if
I'm off-course."

"I will." He studied his compass, then pointed. "See
that crevice in the mountain way off in the distance?"

"Yes."

"Head for that. I think that's a pass through the range.
We should pick up the Overland Trail on the other side."
He turned to her. "I suppose you've been told a thousand
times how beautiful your eyes are."

She blushed—and wanted to say that hearing it from
him meant more than all the other compliments put together. But she kept her silence.

Swerving and turning to avoid the dunes, they raced
across the desert. As the sun rose higher in the sky, it
began to get hot. Jess wondered when they would be
stopping to give them all a break.

Tonio turned to Carl. "Dammit, why don't they stop?
Here it is ten o'clock—and we haven't even had breakfast
yet! The horses need to be fed, as well."

"Maybe Lyle's going to find us a good place to camp
for the day."

"I doubt it." Tonio let out a snort of disgust. "Pretty Boy's so damned full of himself. Much too big for his britches. I wish we didn't have him along."

"He's been a burr under your saddle, hasn't he?"

"Yeah. Right from the start. But your daughter's sure taken with him."

"Dadgummit, she'd better get over that foolishness. Likely to get her heart broken."

In spite of the reins he was holding, Tonio bent his hands into fists. If anyone hurt Jessie, they'd have to answer to him.

Tonio said aloud, "Why the hell don't we stop? Here we are, rushing across the desert, and we'll end up camping out in the scorching heat anyway!"

But when they entered the pass through the canyon, Lyle motioned for Jessie to slow down. He jumped out and knelt down by a little streak of green along the edge of the trail.

Tonio pulled up behind them. "It's about time we stopped!"

Lyle shook his head. "No. We're not stopping here. There's a spring up ahead. So follow me." He climbed up beside Jessie again.

The sweat ran down the horses' flanks and they gasped for breath. But Jessie flicked the whip above their heads, and they took off again.

Tonio fumed with anger as he trailed behind. Slowly they followed the thread of green until they came to a gap in the canyon wall—and saw a little meadow, lush with grass, at the bottom. A small spring gushed forth, forming an oval pool so the horses could drink their fill before they grazed. This shady oasis was protected from the sun by the canyon walls.

"How marvelous," Jessie exclaimed as she climbed down. This lieutenant was not only the most handsome man she had ever seen, but the most capable one by far. "Wasn't Lyle clever to find this place?"

"He sure was," Carl agreed, but Tonio didn't answer.

Lyle helped her start a fire so she could fix breakfast. "I've made quite a study of the desert for army maneu-

vers. Usually there's a good supply of underground water. Occasionally it come to the surface in the form of
springs. It's a question of finding them.''

They ate breakfast, filled the water containers, and
washed themselves. Then they found shady spots to sleep
during the hot day.

After they ate another meal at the end of the afternoon,
Lyle stood up. ''Get a move on, everyone.''

Tonio's eyes snapped. His face turned red. He grabbed
Lyle by the shoulder. ''We don't need you issuing orders,
Underwood.''

''Let go of me.'' Lyle's fist flew out and landed on the
side of Tonio's mouth.

Tonio hauled off and hit Lyle in the stomach. Soon the
two men were hammering each other.

''Papa, stop them!'' Jessie screamed as she grabbed at
Tonio's shirt. This was awful.

Carl yanked Jessie away. ''Dadgummit, leave 'em
alone. They've been itching for a fight ever since we left
Fort Wallace. Let 'em get it out of their systems.''

The two fighters broke contact and warily circled each
other, their fists up and bodies bent. Their beet-red faces
glistened with sweat as they danced around, sizing each
other up. They were well matched, about the same height
and weight.

Tonio feigned and ducked, stepping from one side to
the other to ward off Lyle's fists. He took another blow
on the face, turned to one side to receive a glancing hit
on his shoulder. He waited his chance and threw a ham-
mer fist at the lieutenant's jaw.

Lyle staggered back, slipped on the grass, and fell to
the ground. Tonio dived on top of him, only to be turned
over on his back. Back and forth the fight went. First one
winning and then the other.

But Jessie couldn't stand it any longer. She dropped to
her knees beside the men. ''Stop it! Stop this right now!''
She reached for Lyle's arm—just as his fist flew out and
caught her on the jaw!

The next thing she knew, her father was talking. ''Now

you two men shake hands. The fight was a draw, so no one won.''

Tonio put out his hand. ''You're damned good, soldier. I'll have a shiner for a week.''

Lyle shook his hand. ''You're not bad yourself, Maguire.'' He touched his face and winced. ''My poor nose. One of these days we'll have to put on some gloves and go a few rounds.''

''Now clean yourselves up and break camp,'' Carl put in. ''Lyle, help Tonio round up the horses so we can be on our way.''

He picked up Jessie, carried her to the coach, and carefully laid her out on the backseat. He slid a pillow under her head.

She moaned a little and tried to sit up. ''What happened?''

''Take it easy, Jess. You got a good sock on the jaw. Knocked you out. You had no business butting in.''

She fought back a sob. ''Papa, are they still fighting?''

''Hell, no. It stopped as soon as you were knocked out.''

She grabbed her father's arm. ''Papa, what are we going to do?'' Dread knotted her stomach.

''Do? What do you mean?''

''It's so awful. Them fighting that way—''

''Daughter, you don't understand men at all. That's the best thing that could've happened. Don't you see it cleared the air?''

Jessie had to admit that Lyle was a bit overbearing, and Tonio was building up a head of steam in resentment. ''Were either of them hurt?''

''Tonio has a shiner, and Lyle's nose is a mess. The fight ended in a draw, so nobody's pride was hurt. They shook hands. They'll both have a lot more respect for each other from now on.''

But as Jessie laid her throbbing head back on the pillow, every instinct told her that the rivalry between the men was far from over.

Chapter 7

Nevada, the western section of the Utah Territory, was part of the vast stretches of land acquired by the United States in the treaty of Guadalupe Hidalgo, after the Mexican war.

As their little caravan followed the trail, Jessie felt awed by the land, which was filed with range upon range of dry, gray-green mountains, one folding into the other, lonely and immense. When the setting sun cast long shadows across the land and turned the hills soft pink and orange, it was profoundly beautiful in its own way.

The flatlands and the lower hills were dotted with sagebrush, its small gray leaves especially designed to conserve water. At the base of the bushes was bunch grass, where the horses could graze.

Each day they rose at four in the morning, ate a hasty breakfast, and began their journey again when it was light enough to see. They rested during the worst of the heat, then started out again as soon as they could.

"We'll soon pick up the Humboldt River," Tonio announced one noon. "It drives the horses crazy. They smell the water and want to get down to it, but you can't let them."

"Why not?" Carl asked.

"The water's full of alkali. Makes the animals sick."

Jessie spoke up. "I wonder how they discovered that."

"You can't miss it," Lyle put in, not giving Tonio a

chance to answer. "You'll see the white mineral salt on the banks of the river. We have sinkholes and areas like that in the Utah deserts."

Carl turned to Jessie. "I'll drive. It's going to take strong wrists to keep the team in line."

"Then I'll round up the horses." Jessie swallowed the dread that always rose in her throat when it came time to harness the team. But she'd never let her father and Tonio know just how she felt.

She no longer minded driving them when she was up high in the box. But when she stood on the ground and had to grab them by the halters and back them into their positions on each side of the pole, she still felt shivers of fear.

"Put Prince at the wheel this time," Carl called out.

That made it even worse. Prince was skittish and hard to handle. Apparently he didn't like the wheel position; he always balked when placed there.

"I'll help you," Lyle volunteered.

A rush of admiration for Lyle came over her as they walked out to where the horses were grazing. Even in his fatigues he looked neat and incredibly handsome.

"You're afraid of horses, aren't you?" he asked.

She looked at him in surprise. "How did you know?"

"Because you get so white around your mouth when you have to harness them."

She had never known a man to be so understanding, she told herself. No wonder she had fallen for him so hard.

Lyle took her elbow. "I think your father and Tonio should do it for you. And, by God, I'm going to tell them so."

Jessie grabbed his arm. "Oh, no. No. Don't say anything. They didn't want me to come on this trip. I swore to myself that I'd do my part all the way, so they wouldn't regret it."

"But, Jessie, you're doing more than your share. You do most of the cooking . . . and spend hours driving. It isn't right that you have to harness the team, too. Especially when you're afraid."

"I'll get over this foolishness. I'm lots better than I was."

She walked over to Prince, grabbed his bridle, and tried to make him move. He dug his hoofs into the ground and balked. He was a big roan, nearly seventeen hands. "Come on, Prince. That's a good boy."

"Here, let me try." Lyle took the bridle and yanked the horse's head back with a snap. As the bit cut his mouth, he reared up and neighed in pain and fright.

"Lyle! Stop! You're hurting him."

"You've got to let them know who's in charge. By God, if I had a whip, I'd straighten him out in a hurry."

Shocked, Jessie stared at him, then looked toward the coach. She hoped her father hadn't heard Prince. He never treated his horses so roughly—and he'd be furious if he knew what had happened.

Still shaken by the incident, she chose another wheeler and led the way to the coach. Prince came meekly with the lieutenant. When the team was harnessed, Lyle climbed into the box. Instead of getting up beside him, she walked over to Tonio's coach and pulled herself up on the seat next to the driver's. Of course, army officers had to be authoritative, she told herself. That was their training at West Point. Otherwise, how could they command their troops?

But all the time she watched Tonio, she noticed how gentle and kind he was as he fastened the harnesses. "Atta girl. You're not going to give me any trouble at all, are you? You're a sweetheart." The mare rubbed her muzzle on his chest and whinnied softly.

He loved his horses, just the way her father always had, and the animals sensed it. Perhaps that's why Lyle's treatment of Prince had been so distasteful. Determined to push it out of her mind, she glanced up at Tonio and smiled.

The Humboldt River, its banks frosted with white alkali deposits, wound its sluggish way through the desert. They watched the jackrabbits leap among the sagebrush as they drove by. The wind blew tumbleweeds across the trail. What a desolate, dreary part of the country, she told herself.

When they stopped to fix supper that night, Tonio dug a pit in the ground—one foot wide, two feet deep, and two feet long—in which to burn sagebrush for their fire. When it was filled with chopped-up brush and lighted, it burned down into perfect coals for cooking. The wind didn't blow it out, and it lasted all night and was ready in the morning for breakfast.

Jessie wandered away from the camp to find firewood. She had just reached down to cut a dead piece of sage-brush when she heard a rattling sound. She froze in fear. Before she could draw back, a diamond-patterned snake struck her in the arm. She screamed, and the men came running.

"What happened?" Carl yelled.

"A snake bit me." She pointed to the big snake slith-ering away.

"It's a rattler. I'll get my gun," Lyle said. But first he pulled his scarf off and made a tourniquet around her arm. "Leave her alone, everybody. I'll go get my first-aid kit."

While he ran to the coach, Tonio sterilized a pocket-knife with a match. "I'll take care of it." He made a crosscut over the bite and sucked the poison out, spitting it on the ground. He was sucking on the wound again when Lyle returned.

"Maguire, I told you to leave her alone." Lyle's face reddened with anger.

"Listen, Soldier Boy, the poison could've gone all through her while you were getting your tin box. I've sucked it out, so you put some iodine and a bandage on it now."

Lyle pushed Tonio away. "I'll take over now."

"Watch it. I don't take orders from you."

"Stop it, both of you!" Jessie cried out. Tears washed her eyes. "Hurry up and bandage me, Lyle. And take that tourniquet off. My arm aches."

Carl insisted that she lie down in the coach after Lyle

was through. "You should be as quiet as possible—to give your body a chance to throw off that poison."

"I'll fix supper," Tonio offered.

Later, long after the men were asleep, she lay in the coach with her arm aching, listening to the coyotes howl. Oh, how she wished she were back home in St. Louis with her mother alive and everything normal again.

Apparently Tonio's quick action kept her from suffering any effects from the snakebite. Although they left the Humboldt River, Jessie was beginning to wonder if they would ever get out of desert. Then one day, far to the west, they could see the towering Sierra Nevada range, its highest peaks still covered with snow.

"You're looking at California," Tonio told them when they stopped for lunch. "Except for a small corner that cuts into Lake Tahoe, the whole range lies within California's boundaries."

Carl wiped the sweat off his brow. "There must be some kind of pass through them."

"No, it's a huge chunk of granite about four hundred miles long—with no openings. We have to climb over it."

With his hands on his hips, Carl stared at the high mountains. "Dadgummit, Tonio. How the hell are we going to do that?"

"It's a hard pull. We'll be doing a lot of pushing. You'll get practice in mountain driving, Jess. You'll probably do most of it, while we men push the coach from the rear."

Her stomach tightened with dread at the very thought. Driving over the flat desert trail was a breeze compared to what lay ahead, she reasoned.

As they approached the high range, they turned south to pick up the route the stage lines used between Carson City, in Nevada, and Sacramento, in California. But first they had to ford a river that ran through a fertile valley. In contrast to the brackish, alkali-laden Humboldt, this crystal-clear river was fed from the melting snow in the Sierra.

They camped beside it and, while it was still daylight,

the men explored its banks to find the safest place to ford.

"I'd cross here," Lyle said, pointing toward the water. "It seems to have the sandiest bottom."

Carl looked it over carefully. "I think you're right."

Tonio shook his head. "No, the banks are too steep getting down there. I don't think it'll do."

Lyle's face flushed. "No matter *what* I suggested, you'd be against it."

"That's ridiculous, and you know it!" Tonio snapped.

"Take it easy, Tonio," Carl warned. "Let's see what else we can find."

They finally all agreed on one spot, but Lyle put in, "I still think my first choice is better."

"Listen, Underwood, it's not up to you to decide!" Tonio fought down his temper.

"I've had a lot of training for maneuvers, so I know something about moving equipment."

It was Lyle's very logic that Tonio found so irritating. Of course, he *was* right, but why did it bother him so? Was it because Jessie was falling in love with this soldier? He leaned over and picked up a rock, then sent it skimming across the river. What if she was? What difference did it make to him? Iris was waiting for him in Sacramento, wasn't she?

Tonio watched Jessie set the table for supper. Just as the Indian chief had said, she was too tall and skinny, without much bosom. Her sunburned skin looked like old leather. Yet she had courage and charm. Her big dark eyes were incredible. Dammit, in her own way she was beautiful. He hoped Pretty Boy appreciated her.

The next morning, they got the coaches ready with their strongest horses in the team.

Carl spoke up. "I'll drive, and you younger men can be ready to push—in case the wheels get stuck in the mud."

"Papa, I'm not afraid to drive. That leaves you free to shove if you have to."

"No," Lyle burst out. "Jessie, you shouldn't try to take the coach across this swift river. It's too dangerous."

He turned to Carl and Tonio. "You men expect too much of her."

"No one asked your opinion, Underwood," Tonio retorted.

"I insist," Jessie said. "Come on, let's go."

The men had chosen a crossing where the banks weren't too steep, but still she braced herself against the dashboard with all her might as they headed down. She didn't want to go sliding off the seat onto the wheelers. The men held on to the back axle to keep the coach from going too fast or tipping too much from side to side. Down, down they went, with the wheels rumbling over the rocks.

The leaders stepped into the water, which swirled around their knees. One of them turned his head, as if he were questioning her judgment. She flipped the reins, and they moved forward. The swift current hit the leaders and swingers broadside and pushed them downstream a little.

Finally the wheelers plunged into the river, bringing the coach with them.

Her father yelled, "Crack your whip, Jess. Keep 'em going."

Jessie snapped the whip above their heads.

"Hit 'em on the rump!" Lyle yelled.

But the leaders forged ahead, stumbling over the rocks, yanking and jerking the harness. Tonio and Carl guided the back wheels, turning them when they sank in the sand, while Lyle pushed the coach with all his might.

Now the water swirled around the horses' bellies. They raised their heads, neighing with their eyes rolling back.

"Keep 'em going," Carl yelled again. "The water's deeper than I thought."

Jess cracked the whip again, her stomach tight with fear. She could feel the coach lurch and creak as the swift current hit. They were halfway across the river now. She could hear the horses gasping for breath, the water tumbling over the rocks, and the men grunting as they shoved and pushed. Her teeth chattered with fright in the early morning cold.

The horses struggled with the weight of the coach in the swirling, pounding water, which was getting deeper. Just before they reached the other side, the offside leader, Webster, stepped into a hole. He thrashed around, trying to find ground. Only his nostrils and terror-stricken eyes were above the water. Because he was strapped in the harness, he couldn't swim.

He'll drown! Jessie cried to herself. She had to act fast. There wasn't time to call the men. She threw the reins down and dropped from the dashboard to the pole, now under the surface of the river. The cold water sent a chill to her bones, and her teeth chattered.

Frantically she squeezed herself between the wheelers, balancing herself on the pole until she came to the swingers. The current had jammed them together, so she couldn't get between them. She grabbed the bellyband of the one on the near side and climbed on top of him. Quickly she worked her way to the leaders.

She pulled herself on top of the leader in front of her, reached over and grabbed Webster's bridle, holding his head above the water. With a forceful whack, she dug her heels into the horse's shoulder she straddled. "Come on. Giddyap."

The horse was on solid ground, so she guided him away from the hole, toward the bank. He, in turn, pulled Webster with him. As the team made a sharp turn, the coach lurched, almost tipping over.

Carl yelled, "What's going on?"

Tonio splashed waist-high through the water. "What the hell are you doing?"

Just as she started to explain, Tonio slipped into the hole and sank over his head. He came to the surface, and swam to the bank.

Carl and Lyle waded the rest of the way. Together they got the horses and coach up the side of the bank. Once they were safely out of the river, Jessie told them about her actions to save Webster.

"I was so afraid he'd drown," she concluded.

"Of course he would've. I almost drowned myself." Tonio shook the water out of his hair.

Carl looked at his daughter with pride. "You used your head, Jess."

Lyle spoke up. "I don't think you guys appreciate how brave she was. Fighting the river was hard enough, but handling those terrified horses took guts. Especially when she's afraid of them."

"Oh, Lyle, stop." The last thing Jessie wanted was to have her father know how she felt. "I'm doing all right."

Carl patted her on the shoulder. "You're a real coach-man, Jess. Kept your wits about you."

Lyle put his hands on his hips. "If you'd crossed where I'd wanted to, you wouldn't have had so much trouble."

Tonio looked him up and down. "All right, Lieuten-ant. Since your route is so much better, let's use it."

Carl put in, "It's going to take awhile, so I'm going to unharness my team so they can graze. Jess, you've done enough, so you stay here and get your clothes changed before you catch cold."

Jessie didn't object at all, since she'd had all the ford-ing of rivers she could manage for a while. She turned to the coach, unfastened the boots, and let them air. Fortunately the water had not penetrated the heavy leather. The floor of the coach was wet, so she lifted out the grub box and folding table to let things dry. The bedding, up on the seat, was out of the reach of the river. She found a change of clothes and slipped out of her wet boots and pants.

Once she was changed and comfortable again, she walked down the bank to watch the men with Tonio's coach. From all the yelling and swearing she heard on the way, it was obvious they were having trouble.

"What's the matter?" she yelled.

"We're stuck hub-deep in sand," her father answered. "Look under the driver's seat in my coach and find a rope. Bring it to me."

When she returned with the thick rope, she saw Lyle yank the whip out of the holder. "Your damned horses aren't trying hard enough." With that he snapped the whip through the air and caught the leaders across the rump. They reared up and screamed with fear and pain.

Tonio jumped up from where he was working on the wheel, splashed through the water, and grabbed Lyle by the throat. "You son of a bitch! If you ever strike any of our horses again, I'll kill you!" He yanked the whip away and shoved the lieutenant into the water. Almost purple with fury, he stuck the whip back in the holder.

Jessie started to protest, but her father, who stood in the river below her, put his finger to his lips. "Stay out of this, gal. You'll just make it worse."

Annoyed with both of the younger men, she walked back to her coach.

The men struggled most of the morning. Finally, by hitching two teams to Tonio's coach, they were able to get it across the river.

Jessie had sandwiches ready for their lunch, but little was said while they ate. Tonio glowered at Lyle, but at least he didn't chide him about the crossing spot.

They got such a late start, they had to camp out another night before they reached Carson City, a small settlement in the shadow of the Sierra. It owed its importance to the fact it was a main layover and supply center for the immigrants traveling to California over the Meyers Grade, for the cattle ranchers, and for the miners coming to the silver mines of Virginia City, further to the east.

Sagebrush-covered hills surrounded the town. Already tall poplar trees shaded the clapboard houses on the side roads. Wooden sidewalks ran along each side of the dusty, unpaved main street. There were two general stores, a feed store, barber shop, and a law office. A hotel took up one corner. However, most of the business establishments were combination saloons and gambling houses.

Early that afternoon, they set up camp in a vacant lot next to the livery stable and blacksmith shop at the edge of town. Impatiently Carl barked orders at Jessie as she maneuvered the big coach into place. His hands shook as he yanked off the harness and tossed it under the coach. He reminded Jessie of a racehorse waiting at the gate for the gun.

As soon as he changed his clothes, he said, "Jess, I'm

walking downtown to see what's going on. Don't wait up for me.'' His eyes glowed in anticipation, and there was such an eager expression on his face, she knew he could hardly wait to get to a gambling table. She wanted to beg him not to go, but she didn't dare.

Tonio walked over to her. "What's gotten into your father all of a sudden?"

Jessie hesitated. Should she tell him? But if they were going to be partners, didn't he have the right to know?

She shrugged. "I reckon you might as well know it now as later. He's a compulsive gambler." She felt a little sick with shame. It was like saying that Papa was a drunkard. She and Mama had always kept it a secret from their friends in St. Louis.

"I'll be darned. I knew he liked to play cards, but that was all."

"I've never talked about it before, except to my mother. And, of course, on the trip out, there wasn't much chance for him to really gamble."

"But it's so out of character for Carl. He's such an honorable, upright kind of guy."

"But the minute Papa gets where he can play poker, he changes into a different person. Probably he's got quite a bit of money on him. It's like he can't help himself."

Tonio put his hand on her arm. "I'm awfully sorry, Jess. I know it must be a worry to you."

She nodded and looked away from him. "Mama kind of kept him under control. At least when he was in St. Louis. I imagine he gambled a lot in Springfield, Illinois. That was the end of his stage line, and he had to lay over a day before he started back."

"Maybe you can keep an eye on him."

"I hope so. That's one reason I was so anxious to come with you. I knew what he'd be like on his own. But, of course, I don't have the same influence over him that Mama had." As a surge of grief for her mother came over her again, her eyes misted. She swallowed a big lump in her throat and managed a wistful smile. "I guess everyone has troubles."

Tonio gave her hand a squeeze. "I'm going to take a

couple of my horses over to the blacksmith shop. When
I'm through, I'll mosey downtown and see what Carl's
up to."

Jessie glanced toward the lieutenant, who was sitting
out of earshot—busily writing at a table in the shade next
to Tonio's coach. "Please don't say anything to Lyle."

"Don't worry. We're barely speaking."

When Tonio left with the horses, she walked over to
Lyle. She watched him dip his pen in his ink bottle.
"You look awfully busy."

He glanced up at her and smiled. "I'm working on a
report for Captain Blackston."

"Later on, when you're finished, could we walk downtown?"

"I guess so. Now if you'll excuse me, I'll get back to
work."

Her blood raced through her veins. Hardly containing
her excitement, she unbuckled the boot and took out a
dress box. She'd take a sponge bath and put on her petticoats and dress for a change. She wanted Lyle to see
her as a woman. And a desirable one, at that.

It took her an hour, but when she emerged from the
coach she was wearing a white voile dress with a pink
sash around the waist. Her straw bonnet, with a matching
pink lining, framed her sunburned face. How good it was
to have skirts flipping around her ankles. To be wearing
shoes instead of boots. To feel feminine again.

She and her handsome lieutenant would have a wonderful evening together. Perhaps they could find a cafe
in the hotel and have dinner.

Just as she walked over to the other coach, Tonio came
with his horses and tethered them.

Lyle looked up at her as she approached. "How nice
you look."

Her heart raced and ecstatic shivers ran down her
spine. Her dark eyes sparkled in anticipation.

But he went on, "I'm sorry, but I don't think I can go
downtown, after all. I want to finish this report and put
it in the next mail to Salt Lake."

Tonio saw her face fall in disappointment. She must

be feeling like a fool to be all dressed up and left standing there. How could Pretty Boy do this to her? He'd like to knock him down and rub his nose in the dirt.

He stepped forward. "Such a vision of loveliness. Are my eyes deceiving me? Surely this isn't the young stagecoach driver? In any case, could I have the pleasure of your company for dinner?" He bowed elaborately.

Jessie managed a smile. "Yes, if you'll change your clothes."

In no time, Tonio had washed and changed. He looked quite splendid in brown trousers and a beige shirt with a maroon tie. Did Iris appreciate him? Jessie wondered. Did she know what a treasure she had in Tonio Maguire?

It was still warm in the late afternoon, although Carson City lay in shadow from the vertical, jagged wall of the Sierra that rose so abruptly from the desert. Some of its peaks hit ten to fourteen thousand feet in elevation.

In spite of her disappointment and hurt over Lyle, it was fun walking along with Tonio and feeling like a fragile lady again as she held her skirt out of the dust.

The clapboard houses—with their patches of lawn, lilac bushes, and pansy flower beds—reminded her of her dear, familiar Midwest. She kept her back turned to the frightening Sierra.

They passed a vacant lot where a group of Washoe Indians, with painted faces and colorful clothes, sat in a large circle talking and laughing. They seemed to be playing a game by passing a stick from one to the other.

Tonio turned to her. "You have to admire the Indians. They aren't killing themselves trying to build up a fortune like we white people. The land belongs to everyone—and they all use the same fish holes and hunting grounds."

Jessie glanced over her shoulder at them. "They don't look as scary as the Sioux that kidnapped me."

Tonio laughed and squeezed her arm. "You're so skinny and ugly you're safe. And there's no bear grease in your hair."

"Tonio, do stop it!"

"Anyway, these Indians don't belong to tribes like the

Sioux or Apaches. Just a few families live together in a village, and that's it. But they make the most beautiful baskets you've ever seen. I'm going to take you to a general store where they're for sale.''

When Jessie saw the baskets of all sizes and shapes on a shelf in the general store, she thought they were the most exquisite works of art she had ever seen. She looked them all over, but kept going back to one about ten inches in diameter that was made of soft beige grass with deep brown designs on it. How she would love to own it. But when she saw the price, she gave a little gasp and put it back. They wandered around the store and, while she looked at the calicos and laces, Tonio bought some work shirts.

Soon he took her to the hotel dining room. After they ordered dinner, he reached in his bundle of shirts and handed her a package wrapped in tissue paper. When she unwrapped her gift, she found the beautiful basket she had wanted.

She gasped. "Oh, Tonio, what a wonderful surprise! Thank you. I was dying to buy it."

"I wanted you to have something to remember me by." He took her hands in his and, as he gazed at her, the strangest feeling came over him.

Jessie's eyes filled with tears. "Tonio, you're such a wonderful guy. I could never forget you. Never!"

Chapter 8

Tonio looked over the menu, then put it down. "There's only one thing you should order in Nevada."

"And what's that?"

"Steak. T-bone. Porterhouse. Whatever you want, as long as it's steak. But it'll melt in your mouth."

They started with vegetable-beef soup, then came their plates—filled with the biggest, thickest steaks she had ever seen—with side orders of fresh corn and baked potatoes.

"I'll never be able to eat all this," Jessie declared.

"Don't worry about it. They'll wrap up what we can't eat, and we can have it on the trail."

It was dark by the time they finished their dinner. When they stepped outside and saw all the brightly lighted saloons, Jessie said wistfully, "I wish I knew where Papa was."

Tonio put his hand under her elbow. "Let's go find him."

"I wouldn't dare go into a saloon and gambling house. My poor mother would turn over in her grave at the very thought."

"You can wait outside while I pop in for just a moment."

At the third saloon, which was the noisiest and largest, Tonio spotted Carl right away. He held the swinging door open slightly so Jessie could see her father across the smoke-filled room—with four stacks of chips and a whisky glass in front of him. He was seated at a poker table with a dealer and five other men.

As she watched him study the cards close to his chest, she felt sick with shame.

Some men wanted to enter the saloon, so Tonio took her aside. But whenever the swinging door opened, she could see inside. At tables throughout the room, men were shaking dice, playing twenty-one, or betting on the roulette wheel. Painted women in low-cut gowns, most of them young and very pretty, hung over the gamblers.

"Who are they?" Jessie asked.

"They're called shills. They encourage the men to increase their bets. At least that's one of their functions."

While Jessie watched, one of the girls helped the gambler pick up his winnings, then led him to the stairs to the upper floor. Tonio grinned as he watched his companion blush.

Other men crowded the long bar, their cowboy boots hooked over the brass rail on the floor. A huge mirror, which covered the lower half of the back wall, reflected the busy bartenders in their white aprons, their sleeves held up with bright garters. Above the mirror hung a painting of a reclining nude woman. Jessie's eyes grew round in shock.

"Seen enough?" Tonio asked, trying to suppress his mirth. "Shall I take you home?"

"I'm disgusted with Papa for wanting to spend his time in a place like this. I think it's awful."

He tweaked her nose. "Come off it, Jess. If you're going to live in the Wild West, you've got to be broadminded. Most of those men in there are lonely—and they're just trying to forget their troubles. Where else can they go?" He started to lead her away. "Come on."

"No. I want to talk to Papa. Will you go in and get him? I'll wait here."

"Then you'll have to stay out here by yourself. Because if he's willing to come, I must play his hand while he's gone. Otherwise he forfeits his place—and that'd make him madder than a hornet."

"All right. I'll sit down on this bench. You go get him."

Trying to be inconspicuous, she sat down and put their packages beside her feet. Men who were coming and going stared at her, but no one bothered her.

Soon her father came out of the swinging door.

"Papa, I'm here."

He staggered over to the bench and slumped down beside her. "Wha's the matter?" His speech was slurred.

She put her hand on his arm. "You've been here for hours, so please come home with Tonio and me."

"Leave? Jess, you mus' be out of your mind. Course I won' leave. I'm winning."

"But that's just the time to quit, Papa. I saw all those chips."

"Each one of those dadgummit chips are worth five dollars. Imagine that!"

"Then stop before you lose them all."

"Hell, no."

"I insist, Papa. Come home right now."

As his temper flared, he seemed to sober. He yanked his arm away. "Don't you tell me what to do, daughter! I'm the one who gives the orders, not you!" He stood up, his face red and ugly. He leaned toward her and shook his finger. "Goddamn you, don't ever come after me again! Understand? If I want to play poker, by God, I'll do it. So go back to the coach and mind your own business!" He turned and hurried into the saloon.

Completely stunned, she fought back tears. This couldn't be Papa. Not her kind, thoughtful father whom she adored. He'd never sworn at her before.

Soon Tonio came out. "I couldn't get anywhere with him. He acts like a man obsessed."

"He is. He's not himself." Her voice shook. Her eyes blurred with tears. "He swore at me. I can't believe it. He's never acted so mean to me before."

"I'll take you back to the coach. You'll be all right with Soldier Boy to guard you. Then I'll come back and keep an eye on your father. When he's ready to go, I'll

walk with him. If he has any money left by then, he'll
be too drunk to protect himself.''

"What a good friend you are, Tonio."

"I'll go in and borrow a lantern so we can see."

Soon they were on their way, their path lit by the light
of the lantern and the millions of stars overhead. Tonio
put his arm around her waist as they walked along. How
comforting it was—especially now that she felt so hurt.

"I can't get Papa out of my mind."

"Don't be too hard on him, Jess. We all have fail-
ings."

"But he never turned on me like that before."

"He had your mother then. Probably took it out on
her."

"How awful. Mama was so sweet and good to him.
And so sensitive. If he ever hurt her, she never told me
about it." Just the thought of her mother saddened her.
Her parents had been devoted, of that she was certain.
But maybe her father had been mean to Mama sometimes. He ruled the roost, no question about that. But he
was kind and loving, too.

When they arrived back at the coaches, a light shone
around the edges of the leather curtains, so apparently
Lyle was still up. But for once she was in no mood to
talk to him. After Tonio put his packages in her coach
and left, she undressed and went to bed to nurse her hurt
feelings.

It was very late when her father and Tonio returned,
and Carl was still asleep in his little tent when she got
up to fix breakfast the next morning. But she had a chance
to speak to Tonio alone.

"How did it go?"

"Your father lost it all. Every cent of it. At one time
he must of had three or four hundred dollars in front of
him."

Her stomach tightened with dread. They couldn't afford to lose all that money. "He'll be sore as a bear with
a thorn in his paw today."

Lyle came out, so she couldn't say any more.

As they ate, Lyle asked, "Where's Carl?"

"Well, to be honest, he's sleeping off a night on the town," Tonio answered. "We may have to lay over a day to let him recover."

"Oh, no we won't," Lyle answered. "According to your contract with the army, we have to travel every day. It's imperative I get to Sacramento as soon as possible."

Jessie looked up at the mountains. "I guess I can drive if I have to." Her voice quavered.

"Your father should do it," Lyle said. "I'll walk into town and mail my report. When I get back, I want him up and ready to go."

Tonio saluted. "Yes, sir. Whatever you command will be done." But he thumbed his nose as soon as Lyle turned his back.

After Lyle left to walk to town, Tonio roused Carl, who looked terrible when he came out of his tent. He hadn't undressed the night before and his clothes were rumpled. His bloodshot eyes made burned holes in his unshaven face.

Jessie felt a wave of revulsion. At least her mother had been spared seeing him like this. "Sit down and have some breakfast, Papa."

"Only some coffee." He slumped into a chair by the table and held his head in his hands. "I have a pounding headache. Feels like it's going to explode."

Tonio patted him on the shoulder. "As soon as you drink your coffee, you'd better curl up on Jessie's bed in the back of the coach while we break camp."

Her father was still asleep when Lyle returned. After the lieutenant looked around for him, Tonio snapped to attention, clicked his heels, and saluted. "I'm sorry to report, sir, we couldn't carry out your orders. The subject under discussion is sleeping off a severe hangover in the back of his coach." His eyes twinkled, and he just managed to suppress his grin.

Lyle gave him a disgusted glance.

"Papa's in no condition to drive, so I will," Jessie put in. "You'd better ride with Tonio."

"I've driven these grades before, so I'll guarantee your safety, sir." Tonio clicked his heels again.

"That's enough, Maguire. I'll go with Jessie. She could use some moral support."

"I sure could." She gazed at him gratefully. "Hop up on the box; we're ready to go."

Tonio gave her some final instructions. "There'll be room to pass on the grade if you meet a freight wagon or another coach. But it'll be a close squeeze. And it's one turn after another all the way." He told her again how to make the turns. "Remember, you'll have to swing out, but don't go too far or you'll go over the edge."

She groaned and rolled her eyes. "Pray for me."

Tonio patted her arm. "You'll do fine. We're carrying a light load, so we ought to make it without anyone pushing us. So let's go."

When Jessie gathered the reins and climbed into the box, Lyle said, "Your father put us all in jeopardy by getting into this condition. He's the one with the experience, and he should be driving."

"But Papa never drove over a grade like this before, either. So maybe I'll do it as well as he could."

Tonio led the way through the town to where the road turned toward the mountains. Lyle kept up a conversation, but she barely responded; she was in no mood to talk. Her mind was entirely on the grade ahead.

She had picked two grays as leaders for their strength. Each was over sixteen hands, with powerful shoulders. More important were their steady nerves. This was no time for a skittish, temperamental horse to be in front. She was especially thankful for their blinders—so they couldn't look over the edge of the cliff too much.

They began climbing long before she realized it. Finally they were going up the grade proper. From her perch on the box, she could see the switchback curves going higher and higher up the side of the mountain. She couldn't believe that they had to go so high up or so steep. There was nothing like this in Missouri.

At first she watched Tonio, but when his coach seemed to be on the very brink—ready to topple over—she couldn't bear to look.

Instead she concentrated on her own driving. Take one

turn at a time. Swing out. Watch the leader's rumps in relation to the angle of the curve. Keep the swingers in a straight line until it is time to turn them. Don't let the wheelers cut too short as there is a long coach to get around the curve. She repeated Tonio's instructions over and over, wishing she had his ability and experience.

Way up ahead, she could see a freight wagon with an eight-horse hitch snaking down the grade. They could only pass if she was on a straight stretch, leaving as much room as possible. At least she had the inside lane.

Don't panic. Don't panic. But her blood seem to freeze with fear. She could see Tonio getting into position up ahead, hugging the bank.

After her team completed the turn, she lined the coach up against the vertical wall on the side and made sure the horses in front and back were as far over as possible. They waited for the freight wagon to pass. However, the grade was so steep that the coach kept slipping back—in spite of the fact that the brake was on! The horses bent their knees and dug in their hoofs to hold it back.

Lyle spoke up. "I'll put something under the wheels." He climbed out of the box, grabbed some large rocks, and jammed them in place. He yelled, "I'll stay back here and keep my eye on these horses."

"Good."

Just then, the door of the coach opened. Carl came out. "What's going on?"

"Everything's all right, Papa. We're waiting for a freight wagon to pass."

He walked across the road and looked straight down four thousand feet. "Oh, my God!" He returned to the coach, hung on to the door handle, and vomited.

When he was through, Jessie called down to him, "Papa, will you go up in front of the leaders and hold on to their bridles? They'll feel a lot safer with you there." That was true, she told herself, but it was even more important to save his pride. He must be feeling terribly embarrassed.

Soon he was walking around the team, calling each animal by name and petting them. "You fellows are doing all right. Bet you never saw a road like this before. No, sir, nothing like this between St. Louis and Springfield.''

As she watched him being so sweet and kind, all her hurt and resentment melted away.

The hoofbeats of the approaching freight team, and the jangling of harnesses and wheels, sounded very near. The first pair of massive Percherons swung around the curve. Their huge hoofs, fringed with long hair, gripped the road.

Would they have room to pass? The blood froze in her veins. Her heart pounded against her chest. The team inched past hers. She could hear them huffing, their hoofs striking the ground in unison.

When the big wagon piled with freight came around the curve, the driver yelled ''Howdy,'' to Carl. Appropriately, he was a massive man with bulging arms. When his wagon came parallel with the coach, missing it by inches, he called to Jessie, ''Son, ain't you kind of young to be attempting this?''

''I'm just holding the reins. My father does the driving,'' she yelled, loud enough for her parent to hear.

She leaned over and watched the freight wagon slide past—so close at times she doubted if she could hold the whip between them. When it was safely past, she let out her breath in relief.

Carl walked around the team and stood by her. ''That fat guy knows what he's doing.'' He looked up. ''Move over. I'll drive the rest of the way.''

''Papa, I'm doing fine. Honest.'' She didn't want to turn the reins over to him.

''No, I'll take over.''

He put his foot on the first step plate. What was she going to do?

Lyle, who had been taking the rocks away from the wheels, straightened up. ''Carl, you're in no condition to drive.''

''That's not for you to say, Lieutenant.''

''Well, you're not. Get in the coach.''

"At least I can sit in the box and tell Jess what to do," Carl blustered.

"No!" Lyle stepped forward, opened the coach door, and ordered, "Get inside, Henderson."

Without a word of protest, Carl climbed inside.

When Lyle joined her in the box, she whispered, "Thanks. I didn't know how to handle that situation. But Papa'd make me so nervous if he were up here with us."

"Of course he would. You don't need that worry. You're doing fine."

Jessie gave him a grateful smile as a rush of love for him swept over her. At least Lyle was a real man who took charge, which was needed sometimes. Just knowing that he was beside her increased her self-confidence and gave her courage.

She looked up the mountainside, at all the switchback turns still ahead, stiffened her spine, and gave the reins a flip to get the team started again.

Her arms ached, her legs tensed, and her wrists throbbed as she guided the horses up the steep, endless grade. At least the intelligent animals knew enough to strike the ground at the same time to keep the stagecoach from rocking needlessly. More than once, as they swung around a curve, Jessie held her breath, half paralyzed with fright, and wondered if the wheels were precariously close to the edge, but they didn't go over. Her heart thrashed under her sweat-stained shirt.

Finally they reached the last switchback, which was steeper than ever. The horses were pulling so hard they dropped to their knees.

"Horses have a lot of reserve strength," Lyle said. "You've got to tap it to get the most out of it. You're too soft with them." He reached across her for the whip.

"No. You leave them alone. You get out and push. Tell Papa to help you," Jessie retorted.

Without another word, Lyle jumped down from the box and told Carl to give him a hand.

With the two of them pushing, and the horses straining to the limit, they got the coach over the summit. They were on top of a forested ridge, with plenty of room on each side of the road for a rest stop. Horse troughs filled with water rimmed the turnout. Tonio had his horses there, but as soon they had their fill, he took them away to make room for her team.

"You're a wonder, Jess."

Her knees trembled with relief. "Well, we're over the worst now." She slumped against a lodgepole pine tree, her heart still thrashing.

Tonio looked at her ashen face and shook his head. "We've only gone partway over the range. The big Meyers Grade is still ahead. It's nearly eight thousand feet. . . . But we won't attempt that until tomorrow."

"Papa'll be able to drive then. What do we do now?"

"It's almost noon, so let's have some lunch. That'll give the horses a chance to rest. Then later we'll drop down a-ways to Lake Tahoe. We can go around the lake—to the south end—and camp for the night."

While they ate lunch, Tonio told them about Lake Tahoe. "It's the most beautiful sight you've ever seen. The Indians call it Lake in the Sky. With a sunny day like this, it'll be as blue as the sky. But on a stormy day, it can be gray . . . and rough as the dickens."

"How big is it?" Lyle asked as he took out his notebook.

"It's twenty-two miles long and twelve miles wide. No one knows how deep it is."

The lieutenant wrote the figures down, then asked, "Is it forested?"

"Red fir, lodgepole pine, and aspen mostly. You'll see a lot of green manzanita and bush chinquapin. And huckleberry oak." Tonio grinned. "What are you planning, soldier? An attack on the poor Indians?"

"No, but I have to make note of everything for my reports."

"I just keep it in my head."

After they were on their way, Jessie soon realized that going down a grade wasn't easy, either. The trick was to keep from going too fast. She braked, held the reins tight, and hoped that the horses trailing behind would pull back.

When they came out on a lookout point, they could

see high, snowtipped mountain peaks surrounding a deep blue lake as still as a mirror. Thick forests came to the edge of the sandy beaches. Great granite outcroppings formed cliffs along the east side. A few fluffy clouds floated across the sky. It was all so incredibly beautiful, she wished she could gaze at it longer instead of driving the team down the winding road.

The route around the lake swung out on the edge of the cliffs, cut through the forest with trees towering above them, and crossed over bumpy corduroy roads through the swamps. Finally they came to the south end, and Tonio pulled his coach into a meadow near the water's edge.

"Here's where we'll camp," he called, and waved Jessie into a spot nearby. Everywhere she looked she could see lupine, buttercup, red maids, and cream sac in among the lush grass.

When Tonio came over to help her, she gazed out at the azure lake and said, "You were so right. I've never seen anything as beautiful as this."

As he looked at her eyes, which were glowing with wonderment, her face so filled with delight, he longed to take her in his arms. But he remembered Iris and held back.

When the horses were unharnessed and tethered so they could graze and drink in the little stream that wound its way through the meadow, Tonio suggested they all go swimming.

"You come, too, Carl. That water's cold enough to clear your head."

Soon they were in their swimming clothes and racing to the lake. Lyle stuck his toe in and snatched it back. "It's like ice." He took Jessie's hand. "Maybe if we go in a little at a time we'll get adjusted to it."

But Tonio plunged right into the lake, then rose to the surface, shaking the water out of his hair. "You have to get in fast. You'll soon get used to it."

Little by little Lyle led the way into the clear water. They gazed down at the minnows swimming around their legs and could see the pebbles on the floor of the lake and ripples in the sand. Jessie's legs ached with cold even through her bathing stockings and shoes. But little ripples of ecstasy ran along her spine just being with Lyle. She gazed at his magnificent body and ached with desire for him.

Tonio watched—and couldn't resist temptation. He swam closer and splashed water all over them. Jessie shrieked, but Lyle snarled, "Damn you, Maguire." He let go of her hand and swam after Tonio.

Soon the men were wrestling in the water. Yanking, pushing, and shoving. First Tonio flipped Lyle with such force he sank to the bottom, but he came up and grabbed his opponent by the head and held it under until he squirmed away. On the surface they seemed to be playing, but Jessie sensed they were venting their rivalry and hostility for each other.

Finally she could stand it no longer. She swam over to her father. "Tell them to stop, Papa."

Carl yelled out, "That's enough, fellows. We've got to rustle up wood for a fire."

The wrestlers stopped, but Lyle muttered, "Someday we'll finish this in private, Maguire."

"Any time, Soldier Boy. I'm ready!" But he told himself, God, how I hate his guts. He could hardly wait to rearrange those handsome features.

The next morning, Carl asked Tonio's advice about driving over Meyers Grade. When they were ready to start, he turned to his daughter. "You'd better ride on the other coach, Jess." He grinned a little sheepishly. "You didn't want me to see you yesterday, and I reckon I'd feel better if you weren't watching me." He patted her shoulder. "I hope I can do half as well as you did."

"Oh, Papa, how nice of you to say so." She gave him a quick hug and walked over to Tonio's coach, still relishing his approval.

As they climbed up Meyers Grade, which twisted back and forth up the final barrier, she studied every move that Tonio made. After her experience from the day before, she was able to appreciate his skill.

The west side of the Sierra was a long, gradual slope

to the interior valley. As they passed through miles and miles of forest, Tonio named the trees that he knew. Douglas fir, white fir, and sugar pine. "Makes the finest timber you can imagine. Pretty soon we'll be coming to the incense cedars and Ponderosa pine stands. A lot of the fellows who came out during the Gold Rush of '49 have settled down to be lumbermen."

Jesse marveled at all the knowledge he had acquired about the West—and how her own life had been enriched by his sharing with her. It was fun sitting beside him, enjoying the scenery as they moved rapidly along, with the harnesses jingling and the wheels spinning.

"We'll arrive in Sacramento tomorrow," he said.

"I can hardly wait. I want to find a place where I can make a nice home for Papa. He'll be so well established with you and your cousin." But secretly she dreamed about the time Lyle would fall in love with her and propose. "I'm sure you are anxious to see Iris again. You'll have lots of plans to make."

"I hope so. But you've heard the old saying, 'The way to make God laugh is to tell him your plans'!"

Chapter 9

After spending the night in Hangtown, named after an activity bringing outlaws to justice, they prepared for the final lap of their journey.

Even early in the morning, the mining settlement, which was built in a canyon along the American River, was full of activity. Miners filled the saloons. Freight wagons, headed for the goldfields not far away, crowded the streets. A long line of men holding pouches of gold dust or nuggets waited for the Wells Fargo office to open to deposit their treasure. An armed stagecoach that carried mail took the gold to banks in Sacramento, about fifty miles away.

"Do you want to drive, Jess?" Carl asked as he gathered the reins. "Then I'll take over after lunch to go into town."

Jessie agreed—and was delighted to see Lyle climb up on the box and her father head for Tonio's coach. That meant that she and the lieutenant could be alone. Now that their trip was almost over, every hour together was one to be cherished. She wanted to reach over, grasp his hand, and tell him how she felt. But, of course, she couldn't, as that wouldn't be seemly. She had to wait for him to speak.

Two skewbalds acting as leaders plunged into their collars, their muscles rippling, eager to get started. After the team bunched together, they established their rhythm.

With the coach swinging on its thoroughbraces and the harnesses jingling and creaking, they moved along the hard dirt road.

As they dropped down into the foothills, the timber forests gave way to chaparral, oaks, and digger pine, with the grass dry and golden. There was none of the lush green she was used to, but as Tonio had explained, it didn't rain in California during the summer. Would she ever get used to this strange land that was so different from home?

"It's getting hot." Lyle shed his uniform jacket and loosened his collar. Even so, his handsome appearance made her blood quicken. He reached over and grasped her arm. "I can't tell you what it's meant to know you. I think you're a terrific girl."

Her cheeks flushed. "It's been wonderful having you along." Her voice trembled. She mustn't give herself away and let him know just how deeply she felt about him. She'd fallen in love with him, she realized. No doubt he was beginning to feel the same way.

While he rubbed his hand up and down on her bare arm, little shivers of happiness ran through her. He went on, "I'm going to need transportation when I leave Sacramento on army business. I hope I can persuade your father and you to provide it."

"Of course. I'm sure Papa'll be more than happy to take you anyplace you want to go. I will, too." Her eyes glowed. It wasn't all over for them yet. They'd be together for some time, and surely he'd declare himself.

When they came to a lookout point, they gazed out at a flat valley stretching for miles and miles across to the coast range. The Sacramento River, which wound its way on the valley floor, eventually ended in the San Francisco Bay. Where the American River joined it, the city of Sacramento, which was now the state capital, thrived.

After they stopped for lunch, her father took over the reins, so she climbed up on the other coach.

As they moved along, Tonio said, "When we get to Sacramento, I'm going to take you to Widow White's boardinghouse. I stayed there before Gianni and I moved into our flat. I can sure recommend it. She has excellent food and clean rooms.''

"But will she have any vacancies?''

"I imagine so. She rents her rooms to the legislators, and they're not in session now. If she can take you, you'll have a place to stay until you find what you want.''

"That sounds fine. I won't have much chance to look around for a while . . . because Lyle wants Papa and me to take him where he needs to go.''

Tonio gave her a look of disgust. "And, of course, you're all in a twit. You've sure been bowled over by him. I've seen you staring at him like a sick cow.''

"Oh, stop it! I haven't at all.'' Her face turned scarlet.

"Jess, let me warn you about guys like Lyle. I think you'd better cool off. He's likely to bust your heart smack in two.'' He flipped the reins on the off-side leader to get him back in step.

Jessie drew herself up straight. "Frankly I don't think it's any of your business.''

Tonio looked at her and smiled in his endearing way. "But it is, Jessie. I feel like your big brother—and want to protect you. Pretty Boy is not going to ask your father for your hand. You can count on that. He's one of these handsome guys that goes around making conquests right and left just to feel like some kind of Don Juan. And I'm warning you again. Watch out!''

Jessie turned to face him "Do you know what your trouble is, Tonio Maguire?''

Tonio glanced at her, suppressing a grin. "What's that?''

"You're jealous! You can't stand it because he's handsome and capable.''

"I can't stand him. I know that.''

"So you bad-mouth him. It isn't fair. I'll be so glad to get to Sacramento . . . so we won't all be together all the time.''

"So will I.'' He flipped the reins. "I can't wait to get rid of Soldier Boy.'' He glanced her way. "But not you. I'm glad your father is going to be our partner so I can keep an eye on you. You need a keeper.''

"I do not. I'm quite capable of taking care of myself."
Drat Tonio, anyway. He seemed to be able to look right
into her mind and read her thoughts. But she had to admit
that having Tonio as a friend gave her a wonderful feeling
of security. He was like a big solid rock in this strange
environment. Everything was so different out here in the
West. A swell of homesickness rose in her.

When they reached the outskirts of Sacramento at the
end of the day, her first impression was of all the elm
trees that lined the streets. On each side were large
wooden houses built high above the ground with steps
leading from the sidewalk to a covered porch across the
front.

"Isn't that strange?" she said. "I haven't seen any
house where you walk right from the sidewalk into the
front hall."

"That's because they have floods here. In the late
spring, when all the snow in the mountains melts and
comes rushing down, the rivers overflow their banks.
Even the stores downtown are built high. The Indians tell
how there have been times when the whole Sacramento
Valley's been under water—from the Sierra to the Coast
Range—like a big inland sea. But it's made the soil very
rich. You can grow most anything here."

Up ahead they could see men pouring concrete for the
foundation of the new state capitol building. They swung
around to the south side of the construction site and
stopped in front of a three-story house with big bay windows across the front. A brass sign on the wrought-iron
fence read BOARD AND LODGING.

"I'll see if she's got any vacancies." Tonio handed
her the reins, jumped out of the box, and went up the
steps to the front door.

A plump woman, about fifty, answered the door. From
the way she was giving Tonio a welcoming hug, Jessie
surmised that she must be Widow White.

Tonio came back to the coach. "Yes, she's got some
vacancies. She wants you to come in and look things
over. But I'd advise you to stay here. It's the best place."

Cheerfulness seemed to bubble out of Widow White.

Her dark blue eyes twinkled as she smiled. She shook their hands, led them into the front parlor, and introduced them to the people sitting on the mahogany sofas and high-backed chairs.

"My goodness, but you folks came just at the right time. Some men left this morning on the riverboat, and my housekeeper and I have been cleaning their rooms." She waved her hand around. "This is the parlor, of course, and there's a sun room across the back of the house. It's mighty cheerful and nice in the winter since it faces south. The dining room and kitchen are right across the hall." She led the way to the dining room, which was set with twelve place settings. She tucked a loose strand of hair in her bun.

After the looked over the downstairs, they followed her up two flights to the third floor. There was a big, cheerful room on the southeast corner and two smaller rooms.

Carl spoke up: "I think Jessie ought to have the corner room; she'll be here a lot more than I will."

"It's hot up here on this floor," Widow White admitted, "but it always cools off at night. The breeze comes right up the Sacramento River and makes it as pleasant as can be. My goodness, I've been here for five years, and I've needed a blanket every night."

They worked out the final arrangements, paying a month in advance. "If you miss any meals, I'll give you credit toward the next month. Of course, I have to be notified the day before."

"Widow White'll treat you fair and square," Tonio put in.

"Now," the landlady went on, "if you folks want to get settled and take your rigs to the livery stable, I'll feed you later on. Right now I've got to serve dinner to the folks who are waiting."

They unloaded Carl's coach and carried all the boxes and luggage up the back stairs so as not to disturb the diners. When that was finished, the men left for the livery stable. While they were gone, Jessie undressed and filled the tub in the bathroom at the end of the hall.

As she sank into the water, she let out a sigh, appreciating more than ever the luxuries of civilized living. She thought about how fortunate they were to have made a safe journey and found such a comfortable place to live. It was simply furnished, but immaculately clean.

The future looked so secure and rosy, she told herself. Papa would be well situated in Tonio's stage line as soon as all the arrangements were made. In the meantime, they could take Lyle where he needed to go.

Tonio unlocked the door of his flat and put his satchel in his bedroom. He'd unload his coach in the morning. He'd been told at the livery stable that his cousin had taken some miners to the Northern Diggings, but should be back any day. He was glad to be alone, as he was anxious to go see Iris. He found some cheese and crackers to eat.

After he bathed and shaved, he put on some fresh clothes and walked the few blocks to the Cunninghams' big home on the corner. Even though he was bone-weary and hadn't had any dinner, he could hardly wait to see her again.

Iris opened the door and flew into his arms.

"Tonio! You're back at last."

He smothered her lips, her neck, and the hollow of her throat with kisses. "Oh, how I've longed for you." It felt so good to hold her tiny waist, to feel her breasts pressed against him, to smell the lilac fragrance in her hair. As he hugged her, he rocked her back and forth. "You'll never know how I've missed you."

"And I've missed you." She stood on her tiptoes and kissed his chin. "Now come into the back parlor and say hello to my parents. Then we'll go out on the verandah and sit on the porch swing."

Mr. Andrew Cunningham, chief of staff to the governor, rose from his leather chair and shook Tonio's hand. In contrast to his petite wife and daughter, he was a big, florid man. Wealthy, self-assured, he was the ultimate politician and the power behind the state government.

After Tonio had greeted Mrs. Cunningham, she patted

a place on the sofa beside her. "Iris has been worried sick that we might all be leaving before you got home."

Tonio stared at her. "Leaving?"

"I've been called to Washington," Mr. Cunningham explained. "The head of the Department of the Interior has asked me to serve as his assistant. I'll be in charge of the territories and states west of the Mississippi."

"Congratulations, sir. That's a big honor." But Tonio's heart sank at the thought of Iris leaving.

"Papa was very active in getting California admitted to the Union," she put in.

"As a free state," her father added. "Of course, the South wanted us admitted as a slave state. We felt a great deal of pressure, as there're lots of sympathizers for the Southern cause here. They're stirring up trouble now with all this talk about abolition. Mark my words, there'll be a war over this yet."

"I sure hope not." Tonio shifted uneasily. "When are you leaving?"

"A week from tomorrow. I'm taking Iris and Mrs. Cunningham to San Francisco and putting them on a clipper ship. But I'll take a stagecoach to St. Joseph and then go on to Washington by train, as I'm supposed to get there as soon as possible. Naturally the ladies couldn't stand to go overland by stagecoach."

"No, of course not," Tonio agreed, but he thought of Jessie. She was one in a million. But the news of Iris leaving crowded everything else out of his mind. "Sir, I can't tell you what a blow this is. All the time I was gone I kept planning to ask your permission to court Iris when I returned."

Iris gasped and clapped her hands. "Oh, Papa, please say that he can."

But Mr. Cunningham turned to Tonio. "I think you and I had better have a few words in private. Come into my den."

Tonio followed him. The older man indicated a chair. "Sit down."

When they were settled, Mr. Cunningham went on. "I'm going to talk straight from the shoulder. Iris has had every advantage all of her life. In New Jersey—before we moved out to California—and here. So no one gets my permission to court her unless they can provide her with a lovely home and a high standard of living.''

"Well, of course, my stage line is just getting established.'' Tonio's spirits sank. "I'm afraid I'm not in a position to buy a big home just yet.''

"It's not enough just to provide a home. I don't want Iris grubbing away doing housework, either. You'd have to hire some Chinese servants.''

"Perhaps she'd be willing to start out on a simpler scale.''

"Well, that's not what I want for her. There's no point in her struggling and sacrificing when she doesn't have to. In any case, we insist that she go to Washington with us and have that experience. I want her to see something of our country while she can.''

When they returned to the parlor, Mr. Cunningham turned to his daughter. "You're only nineteen, Iris. There's plenty of time for serious commitments later on. I don't know how long we'll be in Washington, but I want you there with your mother and me.''

Later, when Tonio and Iris sat on the porch swing by themselves, he took her in his arms. But his mind kept returning to the conversation with Mr. Cunningham. He couldn't provide her with a lovely home and servants right away; perhaps he *never* could. Would she be content without them? Or would she soon be dissatisfied and regret that she married him? For the first time, he began to have doubts.

Iris spoke up. "I think Papa's horrid not to let you court me.''

Tonio held her close and kissed the planes of her face. How he wanted her. "What are we going to do? How can we be apart so soon?''

She put her arms around his neck. "I'll write you every day.''

"But it's not the same. All the way across the country I kept dreaming about you and vowing we'd never be separated again.'' He lay his cheek against hers and encircled her small waist with his arms. "I want to keep you right here with me." He loved her petiteness, her beauty, her femininity.

"I know, my dearest. But I'll be back. Especially if war breaks out. Papa says if it does, he'll hand in his resignation and head for home."

They clung together for a long time. Finally Iris said, "We're having a farewell party Saturday night. I prayed that you'd get back in time for it."

"Could I bring my new partner and his daughter? It would be a good chance for them to get acquainted."

"Of course. Bring anyone you like."

"There's also a very handsome young army lieutenant. We brought him out from Fort Wallace in Utah. Shall I invite him, too?" Tonio was determined to introduce him to all of Iris's friends—so he'd find another girl to dazzle and leave Jessie alone!

Iris gave him a squeeze. "All the young ladies at the party'll swoon when they see him in a uniform."

"He'll dazzle them, all right." He nodded his head in satisfaction. "I'm anxious for you to meet Jessie Henderson. She's an amazing girl. I told her all about you as we rode along together."

Iris pushed his arms away. "Tonio Maguire, what are you talking about?"

"Jessie, my partner's daughter. I taught her to drive a six-horse hitch. By the time we got here, she was an expert coachman. You should have seen some of the things she did." He went on to tell her about the steep grade to Lake Tahoe.

"Exactly how old is this amazing Jessie Henderson?"

"Twenty, I think. Just a year older than you."

"And you've been traveling together all these weeks?" A strident, sharp note came into her voice. She pouted. "I don't like that a bit. I'm sure she tried to get her claws into you."

"Oh, Iris, you're being ridiculous. In fact, she was annoyed at me a lot of the time. Once we—"

She put her hands over her ears. "I don't want to hear

about it. I'm surprised you'd bring a woman with you. In fact, I'm shocked." She pulled away from him.

"Iris, her father was with us. And part of the way we had Lieutenant Underwood along."

"You should have left her in St. Louis. Why didn't her father make other arrangements for her?"

"We intended to drop her off with an aunt in Kansas City. In fact, we stopped there, but the old gal was such a mean witch I just couldn't—"

"You?"

"I mean her father and I . . ." He reached for her. "Darling, you're the girl I love with all my heart. Remember? Let's not waste what little time we have left quarreling about such a silly matter."

Iris put her arms around his neck again. "Forgive me, dearest. I'm being a horrid, jealous girl. I'm afraid I want you all to myself." She kissed him. "Besides, this Jessie must be kind of strange to be a stagecoach driver. Probably very plain and masculine."

But Jessie wasn't strange or plain or masculine, Tonio thought to himself. She was amazing, courageous, and charming. And damned attractive, in her own way. Well, she was just—Jessie. But he'd better not talk about her to Iris. He couldn't imagine two girls being more unalike.

He could feel Iris's heart throbbing as he held her against him. He wanted to drown in her loveliness. He lay his cheek against her golden hair, caressed her satiny skin, and inhaled her fragrance. Everything about her was so dainty, like a Dresden doll. He wanted to cherish and protect her. Keep her as exquisite as she was now forever.

Gianni returned the next day. Tonio was showing Carl around the small storefront office on Second Street when his cousin, a man as tall as himself, with the same dark hair and eyes, came in.

The men greeted each other with an enthusiastic hug, then Tonio said, "Gianni, this is Carl Henderson, one of the best coachmen in the West. Carl, my cousin, Gianni Orsoni."

The men shook hands. Tonio went on. "Did you get my letter from Chicago—about having Carl as a partner?"

"Yeah, I did. And it would be great. But there're a lot of angles we'd have to settle first."

Tonio detected a false heartiness in his cousin's voice. Did he object to expanding? "Let's all sit down." He pointed to a chair for Carl and sat in front of his desk. "We've talked about a bigger operation ever since we started. Carl, here, had a stage line out of St. Louis for years. He's experienced, knowledgeable, and has a Concord coach in good condition—*and* twelve splendid horses."

Gianni sat on the edge of his desk. "Those things are all important."

"While I was in St. Louis," Tonio went on, "I looked into Carl's background. Talked to his banker, the livery stable owner, and his landlord. I got glowing reports about his honesty and dependability."

Carl laughed. "I didn't know you were sneaking around behind my back like that!"

"It's just good business to check up on things." Tonio gazed out the window at the stagecoaches going by; they were on their way to the waterfront to meet the riverboats. "We didn't want to take in somebody we didn't know anything about."

"I don't blame you," Carl agreed. "I guess a lot of four-flushers and con men drift out here."

"So far, our operation has been pretty small," Tonio went on. "We've scrambled for passengers to the goldfields like everyone else, and we've done well. But I got some financial backing in Chicago, so we can expand. We need more drivers and coaches—to try and get a regular route established. We should go after a mail contract."

"We'd better not get in too deep just yet," Gianni put in.

Tonio stared at him. What had gotten into his cousin? Ever since they'd started two years ago, it was Gianni who talked about expanding and buying new coaches.

The men visited for a while. Finally Carl got up. "I have to see what the lieutenant has in mind. That gives you fellows a chance to talk things over and decide on the terms."

Gianni smiled weakly. "It gets complicated, doesn't it?"

Carl nodded. "That's right. You'd have to get an attorney and dissolve the partnership, get the books audited, and form a new partnership. At least that's the way they do things in Missouri."

"Same here," Gianni said. "California's been a state for ten years now—and they've come up with more laws and regulations than you can shake a stick at! I've been looking into it ever since I got your letter, Tonio."

After Carl left, Tonio turned to his cousin. "All right, Gianni, out with it. What's sticking in your craw?"

"Well, I don't think this is the time to make any change. We can go on with just the two of us."

"But you're the one who talked about getting someone else."

Gianni's face flushed. "I thought I'd be consulted, at least. Have some say in who we chose." He leaned against his desk.

"Carl Henderson is one in a million. He likes to gamble sometimes, but that's his business. But as far as being a partner in a stage line, he can't be beat."

"I'll admit that he seems okay."

"Gianni, what's got into you? He's everything we want. He's older—and has that rock-solid Midwest background. He's not like some four-flusher or drifter that's come out to look for gold. Every nut in the world ends up here in California. But Carl's different. He'd add so much to our partnership."

"I don't have anything against Carl."

Tonio paced around the room. "Look at this place. It's shabby as hell. These secondhand desks are scratched. The walls need painting."

"How could I fix anything up while I was doing all the driving?"

"I know, I know. I don't blame you. But that's just the

point. If we had three partners in the Valley Stage Line, we could take turns being here in the office and slick it up. It'd make us look like we're an up-and-coming out-fit.''

''Dammit, Tonio, we don't have to take in a partner to do that. We can hire someone. Have a clerk here with the understanding that he spruces this office up when he isn't selling tickets.''

''No one would have the interest of the company at heart like a partner.'' His instinct told him that there was more to Gianni's objections than showed on the surface. He swung around and grabbed his cousin by the shirt-front. ''Now tell me the truth. Why don't you want Carl?''

''As I've said, I don't object to him as a person. It's just that I want to stay as we are. Just the two of us.''

''That's not the way you talked before I left.'' Tonio felt his temper rise. He had to get to the bottom of this.

''I changed my mind when I found out how compli-cated it got.''

''When did you find out?''

''Right after I got your letter.'' He pushed Tonio's hand away from his shirt.

Tonio's temper snapped. ''I sent that letter by pony express. It cost a mint. If you'd changed your mind, why didn't you answer me right away? I'd have let Carl know— so he could've stayed in St. Louis. Instead he closed out everything and came clear out here thinking he had a future with us. Well, I want to take him in.''

''The hell we will! I refuse to have him.''

Chapter 10

If she could only hide in a corner instead of sitting here at the edge of the ballroom listening to a small orchestra and watching the dancers.

Jessie pulled the lace scarf over her tanned arms to try to cover them. Although she had dusted a little rice powder over her sunburned face and peeling nose, it didn't help much. Her calloused hands, with stubby, broken fingernails, looked as if they belonged to a woman who scrubbed the floors here at the Cunningham mansion instead of to a party guest.

How dainty and pretty the other girls were with their pink-and-white complexions, manicured nails, and carefully arranged curls pinned on top of their heads. Even their dresses—decorated with ribbons and bows—were more elaborate than her simple blue one. She felt too tall and terribly plain in comparison with Iris, who was wearing a becoming rose dress that accentuated her dazzling beauty and was everything Jessie herself was not.

As she watched Iris whirl around and around while Tonio gazed down at her adoringly, she felt a stab of raw jealousy so intense it frightened her. How utterly ridiculous, she thought—especially since she and Tonio were just friends!

At the end of the room, Lyle, tall and splendid in his uniform, held court with a bevy of girls around him. That disgruntled her, too. She turned away, regretting that she had ever come to this party.

When the music stopped, Iris led the way over to Jessie and said, "Tonio, darling, would you get Miss Henderson and me some punch while we get acquainted? The evening is flying by and we haven't had a chance to say more than two words." As she settled herself in a chair, some of the other guests moved closer.

"Tonio tells me you're a stagecoach driver," Iris said in a voice loud enough for everyone nearby to hear.

Painfully aware of gasps and suppressed giggles from their audience, Jessie flushed with embarrassment.

"And you drove a six-horse team up the steep grade from Carson City to Lake Tahoe. Imagine that." Iris looked around at the other young ladies, her eyes sparkling with amusement. "I'll bet none of you girls could do that."

"Who'd want to?" one of them asked. The girls exchanged glances and held their hands in front of their mouths to hide their giggles.

Another said, "I don't shoe horses, either." That set off a gale of laughter.

Iris went on. "He told me all about how you were captured by Indians and—" Her voice broke off words hung in the air as Tonio approached with their punch.

Anger boiled up inside Jessie. How could Tonio do this to her? She could just see him with Iris—telling all about the incident with the Indians while they dissolved in laughter. She'd never felt so humiliated in her life.

"May I have the next dance, Jess?" he asked, unaware of the currents swirling around them.

"Yes, of course," she answered, in the sweetest tone she could muster. She could kill him!

When the orchestra played the music for a folk dance, Jessie stood up and grabbed his hand. "Could we walk in the garden instead of dancing?"

They stepped outside to the moonlit garden, and Jessie led the way to a bench by a fountain. "Sit down!"

"What's wrong?"

"How could you, Tonio Maguire?" She grabbed his arm.

"I don't know what the hell you're talking about!"

"You told Iris all about my driving a stagecoach."

"What's wrong with that?"

"You should have been there and seen them all laughing at me. Making fun of me."

"You're just imagining—"

"I am not." She told him what the girls had said.

"Jess, I'm so sorry."

"Even worse, you told her all about the Indian incident. I can just picture how you two howled with laughter when you told how the chief didn't want me because I was ugly. 'Too tall and skinny . . .' " Her voice wavered. "How could you be so hurtful and cruel?" While tears ran down her cheeks, she suppressed a sob.

Tonio took out his handkerchief and wiped away her tears. "Jessie, I swear I never said a word—except that you were captured but released right away. I didn't mention the chief." He took her in his arms and rocked her back and forth, trying to comfort her. Dammit, anyway, the last thing on earth he'd want to do was to hurt Jess, of all people. Sweet, brave, courageous girl. "Yes, I told how you drove the grade because I was so proud of you," he finally went on. "I'd never make fun of you. Never!"

"But why would Iris twist your words so?" she asked.

Anger against his beloved flared up in him. She had twisted his words and had deliberately humiliated Jess. He was surprised at her pettiness. "Maybe she was jealous because I was bragging about you."

"Jealous? Of me? That's ridiculous!"

"Don't underestimate yourself, Jess." He kissed the top of her head. "You're a very special person. Now wipe your eyes and blow your nose. We'd better go inside."

When they went back to the ballroom, Iris immediately claimed Tonio. As she led him away, she turned back and gave Jessie an angry look.

Lyle walked over to her. "They're playing a polka, so
let's dance."

All her hurt melted away as she danced around the
room in Lyle's arms. He squeezed her hand. "You have
magnificent eyes. They're so big and brown. . . . And
such heavy lashes."

Her knees felt weak with love for him. "Thank you.
I've been feeling so plain—with my sunburned skin and
peeling nose! All the other girls here look so lovely."

"Just be your own individual self, Jessie." He smiled
at her. "That's quite enough for me."

Ripples of ecstasy ran through her. He was beginning
to care for her.

"How long will you be here in Sacramento?"

"Until I get all my business taken care of. At least a
month. Maybe longer." He gazed down at her. "I hope
to see a lot of you."

Of course, he would propose before he returned to
Fort Wallace, she convinced herself. Her heart sang with
happiness. They might even be married while he was
here, then she could go with him.

What difference did it make *what* these shallow, silly
girls thought, anyway? If she were Lyle's bride, she didn't
care whether anyone approved of her being a stagecoach
driver or not.

But she felt sorry for Tonio if he ever married Iris.
That girl took such delight in embarrassing her. What
kind of wife would she make for that prince of a man?
What sort of person would she be when her prettiness
was gone? A mean-spirited shrew, most likely.

At midnight, during a lavish supper, Mr. Cunningham
rose and told about his position in Washington and how
they would miss all their friends. "But we'll be back.
Iris will see to that. There's a certain young man here
who's pretty important in her life."

A wrench of regret hit Jessie as she looked at Tonio.

After supper, there was more dancing for the young
people and cards for the older ones.

Later, when it was all over, Carl, Jessie, and Lyle
walked out to the wooden sidewalk to go back to the

boardinghouse. As they strolled along, Jessie glanced behind her. The trees cast long shadows in the moonlight. She thought she saw a dark form with a stiff-legged limp dash from behind one tree to the other as if to hide.

"I think someone is following us," she said in a low voice.

They all whirled around, but no one was there.

"I think you had too much champagne punch," Carl muttered.

Lyle said, "You probably saw the shadows moving with the breeze."

"No doubt that was it." But was it? Jesse gave a little shiver—and was glad she had Lyle and her father with her!

As they approached the boardinghouse, Lyle said, "I'd like to have you take me to the Santa Clara Mission. I understand it's about a hundred and twenty-five to a hundred and thirty miles south and west of here. Not far from the end of San Francisco Bay."

Carl opened the gate. "When do you want to go?"

"Day after tomorrow will be fine. That's Monday. You can come, too, Jessie."

"Fine. I will." Her heart trip-hammered with excitement at being with Lyle.

"No!" Carl frowned at her. "Dadgummit, Jess. I want you to stay here and look for someplace for us to live. Then you're to keep house for me. It's not fittin' for you to be driving a stagecoach and tearing around the country like a man. I promised your mother I'd look out for you, and she wouldn't be pleased at all if she knew what you've been doing."

"But, Papa—"

"Let her come this time, Carl. I was told there were stations all along the way, so we can change horses. That way we can drive all night and not stop over. Jess can help with the driving."

"Well, all right. This time, then. But just as soon as possible, you're to settle down, young lady. Understand?"

"Yes, Papa. Whatever you say."

But she was determined to be with Lyle every minute she could. Besides, driving a stagecoach was lots more interesting than doing housework. There'd be plenty of time to find a flat after Lyle returned to Fort Wallace. And who knew, perhaps she'd be going with him as his bride!

They left early Monday morning and followed the road down the interior valley. Massive oak trees dotted the fields of wheat and corn. Although the day turned hot, there was low humidity, so it was not oppressive. All along the way, they passed other stagecoaches and freight wagons headed for the mines in the gold-laden mother lode that stretched two hundred miles in the Sierra range.

Some coaches and wagons were coming their way as well, so the stations were busy when they stopped to hire fresh horses. They would pick up a team and drop it off at the next stop. Another coach would return it.

Jesse spelled her father with the driving. Every so often, she saw the same horse and buggy behind them as she was driving. When they stopped at a station, so did the other vehicle. She spoke to her father and Lyle about it, but they didn't think it was strange.

When they arrived at the Santa Clara Mission on Tuesday morning, Lyle climbed out of the seat and went inside the office.

Jessie got down as well and walked around to stretch her legs. She stepped inside the chapel and picked up a printed brochure that stated the mission had been established by the Franciscan missionary Father Junipero Serra in 1777. It was one of the sixteen he had personally started along the length of California. She looked at the beautiful Spanish architecture of the mission building and realized how much California had been influenced by Spain and Mexico, the two countries that had settled it.

As she wandered around admiring the gardens, she glanced down the road in front of the mission and saw a horse and buggy half hidden behind an oak tree. There were two men in it. Was it the same one she had seen before? Probably not. They were just likely seeking shade from the hot morning sun.

About an hour later, Lyle came out. "We have to drive another ten miles. I want to go to the New Almaden Quicksilver Mine. They drew a map for me."

Jessie gathered the reins and climbed up on the driver's seat. Lyle sat next to her, with Carl on the outside.

"Just follow the Alameda. It's the street that will take us to the nearby town of San Jose," Lyle said, and showed her the map. "I think we'd better stop there and get a hearty meal and perhaps some sandwiches made for supper. I don't know what we'll find out at the mine."

After their meal, they drove through a narrow valley between hills covered with golden grass as well as an occasional oak tree.

"Dadgummit, I'm curious. Why are we going to this mine?" Carl asked. "I thought quicksilver was used in processing gold."

"It is." Lyle clamped his jaw shut as if he wanted to keep all his secrets deep inside of him. "We're going on army business, of course."

"I see," Carl answered, in a voice that invited more information.

"I guess there's no harm in telling you that quicksilver has other uses," Lyle added. "It's used in manufacturing ammunition. It provides the spark in firing a gun."

"Well, that's reason enough for the army to want you to go," Carl replied, his curiosity satisfied at last.

"There aren't many quicksilver mines in the world," Lyle went on. "Of course, the big one is the Almaden Mine in Spain. Quicksilver comes from cinnabar ore, and they've been mining it there for centuries. But the armed services don't want to be dependent on a foreign country. In case of war, the supply could be cut off by a blockade. That's why I've been sent to this New Almaden Quicksilver Mine to investigate it."

Jessie didn't care why they were going. As she drove, she flipped the reins over one of the leader's flanks. It was enough just to know that she would be with Lyle for the next few days. His thigh rested against hers. Enthralled, she glanced at his handsome profile. Her blood seemed to race through her veins just being near him.

Tonio would be so disgusted if he knew how hard she had fallen for this lieutenant. Just the way Lyle looked at her made a tremor of ecstasy run along her spine. She was sure that he was interested in her as well. How marvelous it would be if their friendship could develop into something serious.

A big freight wagon followed them, but when they made a turn in the road, Jessie looked back and could see the same horse and buggy—with the same two men she'd seen before—coming up behind it. In back of it was another coach and more freight wagons.

Finally she spoke up. "When we go around another curve, look back and see that horse and buggy behind the freight wagon. There're two men in it. I think they've been following us all the way from Sacramento."

Carl smiled. "I think you're having a pipe-dream, Jess. Lots of people come to the New Almaden Quicksilver Mine, I imagine. The lieutenant's been telling us just how important it is."

"That's right," Lyle spoke up. "I had quite a talk with one of the Franciscan monks. He was telling me that the mission owns part interest in the mine. In fact, he wrote a letter of introduction to the superintendent of the mine that will expedite matters for me."

"Won't they have to cooperate with you if you're representing the army?" Jessie put in.

"Not necessarily. Most of the shares are owned by an English firm, the Barron, Forbes Company. They bought it from a Spaniard named Castillero, who was serving in the Mexican army, and General Castro, who had just been appointed governor of California. This was in 1846, before California was a state. Or even before the discovery of gold."

"How did they know that quicksilver was out here?" Jessie asked. "You mentioned how rare it was in the world."

"As I said, quicksilver comes from the ore, cinnabar, which is red. The Indians discovered it in a cave and used it to paint their faces—to ward off evil spirits. In fact, the natives came from all over California to get it. When the missionaries came, they heard about it and realized it could be valuable. Eventually it was mined.''

They reached the Los Alamitos Creek, which had been marked on the map, by late afternoon. They followed the road and entered a small canyon banked on both sides with madrone and oak trees, twisted and distorted by the runoff from the winter rains.

As soon as they came to a large, open ravine, they picked out a spot along the edge of the creek to camp for the night. While Carl and Jessie took the horses out of their harnesses, Lyle walked over to the superintendent's office which was located near the main reduction works.

The horses had to be wiped down, then they were tethered where they could drink out of the creek and graze in the grass growing on its banks.

Carl put up small tents for Lyle and himself, while Jessie fixed her bed on the rear seat. She got the coffeepot going so they would have something to drink with their sandwiches.

It was after six before Lyle returned. He looked jubilant. ''Things went much better than I expected. I'm delighted. They're going to cooperate fully. In fact, I've arranged for us to take some quicksilver back with us— if that's agreeable with you, Carl. Of course, you'll be paid extra.''

''Fine. I've got a good heavy coach. We could carry about eighteen hundred pounds.''

''Quicksilver is shipped in casks that are eighteen inches long and eight inches in diameter. Each one contains seventy-five pounds, so they're heavy.''

Carl took out a pencil and paper and did some figuring. ''We shouldn't try to take more than twenty-four casks then. That is, if we can get them all in.''

After they had their supper, Lyle suggested, ''Let's go for a walk. It's quite an interesting place here.''

But Carl shook his head. ''You young folks go. I think I'll stay here and keep an eye on the horses. Jess, be sure to take a lantern. It'll be dark pretty soon.''

Jessie was secretly delighted to have a stroll alone in the twilight with Lyle. She picked up the lantern and started off with him. First they walked over to a large waterwheel in the creek that furnished the power for the mine.

Next they saw the huge furnaces—they were ten feet high and forty feet long—that reduced the cinnabar ore into liquid quicksilver. Long chutes coming down the side of the hill filled the furnaces with ore. She listened to everything he had to say—just for the sheer delight of hearing his voice!

As Lyle told her how it took fifty hours to reduce the ore, she gazed at him and enjoyed his splendid appearance. They could see the roaring fire inside the furnace and smell the unpleasant odor of the vapor.

"The workers live on top of the ridge. Let's climb up there," Lyle suggested as he tucked her arm in his.

"All right."

"You're such a good sport, Jessie. You're game for anything."

Even small praise from him delighted her.

As they climbed, they could see houses scattered all along the top of the ridge. "Most of the workers are from Mexico, so this is called Spanish Town," Lyle explained.

By the time they reached the church at the top of the hill, they were ready to sit down on the front steps and catch their breath. There was no one around them. Only the gentle darkness and a sliver of a moon in the dark sky above. They could hear the crickets, and the cooing of a mourning dove. She placed the lantern on the step below her.

Lyle put his arm around her. "Even in your boy's clothes, you're very desirable."

He put his cheek against hers, kissed the pulse in front of her ear. She could feel the faint stubble of his beard and hear him breathe. As he leaned her back against the porch, shivers of excitement ran through her.

He fanned his hand under her chin, but with his forefinger caressed her lips until she ached for him to kiss her. Finally he pressed his mouth against hers. At first it was a gentle kiss, then it grew full of desire and longing. She put her arm around his neck and held him close.

Finally they broke apart, but he still held her in his arms. With his fingertips, he ran along the planes of her face . . . the length of her jaw, around the top of her cheeks, and across her eyebrows.

"I think you have the most beautiful eyes I have ever seen," he murmured, and kissed her eyelids. "They're so expressive."

"I've often wished they *weren't* so revealing." For a moment, Tonio came to mind. She always felt he could peer into her eyes and read her very thoughts. Drat him, anyway. It was hard to maintain any privacy with him around!

She turned her attention back to Lyle. Everything about him was so clean-cut and manly. He always looked so neat and immaculate, with every hair in place. He was so well put together, his uniform always looking freshly pressed. How did he manage that? she wondered. He never looked rumpled.

What a contrast to Tonio, with his tousled curls and his shirttail often hanging out! She tried to push thoughts of him out of her mind—because she could imagine how he would disapprove of her now!

She loved the shape of Lyle's well-formed head. She cupped her hand on the back of it, caressed the hair that grew to his collar.

How wonderful to be in Lyle's arms. They seemed to form a magic circle around her—some private world where only the two of them existed with their love. As she brushed her lips against his chin, she wanted to cry out, I love you, Lyle. I love you with all my heart and soul. How she longed for him to declare his feelings. Did he love her as much as she did him?

Lying half over her, he kissed her again. She loved the feel of his body against hers. As he kissed the hollow of her throat, she caressed his back. Every bit of her longed for more. Much more. The color rushed to her cheeks as she realized how wanton she was.

Finally he sat up. "We'd better go back to the coach. Carl will be wondering where we are."

"Yes, of course." She picked up the lantern, and they rose to their feet.

Lyle put his arm around her waist as they walked down the path. "You're a desirable, exciting girl, Jessie. I can't tell you what it's meant to know you."

She leaned against him—and dreamed what it would be like if their friendship could deepen into something more.

By seven o'clock the next morning, they had had breakfast and their gear was put away. Jessie helped her father harness the team so he could pull the coach to the loading platform, where a long line of freight wagons waited for their cargo. The whole area swarmed with people. Mexican workmen pushed wheelbarrows filled with casks along the top of the loading platform. One by one the heavy casks had to be lifted and loaded in the freight wagons, to be taken to the goldfields. Other men were stoking the furnaces. Still others filled the casks when the molten quicksilver was ready.

Jessie walked over to her father and Lyle, who waited in line with the coach. "I'm going to walk up the hill and see the mine."

"You might as well. It'll be another couple of hours before we're ready to go," Carl said.

"I'll watch, and when I see you pull up to the platform, I'll come back."

As she climbed up the hill again, she could see projecting rock formations of reddish stone with deep gullies filled with dense growth between them. Miners carrying picks and shovels entered openings in the hillside.

Off to one side, she could see an aperture in the face of the hill and wondered if this was the famous red cave where for centuries the Indians came to gather the loose ore that furnished the paint for their faces.

She stepped off the path to get a better view of the cave opening. As she stood among the chaparral, she could hear some people coming, so she waited where she was until they passed.

Two men stopped near her. "I'm afraid I've got to rest awhile," one said, gasping for breath. "This damn leg of mine can't stand much climbing."

"Take your time, Eberson. That coach has a long wait to get loaded."

"What I can't figure out is why the coach is taking a load of quicksilver back. If they want to buy some, why not bring it by freight wagon?"

"Maybe the Barron, Forbes Company ain't got that much quicksilver to spare. After all, they must have all their contracts with the mining companies. Guess that army lieutenant put the pressure on."

"Wouldn't cut any ice with Barron, Forbes. They're an English outfit."

Jessie scarcely breathed. They were talking about Papa's coach . . . and Lyle. Her heart thrashed against her chest. She'd have to stay hidden; she didn't want them to know she'd heard them. But she *had* been right. They had followed them down here!

"Guess I'll have to start back," the man named Eberson said. "This game leg's giving me fits."

"You'd better rest in the buggy."

"I want to see how big a load they're going to take on. I'll have to report to the others."

When the men started back, their voices fading, Jessie stepped out of her hiding place in the chaparral. Who were these men? Why were they so interested in Lyle's quicksilver casks? What did they mean by "report to the others"? Was there a group involved? And for what purpose? Something told her that they could be dangerous. A shudder ran through her.

Chapter 11

As soon as they arrived in Sacramento with their load of quicksilver casks, Lyle had them drive to a warehouse, where it was put in storage. After Carl dropped the lieutenant at a government office, he headed for the Valley Stage Line.

"I want to see just where I stand about being a partner," he explained to Jessie.

"Yes, you should."

"By now Gianni'd have all the information he needs. Dadgummit, it can't be that complicated."

An uneasy feeling came over her as she listened to her father. Was this whole deal going to fall through?

As they neared the docks on the wide Sacramento River, other stagecoaches, freight wagons, and buggies crowded the street. They could hear the shouts of the drivers, the pounding hoofs on the hard ground, and the clinking of harness chains. Off in the distance, a paddle wheel riverboat let out a blast, announcing its imminent arrival.

When Carl hitched the team to the post in front of the stage line office, he turned to Jessie. "You come in with me and listen to what they have to say."

"I hope Gianni's here."

He was at a desk in back of the counter, hunched over a ledger, with a green eyeshade on his forehead. He frowned as he looked up. "Howdy. Tonio's not here. He took a party of miners to the diggings out of Auburn."

Carl leaned against the counter. "You're the one I want to talk to anyway. This is my daughter, Jessie."

"Pleased to meet you, ma'am." Gianni rose. "You two had better come in and sit down." He put chairs near his desk. When they were settled, he asked, "What can I do for you?"

After he took off his hat and put it on his lap, Carl said, "Well dadgummit, I want to know where we stand."

"I guess you've always been on your own with your stage line back in St. Louis," Gianni began. "You don't realize what it means to change partners and all." He picked up a pencil and began rolling it between his palms, not looking Carl straight in the eye.

"I know there are certain legal steps to take. But I get the impression that you're not enthusiastic about the deal, Gianni. That's what I came to talk about."

"I'll admit I was terribly surprised when I got Tonio's letter. To be honest, I resented the fact that I wasn't consulted first. The deal was all cut and dried—without so much as a by-your-leave from me." He tapped the pencil on his teeth. "I didn't like being treated that way."

"Tonio understood that you wanted to expand. It'd been damn hard to do much consulting with you out here and us in Missouri. Tonio did write you, and you could've answered in time to kibosh the deal."

Jessie spoke up. "I tried to talk Papa out of coming. After all, St. Louis was our home . . . and it was hard to give up everything and leave."

Carl leaned forward. "That's done and over with. We're here now, and I want to know just where we stand. I'd like a straightforward answer. Am I going to be part of Valley Stage Line or not? If so, what are the terms?"

Gianni ran his fingers through his hair. He looked around the office. "I told Tonio that I didn't think this was the time for us to take in anyone else. And according to the terms of our partnership, both of us have to agree."

"And you don't."

"No, I don't."

Carl's face flushed as he stood up. "And I'm left holding the bag."

Gianni rose as well. "Perhaps later on—"

Carl snorted in disgust. "To hell with it! Come on, Jess. Let's go."

With a leaden heart, Jessie followed her father outside and climbed up on the box beside him. She put her hand on his arm as he slowly arranged the reins in his heavy-knuckled fingers. His long, thin face sagged in disappointment.

"Papa, you can form your own stage line—just as you did back in Missouri."

"There must be a dozen or so here already. You ought to see 'em scrambling for passengers when a riverboat arrives from San Francisco. They swear and bad-mouth each other something awful. Shove the other drivers in the river if they can. Reminds me of a pack of dogs fighting over a bone."

"But Papa, you have this beautiful Concord coach, and you keep it so clean and nice. People'll want to ride in it. Besides that, you're used to dealing with the public. You'll get business. I know you will." She ached for him. He was really hurting.

"Tonio painted such a rosy picture. How we'd eventually consolidate all the small lines and have a regular network from here to Oregon. That's why he went East to get the financing."

She touched his hand. "It's a shame."

"I thought I was all set . . . with an established outfit. Dadgummit, anyway." Looking old and discouraged, he sat with his shoulders slumped. "This is a blow."

"Papa, I'm so sorry. But you'll see. Something will work out for you."

"I'd like to go back in there and beat the hell out of Gianni."

"I wouldn't try. He's a lot huskier and younger than you."

He gripped the reins and got the team started.

"Papa, let's go to the livery stable and I'll help you

with the team. Then we can go to the boardinghouse.
You're dead tired and need to sleep after driving most of
the night. We'll tackle this problem tomorrow, when
you're rested.''

When they finally arrived at Widow White's, she met
them at the door. "My goodness, but you look all tuck-
ered out, Mr. Henderson. I'll bet you haven't had a decent meal since you left.''

"I'm afraid you're right.''

"Then you just sit yourself down in the dining room
while I warm up some food from last night's dinner.''

The widow rushed around, fussing over Carl as if he
were a special boarder. With her cheerfulness, she soon
had him feeling better. She even sat at the table with
them while they ate.

Carl said, "I'm going to be establishing my own staging business. I reckon I'll need a license. Would you
have any idea where I'd go to get one?''

"Try the city hall first. That's where I got mine for
this place. You might have to get a permit from the county
or state for staging.'' She looked puzzled. "But I thought
you were going to be Tonio's partner.''

"His cousin thought otherwise.'' To Jessie's surprise,
her father told the widow all the circumstances.

Widow White shook her head in disgust. "I've no use
for that Gianni at all.'' She got up and filled their iced-
tea glasses. "By the way, when you go for your license,
you'd better take your daughter along. If she's going to
drive for you, she may need a permit, too.''

"Oh, no. I don't want her to do any more driving. It
was all right for her to spell me when we were crossing
the country, but now that we're here, I want her to act
like a lady again. It's not fittin' for a woman to wear
pants and do men's work.''

Jessie put her hand on his arm. "Papa, let me go with
you and get a permit . . . just in case of an emergency.''

"You never know,'' the widow put in. "You might get
sick or something and need her to fill in.''

"Well, I guess so. Just for an emergency.'' He looked

at her and smiled. "I'm much obliged for this lunch. I know you don't ordinarily serve a meal at noon."

"No, I don't. But you looked like you needed a pick-me-up."

"That was right nice of you, Mrs. White."

"Why don't you call me Kitty?" Her eyes twinkled merrily.

"I'd like that. And my name is Carl. My daughter here is Jessie. That's short for Jessica."

Kitty patted his shoulder. "Now you go upstairs and have a nap. And don't you worry about getting passengers. I know lots of state officials who have to make trips upcountry. I'll put in a good word for you."

"Thank you, ma'am. That's mighty kind of you."

Lyle returned later in the afternoon and found Jessie sitting in a lawn swing under a walnut tree. A pitcher of lemonade and glasses sat on a table near her. She poured him a glass. "How did things work out for you?"

He sat down beside her. "Fine. I've been taking care of several things for the army. I'll be free to tell you more about it soon." He sipped his lemonade. "Have you had a chance to rest?"

"Yes, but I've been pretty upset." She told him about their session with Gianni.

"I'm not a bit surprised. Tonio persuaded your father to come out here with a lot of promises, and then he couldn't carry through with them. He's a big bag of wind!"

"Oh, he's not!" she snapped. "He's a fine, sincere man." She didn't like anyone criticizing Tonio, not even Lyle.

"I hope you rise to my defense that quickly." He laughed. "If it weren't for Iris, I'd say something was brewing between you two."

"Well, it's not." If only she could tell him that he was the one she loved with all her heart.

Lyle took her hand and intermingled her fingers with his. "I've been making some exciting plans . . . and you're involved. But don't ask me what they are just yet."

He was going to propose, she knew it. Her heart thrashed wildly—and shivers of ecstasy ran through her.

"Jessie, you're such a special girl. Imagine our meeting out in the middle of the Utah desert." When he squeezed her hand, she felt as if she were soaring, soaring to some special place just for lovers.

But her father came out to join them . . . and the spell was broken.

The next morning, as she and her father started out to get their permits, Carl said, "Jess, I reckon you'll keep my books—just as you did in St. Louis—won't you?"

"Yes, of course."

"You'd sort of be my assistant, as it were."

"I guess so."

"Then I'd better take out my business license in your name, too. If anything came up, you could take care of it."

Delighted, she squeezed his arm. "Papa, I'd like that." All of her life, she'd wanted to be part of something fulfilling. "We'd better buy ledgers, and I'll get your books set up." It would be especially important to have them ready in case she and Lyle were married and left for Fort Wallace.

They spent most of the day taking care of their business. On their way home, Carl said, "I'd like to swing by the livery stable to check on the horses—make sure they're being fed properly. They get better care if the owner keeps a sharp eye on things."

While they were at the stable, Tonio pulled in with his coach. As always, Jessie felt a rush of pleasure when she saw him.

While Carl helped take off the harnesses, he told about their meeting with Gianni. "I'm not blaming you one bit, Tonio. Don't you think that for a minute. But our deal's off, and I'm going it alone."

Tonio kicked at a clod of dirt. "Carl, I feel awful about this. It worried me sick the whole time I was gone. I didn't know how to break the news to you."

"I'm mighty disappointed. I had high hopes about our partnership."

"I did, too. I don't know what the hell's gotten into Gianni. But right now my hands are tied. I can't take you into our company unless he agrees. But I'll throw all the business I can your way. Lots of times we have more than we can handle."

Carl nodded. "I'll manage somehow. Widow White said she'd recommend me, too."

"She's the one who got us started. She knows everyone in the state legislature—and most of the other officials. Lots of them have stayed with her. She'll help you out a lot."

"Then maybe you'll have something to put in your ledger, Jessie, besides a lot of expenses," Carl said. He turned to Tonio. "She took a special course in bookkeeping."

"Gianni does ours. But I wish you'd explain it to me, Jess. I'd like to know more about it."

"I'd be happy to—any time."

While he was still with Tonio, Carl seemed cheerful enough, but as they walked home, his face looked drawn and his shoulders slumped.

As they walked past a saloon, he turned to her. "Jess. I'm going in here awhile. Tell Kitty I won't be there for dinner."

She knew he was going to gamble again. That's what he always turned to when he was down in the dumps. He'd lose a lot of money, and they'd be worse off than ever. She wanted to beg him to come on home with her, but she didn't dare. She just murmured, "Good-bye, then."

Later, when she spoke to Kitty White, her voice showed how disheartened she was.

"Is your father a drinking man?"

"No, not usually. But I have seen him drunk a few times."

"Then it must be cards. Seems like men just have to get rid of their troubles one way or another. My husband was a fine man, but he'd turn to the bottle every time things went against him. Gambling's bad enough, but heavy drinking is even harder to put up with.''

"I never thought of it that way. My mother was so ashamed of his gambling, we never spoke of it to anyone. I was sure it was the worst thing in the world.''

"Honey, you're out here in California, where most anything goes. No one'd think a thing of it if a man gambled.'' She laughed. "So cheer up and quit worrying.''

During dinner she noticed that Lyle was gone as well. Later that evening, Jessie sat in the parlor with the other boarders and tried to make polite conversation.

About eight o'clock, Kitty came to her. "Tonio is here and wants to see you. I sent him out to the sun room.''

He rose when Jessie came in and greeted him. "Gianni's gone, so I thought this was a good time to go over our books. That is if you have some time.''

"I'd be glad to. I was just wondering what to do with myself.''

They had the sun room to themselves, so they sat at a table with a kerosene lamp in the center. "I imagine your books are fairly simple because you don't have a lot of employees.'' She opened his ledger and studied it.

"What I can't understand is why our profits have fallen off so drastically,'' Tonio said.

"But you were gone so long.''

"I've made allowance for that. And apparently Gianni made a lot of trips. I know that because I went over the logs at the livery stable. They keep careful records of when the horses go in and out.''

"You'll have to discuss that with your cousin.''

"It worries me because we're in debt. I established a line of credit in order to expand. I have to pay interest on the money I've already used, and there'll be a payment due in a year. The way things are going, I won't have the dough to pay it.''

"All I can tell you is the way I keep books. I have a general ledger in which I keep the totals for the month. Accounts Receivable on one side, and Expenditures on the other. Then I have a daily journal with the income and outgo for each day. I enter the totals into the general ledger on a monthly basis. I have a spread of different areas. For example, the expenses with the horses would be one area. Livery stable charges. Feed. Blacksmith costs. Veterinarian bills. Under income would be ticket sales and the charge for delivering packages. In Missouri, Papa made quite a bit of money hauling small items from one town to the next.''

They worked together for over an hour. Finally Jessie said, ''I don't understand a lot of Gianni's entries. He seems to have his own special way of keeping books. You'll have to ask him about them.''

Just as they were finishing, Lyle came home. As he walked out to the sun room, Tonio snapped his ledger shut and muttered, ''Don't you tell him any of my business.''

''Of course I wouldn't.''

Lyle greeted them and sat down on a wicker settee. ''I have a proposition that might interest you, Maguire. The government wants certain materials shipped by stagecoach from here to Missouri, and then they'll go on by train to Washington.''

''Materials?'' Tonio asked. ''Then why aren't they using freight wagons?''

''Because it's imperative that as much as possible gets to Washington before winter sets in. Stagecoaches are much faster.''

''Of course, that *is* true,'' Tonio agreed.

''It so happens that the officers at Fort Wallace, under the command of Captain Blackston, are in charge of the whole project. I'm responsible for the route west of the fort, and another lieutenant has the eastern end. We're planning to ship the materials in convoys . . . with soldiers guarding them.''

''If it involves the army, it must be important,'' Jessie said. The quicksilver's part of it, she thought. She remembered of the quantities that were on the way from the New Almaden Quicksilver Mine to Sacramento.

''Believe me, it's important, all right.'' Lyle nodded.

Tonio's eyes narrowed. ''I'll bet it's gold for the Union army. They're getting ready for war.''

"I'm not at liberty to tell you. But don't you start spreading rumors, Maguire."

"I don't intend to," Tonio snapped back, as his face flushed in annoyance.

"Let me explain how we're going to set it up. One convoy will take a shipment from here, over the Sierra, to Carson City. There it will be unloaded and put in another convoy, which will go to a midpoint in Nevada. The next one will bring it on to Fort Wallace, and so on across the country."

"How many coaches'll be in a convoy?" Tonio asked.

"We've decided on five. That way, not too much is concentrated in one shipment in case there's trouble."

Jessie thought of her father, then asked, "How are you getting your drivers?"

"We're putting it up for bid. Hopefully several staging companies'll bid on it. The company that submits the lowest price will get the contract. It will be up to them to get the other drivers and coaches. I'll send out the notices tomorrow. They can pick up the forms at the post office."

Later, when Tonio walked to his flat above his office, he decided to submit a bid for his stage line. They needed the money, and he could see another big advantage. If they performed well for the government on this project, perhaps it would help them get a mail contract when they established their route to Oregon.

The stage lines that carried the mail were the most highly respected and lucrative ones. He could just see the words U.S. MAIL, with an eagle insignia underneath, all painted in gold on the door of his coach. The stationmasters on the route stepped lively when a mail coach pulled in. The drivers with mail on board were regarded with awe, the horses were changed in double-quick time, and the coach was sped on its way. He smacked his fist on his other hand and declared aloud, "I'm going to get that contract. Nothing's going to stop me."

After Tonio left, Jessie sat at the desk in her room with a pencil and a sheet of paper. She wrote some figures down, scratched them out, and wrote them again. She knew as much about the finances of staging as Papa did. Tomorrow, she'd tell him all about the project, and they could go to the post office and get the forms. They had to win the contract. Now that the deal with Tonio had fallen through, they were desperate for work. If they could just get this army contract, they'd be all set for a while.

She heard her father come in long after she'd gone to bed. How she wanted to get up and talk to him about the bid, but she didn't dare. What if he'd lost at gambling and was in a bad mood? No, she would have to wait until morning.

At eight o'clock the next morning, Lyle appeared at a printer's shop. The owner had worked until late getting the notices about the project, and the bid forms, ready for the army.

As soon as Lyle got the printed material, he walked to the post office, put a notice on the bulletin board, and gave the bid forms to the postmaster. He'd spend the rest of the day calling on the various stage lines, explaining the project and urging them to bid. He didn't notice that a man with a stiff-kneed limp followed him—and watched every move he made.

When Jessie saw her father at the breakfast table—joking with Kitty and seemingly in an excellent mood—she sighed with relief. Apparently he'd won the night before.

The breakfast of fresh peaches, followed by scrambled eggs, sausage, and muffins, tasted unusually good. When they were finished, and ready to leave the table, she turned to him. "Papa, I need to talk to you."

"Well, then, let's walk out to the garden."

When they were on the lawn swing, she told him all about the army project. "Papa, think what it would mean if we won the bid."

"But didn't you say he was telling all this to Tonio?"

"Yes. But what difference does that make?"

"Would it be fair for us to butt in on something Tonio might want?"

"But, Papa, it's going to be open to all the stage lines. Anyone can submit a bid. We have just as much right to do so as the next person. Think what it'd be like to have steady work until it snows in the mountains."

"It'd be wonderful," Carl agreed. "And I could do it, all right. Going up and down that grade isn't the easiest run in the world, but I'd get used to it."

"Of course you would. I'm sure you could round up three other coachmen with their rigs."

"Three? I'd need four."

"If you could rent or buy a used coach, I could drive it."

"No, Jessie. I vowed when we got out here, I'd—"

"Papa, I know you did. But the only way we'll get that bid is to cut it to the bone. I can drive just as well—and save the wages of another man. And the job lasts less than three months. Only until the snow flies."

"I realize that. But it means everything to me to see you wearing pretty dresses and looking like a lady, just as you do now. Dadgummit, when you've got on pants, I keep thinking about your mother and what she'd say."

"Mama had a lot of common sense. She would have approved of my driving under the circumstances."

Carl looked at Jessie, his eyes sad. "I should have tried harder to make arrangements for you to stay in St. Louis. Placed you with a parson's family, or something like that."

She put her hand in his. "Papa, I wouldn't have missed this experience of coming West for the world." And she meant it, too, she realized in surprise. It'd been the most exciting time of her life. "Now let's go down to the post office and get those forms. Then we can come home and work on the bid. They have to be in right away."

At the post office, Carl had to fill out an application form giving his license number, type of equipment, and previous experience. "Jess, there's a section here that asks for three references. I hardly know anyone here."

"Put down Lieutenant Underwood. And Tonio. He's an established businessman. And Kitty White."

The postmaster read over the application and handed Carl a bid to complete.

When they returned to the boardinghouse, they worked the rest of the day on the bid to make sure they didn't miss anything. There was so much to consider. Livery stable fees. Renting horses at the stations along the way. Veterinary fees. Insurance. Repairs on the coaches. Meals and lodging at the various stops. And, of course, the wages for the three drivers—and reimbursement for the use of their coaches. According to the specifications, they had to make ten trips with the shipments. When they were finished completing the bid, they went back to the post office to submit it. The sealed bids would be opened the next Saturday.

In the meantime, Kitty White got Carl a job taking an engineer to his new position at a quartz mine in the mother lode.

Saturday afternoon finally came. As Carl and Jessie arrived at the hall where the bids were to be opened, they saw Tonio on the sidewalk.

"I didn't know you folks were going to try for this," he said, looking surprised.

Carl answered, "I wasn't going to, but Jessie persuaded me to. Said it was open to all."

"Of course it is." But Tonio felt a little uneasy as he sat down. Carl could afford to bid low. He wasn't maintaining an office like the rest of them were.

Lyle stood behind a table and called the meeting to order. Just watching him take charge sent a wave of admiration through Jessie. How handsome he looked in his uniform. The postmaster sat beside him, ready to record the bids. "Nine bids were submitted, and I thank all of you," Lyle began. "I'm sure each one of you would do a fine job for us. You are all well qualified. So on with the business at hand."

The postmaster handed him a sealed bid, which Lyle opened and read. "Sacramento River Stage Lines—four thousand, one hundred and eighty dollars." Jessie gave a little gasp; theirs was nearly nine hundred dollars cheaper!

"Delta Stage Line—three thousand, eight hundred and ninety-five dollars," Lyle read.

The next three were between thirty-six and thirty-nine hundred dollars. "Valley Stage Line—three thousand, five hundred and fifty dollars." Everyone groaned. The next two were higher than Tonio's. Carl's bid was read last of all. "Henderson Stage Company—three thousand, two hundred and ninety-five dollars. That is the lowest, so the contract goes to Mr. Carl Henderson. Please stand up so we can give you a round of applause."

Carl stood up. "I'm going to need extra drivers and coaches, so if any of you are interested, please see me now."

As some of the men crowded around Carl, Tonio and Jessie moved out of the way.

"Well, congratulations, Jessie. I hand it to you." His eyes snapped with anger. She could tell he was furious by the way he ran his fingers through his curls in quick, vicious stabs.

"What do you mean?"

"It must have been a great advantage to you to have studied my books and know all my business before you figured your bid."

"Tonio, I swear . . . I never even thought about your ledgers when Papa and I were figuring our costs."

"Really? Then it's quite a coincidence that your bid was two hundred and sixty-five dollars lower than ours—which is just what running our office will cost." He turned on his heels and walked out.

Chapter 12

As Jessie walked out of the hall with her father, she felt heartsick about Tonio and his accusations. It took all the joy out of their winning the contract. How could he think she'd take advantage of him that way?

Lyle caught up with them. "I'd like to take you to lunch to celebrate. I've heard about an excellent Chinese restaurant near here."

"Thanks, I'm game," Carl said. "How about you, Jess?"

"Of course. It'll be fun." She tried to sound enthusiastic, but hurt and despair welled in her. Finally she pushed her worries over Tonio to the back of her mind and smiled. "I've never been to a Chinese restaurant before." In fact, she had seldom seen an Asian in Missouri.

As they entered the strange restaurant, which had gold dragons painted on a red wall and was filled with the odor of incense, she felt uneasy and moved closer to Lyle. He took her arm and tucked it under his.

Red-and-gold lanterns with long silk tassels hung from the ceiling. The dining area was partitioned into separate booths, curtained off with strings of glass beads. An Oriental, wearing a black coolie jacket and pants, took them to a booth and handed them a menu, which she couldn't read. Chopsticks took the place of silver, and they were all so intent on trying to learn to use them, they didn't otice that two men entered the restaurant, one with a limp.

The men silently followed the waiter, but pointed to he booth adjoining the one Carl, Jessie, and Lyle occupied and slipped into the padded seat, where they could out their ears close to the wall.

Everything was so different here, Jessie thought, as she pulled off her gloves. A shiver of apprehension ran hrough her. She wished they had gone to a regular cafe. What kind of food would they serve here? She probably wouldn't be able to eat it.

Lyle ordered their meal and, as they waited, he said, 'It's great that you got the contract, Carl. I'm delighted. Did you get your other drivers and coaches?''

"Yes. Three drivers and their rigs. One had an extra coach I'm renting. Jess'll drive the one I own.''

"Sounds like we're all set.''

"I'm afraid Tonio was real put out,'' Carl said. "I think he was counting on the contract. I feel kind of bad about it.''

So do I, Jessie told herself with a sinking heart. All her remorse came rushing back. Papa's instincts had been right. They shouldn't have submitted a bid.

"To be frank, I'm relieved he didn't win it,'' Lyle said. "We don't see eye to eye, and it would be difficult for us to work together. So I'm glad you got it, Carl.''

"Tell me exactly what my schedule will be.'' He took out a notebook and pencil.

The men in the adjoining booth took theirs out as well.

Lyle went on. "I want to have all the coaches brought to the Capitol Warehouse on Front and J streets at two o'clock on Monday afternoon. There's plenty of room in the back lot for them. Our shipment will be loaded there. And, of course, we'll have guards stationed day and night.''

"I'll go there after lunch and look things over.''

"Then, on Tuesday morning, be ready to start out at six o'clock. I've made arrangements for the convoy to spend the night at Everett Springs Station. The next day you'll go on to Meyers Station near Lake Tahoe. Then on to Carson City on Thursday. The other convoy will be there to meet you. You come back on your own, but I want your coach at the warehouse at two o'clock every Monday to be loaded."

"That doesn't give us much layover time."

"The one thing we *don't* have is time, Carl."

When the food came, Jessie found—to her surprise—that it was delicious. Soup with something in it that sizzled and crackled. Crispy egg rolls filled with bean sprouts. Then came dish after dish, piled high with such treats as sweet-and-sour pork, bits of chicken with cashew nuts, and spicy beef with broccoli and black mushrooms. Everything had been chopped into bite-size pieces before it was cooked. Lyle showed them how to use the chopsticks.

After they were through eating and had walked outside, Carl said, "I'm going to the warehouse now. Then I'll contact the other drivers. I won't be home for dinner; I've eaten enough for the whole day!"

He'll be gambling, of course, Jessie thought in dismay. She turned to Lyle. "Thank you so much for the wonderful meal."

"You were reluctant to go into the place," Lyle teased. "Thought you'd be sold into white slavery or something."

Her neck reddened. "I did not."

"I have the rest of the afternoon free. Let's walk around." He took her arm.

"Oh, I'd love to." She held up her skirt to keep it off the dirty sidewalk. All of her concerns melted away as she glanced up at him. How handsome he looked in his summer uniform. Every feature of his face was in perfect proportion. She loved the way his hair came down below his cap. His shoulders filled his jacket, and his torso narrowed to slim hips. She felt weak-kneed with love as she strolled beside him.

Between the busy riverfront and where the capitol building would be, the streets were filled with general stores, barber shops, rooming houses, cafes, saloons, and hardware stores that sold mining supplies.

They caught a horse trolley, rode to the end of the line, and walked to Sutter's Fort. The camp now lay in ruins, the adobe buildings falling apart and weeds growing everyplace.

"I feel sorry for poor John Sutter," Lyle said. "I've read that he came from Switzerland and the Mexican governor gave him eleven square leagues of land in this valley. That'd be about thirty square miles. Anyway, he built his fort, and for nearly ten years reigned as sort of a monarch over his kingdom—with the Indians doing all of his work. Then disaster struck."

"What happened?"

"He had a sawmill built on his land, up the American River. That's where gold was discovered. Within a year, hundreds of thousands of gold seekers came from all over the world. They trampled over his crops, stole his cattle and his land. The poor guy is ruined."

"Why didn't he go up and get the gold for himself? Especially since it was on his land."

"I don't know. I've often wondered about that."

While Lyle and Jessie roamed around the remains of Sutter's Fort, eight men gathered in the back room of a saloon. They fell silent when their leader, Ross Eberson, from Atlanta, Georgia, limped into the room, took the seat saved for him, and stretched out his leg to ease the pain. He had fallen from a horse a few months before, and the broken bones had never healed properly. His dark, intense eyes looked around at his followers.

He greeted them and began speaking in a voice so low everyone leaned forward to hear him.

"They're all set to ship gold and quicksilver to Washington." He took out his notebook and shared the plans he had overheard in the restaurant.

"We've got to get some of that gold for the Southern cause," one of the men declared.

"That's right," Eberson agreed. "War's coming. We all know that. It's just a question of when it will start. And the South will need money to finance our side."

"But you said that the soldiers are going to guard the

convoy," a heavyset man spoke up. "How'll we be able
to get our hands on the gold? It ain't going to be easy."

"It means we've got to outfox them."

"Just how are we going to do that?" another asked.

"I don't know. We'll have to put our heads together."

A small, bearded man who had accompanied Eberson
to the restaurant added, "Henderson said that Jess would
drive his coach and he would have the rented one. I
couldn't figure out who Jess was because they also called
that girl with them Jess or Jessie."

Eberson rubbed the stubble on his cheek. "When I
saw them at the New Almaden Quicksilver Mine, there
was a boy driving the coach. Looked a lot like Henderson. I figured they were father and son. Now that you
mention it, I heard the young fellow being called Jess.
So you suppose they're one and the same person?"

One of the men slapped his thigh. "A female driving
a stagecoach? You must be looney. Ain't possible."

"Hell, no," another added, and guffawed. "Why ain't
it a headline in the *Sacramento Union*: STAGECOACH
WOMAN HANDLES SIX-HORSE HITCH!"

Ross Eberson got them back to order. "Whether this
driver is a woman or a young boy doesn't matter much.
He or she will be the weak link in the convoy. That's the
person we should concentrate on. The one who'll be
driving the coach with the words 'Henderson Stage Company' painted on it.

The other men nodded. One asked, "Do we go after
that coach on this first trip?"

"No." The leader shook his head emphatically. "Let
'em go a few times, get a sense of false security. Our
people on the other end can get 'em before they reach
the Mississippi. I'll let you know when we're to strike.
It'll have to be carefully planned."

"But it'll be too bad for Jess," one man added.

As Jessie strolled with Lyle along the tree-lined streets
in the residential section, she felt as if she were walking
on big puffy clouds instead of hard-packed dirt sidewalks.

A water-sprinkling cart, pulled by two swaybacked horses, came along to settle the dust. The pungent odor of freshly dampened earth hung in the warm air.

Lyle spoke up. "Now that you're out here in California, you'll probably never want to leave."

Was he sounding her out? Seeing if she could adapt to the life of an army officer's wife?

The words tumbled out. "Of course I could leave California."

"Under what circumstances? Your father talks as if he's going to settle here regardless of the raw deal he got from Maguire."

She didn't want to argue with him about Tonio. She weighed her words carefully. "If I ever marry, I would go wherever my husband's work took him."

"And a girl like you could be happy no matter where she had to live?"

"Of course." She looked up at him. "When a girl loves a man, she'd go to the ends of the earth with him."

Lyle squeezed her arm. "I'm glad to hear that. The girl I marry would have to be flexible and courageous. Able to make a home for us anywhere. She'd have to be healthy and strong. Army life is no place for a weakling."

She ached to remind him that she had all of those qualities.

Finally Lyle went on. "She'd have to be a girl like you."

Jessie shivered with excitement. That was the next thing to a proposal, wasn't it? No doubt he was waiting to speak to Papa.

By the time they returned to Widow White's, it was late in the afternoon. Jessie rushed up to her room, poured water from the pitcher into a big washbasin, and gave herself a sponge bath. She patted some lavender cologne on her neck and arms, then put on a pale green dress that looked refreshing and cool.

Nearly all the boarders had gone out for the evening. After Jessie and Lyle ate, they went outside and sat in

the lawn swing to enjoy the balmy evening and feel the
breeze off the river.

Finally dusk gave way to darkness and stars pinpointed
the sky. Soon the moon rose over the horizon.

Lyle put his arm around her. "We'll always remember
today, won't we?" His voice sounded caressing, with a
note of tenderness she had never heard in it before.

His long, tapered fingers cupped her shoulder. She
pressed her cheek against them. She loved his hands, so
free of imperfections, his nails filed and clean. They
weren't at all like her father's big-knuckled ones—or
Tonio's calloused palms.

With his other hand, Lyle turned her face toward him
and brushed his lips on hers. It only lasted a second, like
the brush of a butterfly wing, but a tingling sensation ran
to the very marrow of her bones. She could hardly
breathe; her heart pounded.

"You're a beautiful, lovely girl," he murmured, and
kissed the hollow of her throat.

Her arm crept around his neck; she buried her face in
his hair so she wouldn't cry out, I love you, I love you
with all my being. She could feel his heart pound as he
pulled her against him.

For a long moment, neither spoke. It was as if they
wanted to savor their nearness in the soft darkness. The
sweet notes of a nightingale soared in the air. A palm
tree rustled.

He cupped her face with his hands and bent his head
to her. "You're so desirable. So lovely," he murmured.
He kissed her slowly and tenderly and then with demanding passion. Her whole body throbbed in response
to him.

Widow White began turning off the lamps in the big
house.

"We'd better go in," Jessie said, and pulled herself
away from him. "She's getting ready to lock up."

They hurried into the house and up the stairs. When
Jessie got to her room, she said a quick good night and
slipped inside. She didn't dare stay with him any longer.

As she leaned against the back of the door, her face

flamed as she thought of their ardent caresses on the lawn swing. But he wanted her. He'd called her desirable. The strangest curling sensation in the pit of her stomach warned her that she desired him as well.

Her breath came in little quick gasps. Her hands trembled as she took off her clothes, hung them up in the tall wardrobe, and put on her nightgown and robe. Hardly aware of what she was doing, she pulled back her bedspread, folded the blanket out of the way, and turned down the sheet.

As she walked out of her door and started down the hall, Lyle came out of the bathroom in his robe. Without a word, he held his arms open . . . and she stepped into his embrace.

Every shred of conscience implored her to leave while there was time. Danger! Danger! But she clung to him desperately. She couldn't tear herself away.

"Oh, my darling," Lyle murmured in her ear. "I want you so much." He held his body against hers, ran his hands down the curves of her back, pressing her closer and closer. A hunger, like an intense, physical pain, pierced her.

"The other roomers are gone," he whispered. "We're all alone up here."

"I know."

"I want to make love to you. Do you understand me?" he asked.

Her heart pounded and her cheeks burned. Refuse! Refuse! her conscience clamored. But she had passed the point of no return. Finally she whispered, "Yes."

He half carried her into her room and locked the door. After he turned down the lamp, he took off her nightclothes and carried her to her bed. Since he had nothing on under his robe, he was beside her in a moment.

The moon shone through her window as they lay together. Lyle traced her lips with his finger, then kissed them. "Oh, my dearest. I've dreamed of us being like this. Did you know that I've desired you right from the start?"

"No, but I've cared for you ever since we met."

He kissed the hollows of her cheeks and felt the planes of her face with his fingertips. "You're so lovely. So ethereal here in the moonlight."

With infinite tenderness, he caressed her body, her breasts, and her thighs. "Sweetheart, my love . . ." he whispered over and over. She felt the faint tremor in his fingers, the quickening of his breathing. His mouth sought her lips, again and again, tender at first, then urgent and demanding.

Nothing mattered except that she be possessed entirely. She cried out in ecstasy when that time came, and suddenly she was more alive than she had ever been before. As a vital woman, every instinct took over. She matched her rhythm to his until they soared beyond anything she had ever known before to reach an explosive climax.

Afterward they lay together, their legs entwined, engulfed in a delightful lethargy, savoring their love. Lyle nuzzled her neck and kissed her bare shoulder. How she adored him. She should be ashamed of herself, but how could she be when they had longed for each other so much? And they would be married soon, she was sure. Completely happy, she dozed off to dream of their lovemaking.

Suddenly someone pounded on the door. "Jessie, wake up! I've got something to show you!"

Jessie jumped up with a start.

"Open the door!"

"Who is it?" Lyle whispered as he sat up.

"Oh, God. It's my father." She called out, "Yes, Papa. Just a minute."

She climbed out of bed, slipped on her nightgown and robe, and whispered to Lyle, "I'll go to his room. That will give you a chance to slip out."

As soon as she opened the door, she saw her father in the hallway, holding a lantern. "You won't believe this. Just wait until you see!" His speech was slurred.

He's been drinking, she told herself. "Come on, Papa. Let's go in your room. Then you can show me what you have."

Carl put the lantern on the floor by the door and got out his key. He tried to insert it, but kept missing the keyhole.

"Here, Papa, I'll do it." She unlocked the door and led him inside. Soon she had the lamp lighted.

Carl stood by his bed and reached in his pocket. He flipped a twenty-dollar gold piece on the bed. Then another . . . and another.

"Papa, how wonderful!"

Her father stood with his back to the door, but she could see around him, could watch her room across the hall. Her heart thumped. Get out, Lyle. Get out now, she kept crying inwardly.

Carl chuckled in glee as he tossed the gold coins on the bed one by one. "I won tonight. Guess how many of these I have."

"About eight."

"Eight? You're way off. Dead wrong! Guess again."

"How about twelve?" She peered around him at her door across the hall and saw the door open slightly.

Carl's voice rose excitedly. "There are twenty-five of these golden babies. I won five hundred dollars! Imagine that! Five hundred!" He threw the rest of the coins on the bed in a shower.

Jessie watched Lyle leave her room and start for his own. Suddenly Tonio stepped out of the shadows.

"Tonio!" she screamed.

"Yes," her father said. "He walked home with me. Wasn't that good of him? He was afraid someone would knock me over the head and take all my money away." He reached down on the bed and grabbed the gold coins, tossed them into the air.

This has to be a nightmare, Jessie told herself. Surely she'd wake up and find out it wasn't true.

In the hall, Tonio reached out and grabbed Lyle's robe. "You damn skunk! I saw you coming out of Jessie's room. You seduced her." He made a fist and punched the lieutenant in the stomach. Lyle bent over, then came up with a blow of his own.

Jessie ran out. "Don't fight. Please don't cause a

ruckus and get Kitty and the others up here.'' She kept her voice low, but her face was ashen.

Tonio turned to her. "Stay out of this." His jaw stuck out. His eyes snapped in anger.

She grabbed his arm. "Tonio, it was my fault, too."

He pushed her arm away—and gave her a look of such disgust it seared her very soul.

"Please go on home and leave this be," Jessie pleaded.

"Like hell I will."

She glanced over her shoulder with panic-stricken eyes. "Please go, Tonio. I beg you, go!"

But Tonio looked at Lyle. "We've got a score to settle, you bastard, and we're doing it right now. Get your clothes on. I'll be waiting for you across the street." With that he turned and left.

"Lyle, don't go out with him," she begged.

"Don't worry. I can take care of myself. I've been itching to have it out with him."

Carl stuck his head out the door. "What's going on?"

"Nothing that concerns you, Papa." She walked into his room. "Now tell me all about how you happened to win so much money."

Her father seemed satisfied. "This is my lucky day. First the contract, and then this. I know you don't cotton to gambling, but you'll have to admit that five hundred dollars is a lot of money." He went on to tell her how he'd won it.

All the time he talked, she felt as if she were in a trance. All she could think about was how wanton she had been, how she had sinned. Now neither Lyle nor Tonio would respect her. Still, if she and Lyle loved each other, was it so terrible? They would be married before very long.

Tonio fumed with anger as he walked across the street to where the capitol building was being constructed. He'd been itching for another fight with Pretty Boy. One that would settle things between them once and for all.

Now that Lyle had added Jessie to his conquests, he could hardly wait to get his hands on him. He felt sick about Jess. Deep inside he felt this ache, almost like

grief. She was besotted with the lieutenant. Every time
she was around him, she became radiant and alive. Those
glorious eyes of hers glowed. Why did it hit him so hard
that she had succumbed to Soldier Boy?

After he walked around the grounds, he chose a roomy
spot on the east side, near Fifteenth Street. The big moon
shining overhead enabled him to look it over carefully—
to make sure it was free of any construction materials or
machinery.

"All right, Maguire. I'm here," Lyle said as he
stepped out into the cleared area.

Tonio grabbed his arm. "One thing I want to know—
Do you intend to marry Jessie?"

Lyle yanked his arm away. "That's none of your business. What's it to you, anyway?"

"Because she's a decent, lovely girl, and she cares for
you. You had no right to take advantage of her, you
s.o.b."

"Well, she was more than a willing partner, so you
don't have to get up a head of steam over it."

"You despicable louse. All she means to you is another notch in your belt." Tonio's fist flew out and hit
Lyle.

Soon they were on the ground, rolling over and over,
hitting each other. Lyle landed a blow to Tonio's ribs that
nearly knocked the breath out of him, but he wrenched
himself away and got to his feet.

Lyle rose slowly, and the two men sparred around each
other, throwing in a fist and dancing back and forth. They
eyed each other carefully, trying to get the slightest advantage, to find the other off-guard for a second.

Like lightning, Tonio's fist landed on Lyle's upper lip,
splitting it in two. Blood trickled down his chin. Furiously he went after his opponent and hit him on the jaw-
bone. Tonio staggered back, almost fell.

The two men came together again, locked and twisted,
trying to make the other give way, huffing and gasping
for breath. Lyle reached up and grabbed Tonio's hair and
pulled his head back with a jerk.

With that, Tonio landed a blow to Lyle's solar plexus

that forced the lieutenant to let go. They stumbled over each other's feet and fell to the ground. Over and over they rolled, grasped in a macabre embrace. Tonio tasted the dirt in his mouth. He spit it out, got his arm free, and whacked his opponent in the ribs. He could hear Lyle gasp in pain.

Back in Carl's room, Jessie forced herself to act calm. But a knot of panic clutched at her insides. What were the men doing? Would they get badly hurt? She had to see how they were getting along for herself. Perhaps she could stop them.

"Papa, I think it's wonderful that you have so much money. I have a little box we could put it in, and then on Monday we could take it to the bank. It will make a wonderful nest egg for your stage line. With that kind of money, you could rent a little office space, where people could buy tickets. I'll go get the box."

"Naw, I don't need it. Just put it in my coat pocket. I'm going back tomorrow to win some more."

She didn't dare oppose him too much. "Let's compromise, Papa. You're on a real winning streak right now. Everything's going your way. You can win some more with just part of your money. You don't need to take it all."

"Well, I guess you're right. Get your box. You can keep a little of it for our nest egg."

Jesse hurried across the hall and found a small box with handkerchiefs in it. She emptied it and returned to her father's room. While he was looking the other way, she gathered up most of the coins. "Well, good night, Papa. I'm going to bed now." She rushed back to her room to wrap a camisole around her box and hide it in the back of her bottom dresser drawer.

Now to see if she could stop the fight. She put some clothes on, tiptoed down the stairs, and slipped out a side door, leaving it slightly ajar.

The men were rolling in the dirt again when she found them. Over and over they tumbled, freeing themselves enough to land an occasional blow. But they were both gasping and acting as if they were tired. "Stop it!" she cried. "Right this minute." She grabbed Tonio's arm. "Let go of him. Lyle, get up and go over to the house. I want to talk to Tonio."

The lieutenant pulled himself together and got to his feet. "The fight was a draw."

Jessie said, "Of course it was. Now leave."

Tonio got up and brushed himself off. "I hate his guts. I'm warning you, Jessie. He has no intention of marrying you. You were a darn fool to throw yourself away on a guy like that. You're likely to have a baby, and then what are you going to do?"

"Lyle's going to marry me. I know he is." But her voice quavered.

Tonio gathered her in his arms, his heart aching for her, and held her close to comfort her. She felt sick with remorse as she leaned against him.

Chapter 13

On Monday morning, Jessie took the box loaded with gold coins to her father's room. "Papa, don't you think we should put this in the bank? It would be much safer than leaving it here while we're gone."

"You're right, of course. In fact, I should get all my assets in an account. We'll have expenses to pay for the convoy as we go back and forth."

If she could only get him to put her name on the account so she could write checks if necessary. . . . Somehow it seemed so demeaning to always be asking for money, having him hand it out a little at a time.

"I'll put my hat on and we'd better go right away. We'll be busy taking the coaches to be loaded this afternoon."

"You don't have to bother going with me, Jessie." He waved his hand in dismissal.

"Please let me, Papa. If I'm going to keep the books, I want to know exactly what figures to deal with."

"Well, all right, then."

All the way to the bank, she wondered how to tactfully ask him to put her name on the forms as well. He glanced at her with such a kindly expression—and she knew he was devoted to her—but it was hard for him to share any authority.

When they saw the bank ahead, she screwed up her courage. "Papa, as long as you're getting your business taken care of, wouldn't it be wise to plan for the time when you have a regular company again? After all, this army contract will only last a few weeks."

"I intend to open my accounts in the name of the Henderson Stage Company."

"And you will put aside some in savings so you can rent an office later?"

"Yes. Why do you ask?"

"Well, you said I was your assistant. I'll be running your office while you're out with the coach. Wouldn't it make sense to have my name on the accounts—so I can take care of your business when you're gone?"

Her father didn't answer. She remembered her mother's advice about not arguing a point: "He has to digest a new idea. Think it over. If you push too hard, he just says no, and he won't change his mind."

However, when he talked to a teller in the bank, he said, "Better put my daughter's name on my accounts. Then she can handle my affairs when I'm out of town."

On Tuesday morning, Jessie sat on the driver's seat with the reins in her hand. The casks of quicksilver were loaded inside the coach so their weight was evenly distributed. The locked containers of gold rested on top of them or were packed in the boot under the driver's seat. She wondered how large a fortune was placed in her care.

Lyle moved from one coach to the other, getting the convoy organized. A cavalryman rode at the head on a big black horse. Her father came next in the coach he had rented, then came one of the other coaches.

"I want you in the middle," Lyle told Jessie, so she got her coach in line.

The other two stagecoaches followed with another cavalryman at the end. Everyone in the convoy was armed with a pistol in a hip holster and a rifle on the seat.

Just before they pulled out, Lyle came over and climbed up beside her. "Good-bye, my dearest. We'll have dinner together when you get back. We'll have a lot to talk over." He squeezed her hand and got down.

A rush of happiness surged through her as she watched him move out of the way. In spite of his swollen lip and some bruises on his face from the fight, he was still wonderfully handsome. He was going to propose when they had dinner together, she told herself. Of course he was. Hadn't he said that they had a lot to talk over?

As the convoy moved down the street, away from the warehouse, two men watched from a second-story window. One of them shook his head. "Look at that. They might as well put a notice in the newspaper and tell what they're carrying."

Ross Eberson nodded. "Notice the coach in the middle with Henderson Stage Company painted on it. That's the one we'll target."

"The driver, he or she, looks like a young kid."

"But surprisingly skilled at handling the team. Notice how the horses are all bunched together with their hoofs striking the ground at the same time." Eberson's voice sounded respectful.

"I wish we were going after them this trip."

"It'd be suicide. They're all alert and on their guard. It's best to wait."

Jessie felt a real sense of satisfaction as she managed the reins. They'd been called upon to perform an important task for their country, and she, for one, was going to do her best. But she wished that Tonio was along with his coach. He had made the trip over the grade several times, and he knew what he was doing. But since he'd lost the contract, he'd refused to have anything to do with the project, and she couldn't blame him.

They changed horses at every stage station, which were fifteen miles apart. With fresh horses, they were able to move at a lively clip, especially across the valley.

Going from west to east over the Sierra, the grade was long and gradual. But when she thought of the hairpin turns dropping from the summit straight down the other side, a ball of dread formed in her stomach.

When the time finally came to go down the precipitous grade, she imagined that Tonio was sitting beside her. She could almost hear his words: "Keep the leaders going straight until their tails are in the center of the turn, then make it slow and easylike. In the meantime, keep the

swingers straight—until they're centered just so—before
you pull the reins. The wheelers mustn't cut too soon,
either.''

Back and forth, back and forth, around each hairpin
turn she guided her team, braking to keep the coach back.
The weight of the load, and the way it was distributed,
helped as well. She was too busy to look over the edge
at the drop straight down.

By the time they reached Carson City, she was more
than happy to turn the precious load over to the convoy
that was waiting.

Carl congratulated the other three drivers. ''Now
you're on your own. Just so you show up at the warehouse in Sacramento at two o'clock Monday afternoon.''

''Are we allowed to take passengers back?'' one of the
other drivers asked.

''Sure, if you can find them!''

After Jessie and her father finished dinner at their hotel, she asked, ''Is it all right with you if I put up a sign
on the bulletin board saying that we'll take passengers to
Sacramento?''

''Yes, if you want to.''

''If we get any fares, I want to put the money in the
bank for your stage line, so you can equip your office.''

Carl reached across and took her hand. ''Jessie, what
would I do without you?''

She stared at him in surprise. Papa wasn't sentimental.
When Lyle and she got married, he'd have to get along
without her.

He went on. ''I'm hoping to find a partner who'll go
in with me, so we could take turns staying in the office.''

''I could keep the books there instead of at home.''

''No, I want you out of it entirely. A stage office is no
place for a female.''

Resentment flared up in her. ''Papa, I don't want to
be out of it. I'd like to be part of your stage line. I could
sell the tickets—and even drive if necessary.''

He shook his head. ''No. That's not to say I haven't
been right proud of the way you've taken hold and learned
to drive like a real knight of the road. There's many a

whip that'd hesitate taking a six-horse hitch down those grades. I've been amazed at you. But you're a female, and it's not fittin' for you to do men's work. Your mother wouldn't approve of it at all."

Well, there was no use arguing with him. When she and Lyle were married, she'd be leaving, anyway.

Carl took out his wallet. "Well, I guess I'll find a card game. I'm having a lucky streak now."

"Be sure you have your gun with you, Papa. You ought to have some way to protect yourself if you do win again."

He patted his holster. "You're right, Jess. I made up my mind to that the other night when I won. I determined then I'd better take my revolver with me whenever I play cards. There're always low-down skunks watching a winner as he leaves a saloon."

Later, as she wrote out the notice about the passengers, she thought again how interesting staging was. Every trip was a separate challenge. A man with a lot of initiative and gumption like Tonio could eventually make a fortune.

The next morning, seven passengers waited outside the hotel for transportation to Sacramento. She collected the fare in advance, and put it in her satchel to bank later. Three of the men rode with her and four with her father.

"You lead the way, Jess. That way I can keep my eye on you and know you're safe."

The trip back over the grade was not so frightening now that she was more experienced. All she could think about was getting home and having dinner with Lyle. Of course he would propose.

But when she arrived back at the boardinghouse, she found a note on her dresser dated the day before:

I'm so sorry, Jess, but I can't have dinner with you when you return. I have to take the riverboat to San Francisco tonight. I have some business for the army to take care of at the presidio there. I've left instructions so the convoy will be loaded and guarded just the same.

She ached with disappointment, but she reminded herself that if she was going to be a lieutenant's wife, the army would always be first.

She bathed, then dressed in her feminine clothes to have dinner at the boardinghouse.

Carl left the house as soon as he finished eating. He could hardly wait to get back to the poker table at the saloon. Lady Luck was riding on his shoulder these days. First the contract, and then the five hundred dollars. In Carson City, he'd won fifty-five dollars, which was nothing to sneeze at, either.

By the time Carl got to his favorite saloon, all of the seats at the poker table with the official dealers were taken. He stood in back of the players wishing he could be part of the action. Two other men watched as well.

Finally one of the bystanders, a heavyset, bearded man with a gold chain across his plaid vest, turned to Carl and said, "Not much chance of getting in this game. How about having our own table?"

"Sure."

A third man agreed to join them, and soon they were seated at a table in the corner.

Carl introduced himself.

The stout man put out his hand. "Fats Oberheimer's my moniker. I'm out here from New York."

The third man had a fringe of rust-colored hair around his bald head, a spattering of freckles, and a handlebar mustache. "Red McNalley. I've staked a claim up in the north mines near Rough and Ready."

The men shook hands. A bartender came over and took their orders. They bought chips and a new deck of cards from him.

"Let's play Down the River," Fats suggested.

Carl nodded, as it was his favorite game—seven-card stud poker, a real challenge. It required card-reading ability, recall of cards that had been folded, and attention to probabilities.

"Let's outlaw check and raise and other forms of sandbagging," Red put in.

Carl added, "We should fold in turn only, and all cards

should be exposed before doing so." He had a good memory for the cards that were folded, but he wanted a chance to see them.

"All right."

Fats agreed, then suggested, "How about making it interesting? A limit of twenty-five cents on the first bet, fifty cents on the second and third bet, and a dollar on the last two bets."

Carl gulped. Those were high stakes, but Red agreed, shoving the cards toward him, so there wasn't much he could do but go along.

Carl dealt three cards—two down and one up—before the first bet. He had a pair of sevens down and a king up, so he shoved in his quarter chip. The next three deals brought him another seven. The last round was down, and when he looked at his card, he had another king, which made a full house. So he won that round.

At first, Carl won every hand, so he knew his lucky streak was continuing. However, before the evening was over, he noticed that every time Fats dealt he won. Somehow the big man managed to get flushes, straights, or a full house.

Carl studied Fats's hands as they handled the cards. They moved with lightning speed, but finally he was sure that the big man dealt to himself from the bottom of the deck.

"Damn you! You're cheating!" Carl cried out.

Fats reached in his pocket and pulled out a gun.

In a flash, Carl had his gun out of the holster. Hardly aware of what he was doing, he fired it. Fats slumped forward, blood oozing out of a fold in his stomach.

Everyone shouted at once, then crowded around. The bartender rushed to the table. "What's going on?"

"This guy was cheating. Dealing from the bottom. When I challenged him, he pulled a gun on me." Carl's heart thumped crazily. Fear, anger, remorse pulsed through him.

The bartender said, "I'll go get Mr. Dumont. He's the owner. He ain't going to like this one little bit. You wait here."

"You'd better send someone for a doctor," a bystander shouted after him.

"Yes, I will."

While they waited, another man yelled out, "Here's the bullet. Jammed right here in the floor."

Carl dropped into a chair in relief. It was just a flesh wound then.

Mr. Dumont, a giant of a man, strode angrily through the crowd carrying a bath towel. When he reached the table, he pressed the towel on the injured man's stomach. Fats was still slumped over the table.

He glowered at Carl. "I run a decent, law-abiding saloon, and I don't allow any rough stuff like this. Why did you shoot him?"

"He was cheating. Dealing from the bottom."

Fats Oberheimer raised his head. "I was not."

Mr. Dumont went on. "You could've told him to stop it. Dammit, you didn't need to shoot him down like a dog."

"He pulled a gun on me."

"You're a liar," Fats protested. "All I got is this little derringer. It's still in my pocket."

"Red McNalley saw you, too." Carl looked around, but he couldn't see his gambling partner. "You pulled your gun first."

"That's a lie and you know it."

The saloon owner took hold of the injured man's arm. "I've sent for a doctor. Come on into the back room." He nodded at Carl. "Take his other arm."

After they got Fats on his feet, Mr. Dumont turned to his bartender. "Get the crowd back to the gaming tables and the bar."

They soon had the injured man laid out on a cot in the back room.

The bartender stuck his head in the door. "Here's Dr. Whitney."

The doctor looked as if he were recovering from a hangover with his bloodshot eyes, disheveled clothes, and shaking hands. Carl noticed the physician's dirty fingernails as he pulled down Fats's pants and examined the torn flesh.

"It's just a flesh wound," the doctor muttered. "But I'd better sew it up." He opened up a battered bag and found what he needed from the jumbled interior.

When the doctor was finished and ready to leave, Carl handed him a five-dollar gold piece. The saloon owner added another one and said, "Just keep your mouth shut about this. Okay?"

"Sure. I get the usual free drinks, don't I?"

Dumont nodded, and the medical man left.

Fats spoke up. "Aren't you going to send for the sheriff?"

The saloon owner shook his head. "I run a decent place here, and I don't want to call in the law. The less I have to do with them, the better."

"But this guy shot—"

Mr. Dumont turned to Carl. "Are you a local man?"

"Yes. I have a stage line. Right now I'm doing some work for the army."

The saloon owner took a notebook and pencil out of his vest pocket. "What's your name and address?"

Carl told him. Dumont seemed impressed when Widow White's place was mentioned.

Fats half sat up on the cot. "Dammit, I was shot. I could have been killed. You ought to have this man arrested."

Mr. Dumont looked down at him. "I haven't the slightest doubt that you cheated."

"That's not true."

"Oberheimer, you're a regular card shark. I know your type, and you're not welcome here anymore. And I suggest that as soon as you're able, you take a riverboat to Frisco—because I'm going to warn all the other saloons about you."

Later, when Carl went back into the game room, he felt a great sense of relief. He was lucky to get out of that sticky situation as well as he did. He looked around for Red McNalley, but couldn't see him, so he dismissed him from his mind then and stopped to shoot dice.

Their coaches were loaded the next day, and they were ready to start out again the following morning. As usual, Lyle was there getting the convoy organized. A sergeant worked with him.

Before they pulled out, Lyle went over to each driver. "This is Sergeant Winter from the presidio in San Francisco. He'll be stationed here in Sacramento and will have charge of our project at this end. I'm going to be working out of Carson City for a while."

When he spoke to Jessie, he added, "I'll be riding with you."

When Lyle finally climbed up on the box after storing his gear in the back boot, he reached over and patted Jessie's arm. "I'm so sorry we couldn't have our dinner together, but I was in San Francisco. We'll have to make up for it in Carson City."

Jessie's spirits soared. After being so disappointed, she felt like shouting with happiness. They'd be together this whole trip. Then they'd have their dinner in Carson City . . . when he surely would propose.

The convoy started out with the harnesses jingling and the horses' hoofs clattering along the way. She guided the team through the heavy waterfront traffic.

But once they were safely on their way, she glanced at him just to enjoy his handsome appearance again. When he turned toward her, their eyes met.

"You're a lovely girl. You look so pretty this morning."

He cared for her, of course he did. Besides that, he was an honorable man. Now that they had made love, he would want to make everything right between them. They shouldn't have been so wanton, but how could they resist each other?

As if he could read her thoughts, he said, "I've been worrying about something, dearest."

"What is that?"

"You're not in the family way, are you?"

The color rose in her cheeks as she shook her head.

"You're sure? You've had your female monthly since then?"

She flamed in embarrassment. "Yes. Everything's all right." Why was it that she had been so intimate with him, but couldn't talk about it?

He let out a long sigh of relief. "I feel a lot better. I'll bet you do, too."

"Of course." She had been freed from anxiety, but if they were married right away would it have mattered so much? Perhaps he wanted her to get adjusted to the life of an army post before she had the care of a baby.

She cherished every minute they rode together. That afternoon he sat with her father. Was Lyle asking Papa's permission to court her? She hoped so. And Papa would give it, she knew.

The next day, the lieutenant rode with each of the other three drivers for a while, which disappointed her. She didn't want to share Lyle with anyone. But they did take the last lap together.

When they arrived in Carson City, it took some time to transfer the load to the other coaches and get the horses settled in the livery stable. At the hotel, however, she managed to get a bath before she changed. She whirled around in front of the mirror, enjoying her appearance as a woman. It was worth the trouble of bringing her clothes and hairpiece with her.

When she met him in the lounge, he took her hand and squeezed it. "You look so lovely in that lavender dress. I can't believe you're the same person as that very skilled driver you are all day long."

"It's so good to feel like a woman again."

"We might as well eat right here in the dining room. All the other places are in gambling houses or saloons. Or else they're greasy-spoon joints not fit for ladies." He took her arm.

When they were seated and the waiter had taken their order, she said, "I'm going to miss you now that you're here instead of at Widow White's."

"But I'll see you every time you come over the hill. It'll be about the same. Besides, I don't think we should spend too much time together right now. I don't want things to get out of control again."

How she wanted to add—until we're married. While she sipped her wine, she waited for him to say something about their future. Would he ask her if she would be willing to live here in Carson City and later at Fort Wallace? She could hardly wait to assure him that she would. Actually she liked this little town nestled against the Sierra range.

She leaned forward eagerly, holding her breath. Surely he would hint about their life together. How she would have to follow him wherever he was stationed. About the children they would have.

He reached over and took her hands in his. "Jessie, I have some plans. But I'm not ready to speak about them just yet. I hope you understand."

Slumping back, feeling completely deflated, she expelled her breath. "Of course," she murmured as she swallowed the lump in her throat. So he was postponing his commitment once again. But he did say that he had some plans. She'd have to be content with that.

After they ate their dinner, he said, "You'll have to excuse me, Jess. I must work on a report."

He walked her up the stairs to her room and said good night. She went inside and took off her dress, her two petticoats, her corset and underwear. She put on her nightgown and crawled into bed, feeling neglected. Finally she came to the conclusion that she'd just have to be patient. She didn't know anything about his army orders. Lots of secret things went on in the military, such as shipping this gold and quicksilver to the East Coast. Lyle was just waiting for the right time to propose. Finally she dropped off to sleep.

They had passengers waiting for them the next morning, so she had more money to add to their savings.

They made the trip back to Sacramento without incident. When Jess pulled into the livery stable late in the afternoon, she saw two policemen talking with the owner.

By the time she'd unharnessed the team and wiped the horses down, her father had pulled in. He climbed down from the box and started to unhook the harnesses.

The policemen walked over. One of them asked, "Are you Carl Henderson?"

"Yes."

Jessie joined the men. "Papa, what's going on?"

"I don't know."

One policeman pulled Carl's hands behind his back while the other snapped a pair of handcuffs over his wrists.

Jessie cried out in protest; the color drained from her face. This must be a nightmare.

"You're under arrest!"

Carl's mouth gaped open in astonishment. "What in hell for?"

"Murder."

"My father didn't murder anyone," Jessie cried. "There's some mistake. We just pulled in from Nevada." This wasn't real. It couldn't be happening.

Just then Tonio drove into the livery yard. Jessie ran toward him, her face ashen, her eyes huge with horror. "Tonio, come here! We need you!" Her voice shook.

Tonio jumped down from the box. "What's going on?"

"Those policemen are arresting Papa!"

Tonio and Jessie hurried back to the group in time to hear one of the officers say, "We'll have to take you to the station."

"Now just a minute!" Tonio spoke up. "His daughter deserves an explanation."

One of the officers turned to Jessie. "Well, ma'am, a week ago your father shot a man in the stomach when he was gambling."

"Papa!" Jessie couldn't believe what she was hearing. "Is that true?"

"Yes, I'm afraid it is." Carl looked at her, his eyes pleading with her to understand. "He was cheating. Dealing from the bottom of the deck. I called him on it, and he pulled a gun on me. I guess I acted too quick. I yanked out my Colt revolver and shot. It was just a flesh wound. Didn't amount to much."

Jessie turned to the policeman. "But you said it was murder."

"Ma'am, the wound became infected. Mr. Oberheimer died at ten o'clock today. That makes it murder." The officer tightened his grip. "You'll have to come along with us."

"At least let him take his satchel." Jessie ran to the coach. Tears ran down her cheeks as she returned with it. "Oh, Papa." She kissed him good-bye.

Carl turned to Tonio. "Better get me a lawyer."

The policemen escorted Carl out to the street and put him in the police wagon.

Tonio took Jessie in his arms while she sobbed. "There, there. It's going to be all right. Now don't you be so upset. We'll find him a good lawyer."

"Thank God you came along. What if I had to deal with this all by myself?" For a long moment she leaned against his shoulder for comfort. What a dear, dear friend he was. "I can't believe this has happened. He's the last person who would do such a thing. What am I going to do?"

"Let's unharness the horses and get them settled. Then we must go talk to Kitty White. She'll be able to help us."

Later, when they sat in Kitty's garden in the twilight and told her all about Carl's dilemma, she slumped back in her chair in shock. "I can't believe it. He's one of the finest men I've ever known. I feel so sorry for him."

Tonio asked, "Do you know a good lawyer? One who handles criminal cases?"

"I'd recommend Bob Grist. He's the best in town. We've been friends for years. You can see him in the morning."

"Come with us, Kitty," Jessie implored.

"All right, I will."

When it was time for Tonio to leave, Jessie walked out to the front gate with him. Just as he was saying good-bye, she let out a gasp. "The convoy! Oh, my Lord, what am I going to do without Papa? This is awful!"

Tonio put his arm across her shoulders. "Would you like me to take your father's place?"

"Oh, Tonio, please do. That would be wonderful. I didn't think you'd consider it."

"Well, I owe you something after getting your father to come out here to California and not taking him in the stage line. Gianni can get along without me for a few weeks. Serves him right."

She told him about how the coaches had to be loaded the next day.

"I'll be there with Carl's rig."

"Tonio, you're one of the nicest guys I've ever known."

He kissed the top of her head. "Now get some rest and quit worrying. We'll work things out."

The next morning, Bob Grist agreed to take the case. "Let's walk over to the jail and see my client."

They waited in a small conference room. When her father came into the room in his jail garb, it was all she could do to control herself. How dreadful he must feel.

The men shook hands. "Now tell me the whole incident. Even the smallest detail."

When Carl finished, the lawyer said, "If this Oberheimer drew his gun first, you could plead that you shot in self-defense. That is if we can find the witness, Red McNalley, and he testifies in your behalf."

"He said he had to stake a claim somewhere around Rough and Ready. But there are hundreds of prospectors up there. It'd be like finding a needle in a haystack." Carl shook his head in discouragement. "Tonio, would you have time to search for him?"

"No, Carl. I'm going to take your place in the convoy."

"Thank God for that. I've been worried sick about what we were going to do."

Kitty took a piece of paper out of her purse and found a pencil. "Tell me about this Red McNalley."

As Carl described him, she sketched a man with a bald head, a fringe of hair, and a big handlebar mustache.

"That looks quite a bit like him. But his cheeks were fuller."

She made the cheeks rounder.

"Dadgummit, if that isn't a perfect likeness! But there's no use getting our hopes up. The chances of finding him are one in a million."

"But we should try." She folded the sketch carefully and put it in her purse.

Chapter 14

Jessie dreaded explaining what had happened to her father to Sergeant Winter. When she drove her coach into the loading yard, she saw him standing ramrod-straight, a stern expression on his face, supervising the workmen.

Should she tell him the truth . . . or make up some excuse? Would he take the contract away from them now that her father was in jail? But she needed every cent of the money—to pay the lawyer for her father's defense and to support herself. She grieved thinking of poor Papa incarcerated.

Finally she decided it was best to tell the sergeant the truth. What if the *Sacramento Union* should run a story about the shooting? Then she would certainly be in trouble!

She climbed down from the box, swallowed hard to calm herself, and walked over to the sergeant. Her voice trembled as she began. "We have a problem, but it's all going to work out all right." She told him the whole story. Just as she finished, Tonio drove in. "I've asked Mr. Maguire to take my father's place," she added when he walked over.

The sergeant scowled. "I have no authority to let some stranger take Mr. Henderson's place."

"I can understand exactly how you feel," Tonio spoke up. "I respect your caution. Of course you have to check me out." He put out his hand. "My name is Tonio Ma-

guire, and I am a partner in the Valley Stage Line." He
reached in his vest pocket and took out a business card.
"I have been in business here in Sacramento for three
years." He nodded toward the other drivers. "They all
know me, so why don't you talk to them?"

"I'll do that." The sergeant went to each of the drivers
and showed them the card. When he returned, he said,
"They all vouch for you, but I don't know what to do.
I've never had to deal with a situation like this. Lieutenant Underwood's orders are that only drivers authorized
by him can be in the convoy."

"Lieutenant Underwood knows Mr. Maguire very
well," Jessie put in. "In fact, we all came out together
from Fort Wallace. I know he would approve." The two
men didn't get along, but Lyle certainly respected Tonio's ability as a driver, she told herself. How tactfully
he was handling the sergeant, she thought.

The soldier looked at Tonio. "So you were in Fort
Wallace?"

"That's right." Tonio described the fort, the square
miles it covered, and the total number of men stationed
there. He told about the Indian artifacts in the officer's
mess.

The sergeant nodded. "I've been in Fort Wallace, and
it's obvious you have."

"We had lunch with Captain Blackston," Tonio went
on. "He has sideburns that almost reach his mouth."

Finally Sergeant Winter smiled. "I'm convinced. Either I let you take charge of the convoy—or hold everything back while I send word to Lieutenant Underwood."

"It would take at least four days to hear from him,"
Jessie put in. "He emphasized how important the time
factor was. We have to get the shipments on the way
before the snow closes the road over the Sierra."

"That's right. No offense, ma'am, but I certainly won't
put you in charge . . . because you're a woman. In fact,
I don't approve of you being one of the drivers. However,
Lieutenant Underwood insisted. I don't know why."

"Well, I do." Jessie squared her shoulders and drew
herself up to her full height. "It's because I am just as

skilled as a man. I'm capable and reliable. Mr. Maguire
and my father trained me so I can handle my team as
well as anyone.'' If Papa were only here to stand up for
her.

"No offense, ma'am.'' The sergeant's neck turned red.
"You can unhitch your teams and take them back to the
stable while we load the coaches.'' He nodded toward
the building at the back of the property. . . .

The hearing was to be held that afternoon. Jessie and
Tonio hurried to the courthouse and found a seat next to
Kitty.

She leaned toward them and whispered, "The lawyer
says we've drawn Judge Lundstrom, and he's the toughest
one of all.''

The bailiff led Carl into the courtroom, and Jessie
looked at her father's stricken face. It was all she could
do to keep from rushing to him as he sat down next to
his lawyer. Tonio squeezed her hand.

Soon they were told to rise as the bearded judge entered the courtroom. When it came time, the prosecutor
presented his case. Carl's lawyer pleaded "Not guilty.''

The judge listened to the proceedings and banged his
gavel. "The prisoner will be held without bail until his
trial on October twentieth.'' Carl was led away.

Out in the hall, Bob Grist said, "Holding him without
bail is ridiculous. He's no danger to society.''

"I hope we don't get Judge Lundstrom for the trial!''
Jessie spoke up.

The lawyer shrugged. "We have no control over that.''

Widow White worked at her desk, copying the sketch
she had made of Red McNalley. She made ten copies,
tucked all but one in a pigeonhole in her desk, and walked
out in the backyard to talk with her handyman, who was
pulling weeds.

"Amos, don't bother with those weeds now. I want
you to find someone for me.''

While the middle-aged handyman stood up and brushed

his hands on his overalls, Kitty gave him her sketch of Red McNalley and told him the circumstances.

"You'll have to go to the northern mines out of Rough and Ready. Apparently he staked a claim up there."

Kitty knew Amos Steinhuss would do anything for her. Although he was not too bright or ambitious, she felt confident he'd go up to the mines and do his best. He was patient and tenacious and if anyone could find McNalley, he would.

"You go hire a horse and buggy and get yourself ready so you can leave at daybreak tomorrow morning. If you find this McNalley, tell him I'll pay him one hundred dollars to come here to Sacramento and talk to a lawyer. I'll even give him his room and board. If possible, bring him back with you."

Amos nodded and headed for his room and small bath in the basement.

She returned to the house and put on her hat; today she would go to the newspaper office to insert advertisements offering a reward for information about the missing witness. Tomorrow morning she intended to visit all the saloon keepers and leave her sketch with a notice of her reward.

When Jessie reported to the warehouse on Tuesday morning, Sergeant Winter met her and said, "You're to take a passenger headed for Fort Wallace as far as Carson City."

"A passenger? I thought that was absolutely against all regulations when we had our shipment on board."

"These are my orders, ma'am. The passenger arrived on the river steamer early this morning."

"But you're asking us to take on this extra responsibility. That's not part of the contract."

"Ma'am, I bent the rules yesterday to accept Mr. Maguire as the one in charge. So if I were you, I wouldn't have too much to say about the terms of the contract. Follow me to the office and meet the passenger."

Jessie felt she had been put in her place. "It's out of my hands then. I don't know what Lieutenant Underwood will say."

"He knows about it and is agreeable."

She followed him into the office . . . and there sat a pretty, charming young lady surrounded by boxes, satchels, and a small steamer trunk. She wore a straw bonnet over her red-gold hair.

The sergeant said, "Meet Miss Elizabeth Foxworthy from New York. This is one of our drivers, Jess Henderson, or actually Miss Jessie Henderson." His voice showed his disapproval.

Elizabeth put out her hand. "So you're a girl. How wonderful! And you can drive a stagecoach? That's amazing." After shaking hands, she stood up and reached for some of her luggage. "I'm afraid I've brought too many things. But I came by *The Flying Cloud*, a clipper ship traveling around the Horn, so I had plenty of room."

"I'll ask the drivers to help you load your things," Jessie offered. "Actually we have plenty of room for them, so don't worry."

This lovely girl had come out to marry one of the young officers at Fort Wallace, Jessie decided. She was adorable. Some man was going to be fortunate to have such a charmer as a bride.

When they got outside, the sergeant said, "I'll help you get up on the seat of the first coach. You'll have to ride with the drivers, as the inside of the coaches are full."

Elizabeth gave Tonio a dazzling smile. "This will be a wonderful new adventure. I've never ridden next to the driver before."

Soon all of her luggage was loaded and they were off.

Watching the proceedings from their small office across from the warehouse were Ross Eberson and his group of Southern sympathizers.

"They're taking a passenger," one spoke up. "Wonder what that means."

Eberson shook his head. "I don't know. But it's a good thing we didn't plan our strike for this trip."

"Yes, it would complicate things," another said.

As soon as the convoy was out of sight, Eberson indicated that they were to gather around the table, which was covered with maps. "Their next trip is when we strike. I'll go over my plans with you. Remember it's the Henderson coach with that female driver that's the vulnerable one."

When the convoy stopped at the designated stage station for lunch, Elizabeth rushed over to Jessie. "We had a marvelous trip here. We sang folk songs all the way. It was so much fun."

In spite of herself, Jessie felt a twinge of resentment. Somehow singing with Tonio while they rode along seemed her own private prerogative. But she told herself not to be silly. And who could be annoyed with Elizabeth, who bubbled over with good spirits and charm?

Tonio brought his guitar into the dining room, and, as the others ate, he sang "Sacramento."

A bully ship and a bully crew, doo-da, doo-da!
A bully mate and a captain, too, doo-da, doo-da-day.
Then blow ye winds, hi-oh, for Cal-i-for-ny-o!
There's plenty of gold, so I've been told,
On the banks of the Sac-ra-ment-o.

He sang all the verses in his beautiful voice before he sat down to his own lunch. "Actually they discovered gold on the American River, which we follow today, but it's a tributary to the Sacramento," he explained to Elizabeth.

She gave him a grateful smile and looked around at all the drivers. "I'd like to take a turn riding with each one of you, if I may."

Elizabeth rode with Jessie the last day. They came around Lake Tahoe, which thrilled her with its beauty. "I've never seen anything so magnificent," she exclaimed over and over. "I'm so excited about everything."

Jessie's own anticipation was beginning to grow. She would see Lyle this very evening. They'd have dinner together and, of course, he'd propose. He'd said that he had plans he would tell her about. She thought of the pretty green taffeta dress she had brought for the occasion.

She glanced at her passenger and saw how radiant she looked. "Elizabeth, I have a hunch you're going to Fort Wallace to be married. You look like a bride."

The other girl giggled. "You're right, of course. Did I give myself away? I wasn't supposed to say a word to anyone."

"Maybe the men didn't notice. But I've sensed it ever since we started. Where did you meet your fiancé?"

"We live in a small town on the Hudson River, right near West Point. Bert was attending the academy, and we saw a lot of each other."

"That sounds very romantic." She wished she had known Lyle while he was going to West Point.

"When Bert came out to Fort Wallace, he wrote me a letter. We corresponded back and forth and finally he asked me to come out and marry him."

By now they were around the lake and on the grade dropping down to Carson City.

Elizabeth squealed as she looked down the sheer drop. They were on the outside, so she could see the thousands of feet to the canyon below.

"Don't look down, Elizabeth," Jessie warned. "It isn't so scary if you keep your eyes on the road."

"I don't see how you can drive your team around these curves."

"I've learned how to." To distract her passenger, Jessie said, "Tell me about your wedding plans."

"For one thing, I want you to be my maid of honor. I don't know another girl in Nevada."

"So you're getting married in Carson City. I thought you were going to Fort Wallace."

"We will eventually. But right now Bert's in Carson City."

Lyle must have an assistant to help him with this shipping project, Jessie told herself. "Fortunately I brought my nicest dress with me. I'd love to be your maid of honor." A wedding would be the perfect atmosphere to encourage Lyle to propose, she told herself.

"And I want to have Tonio sing at our wedding."

Jessie smiled. "If I ever get married, I hope he can sing at mine."

"I thought perhaps you and Tonio—"

"No. He has a girl he hopes to marry." As she carefully maneuvered the big coach around a curve, she told Elizabeth about Iris. As always, she felt a pang of resentment and jealousy when she was reminded of Tonio's girl and the party at the Cunningham mansion.

The steepest part was coming up, so she would have to keep her mind on what she was doing. "If you want Tonio and me to take part, you'll have to get married tonight. We start back tomorrow morning."

"I think that will be all right."

The worst curve of all was at hand. Jessie kept her leaders going straight ahead as long as she could. She climbed the reins to get them to turn just right. Then came the swingers. The coach was getting too close to the edge, she realized.

Elizabeth spoke again. "I imagine Lyle was planning the wedding for tonight, anyway."

Jessie's heart constricted. "Lyle?"

"Yes. Lieutenant Lyle Underwood. That's the man I'm marrying. I sometimes call him Bert because his first name is really Albert."

For a moment, Jessie's mind went blank with shock. The right wheels spun over the edge. The coach teetered back and forth and almost tipped over. Elizabeth screamed. Instinctively Jessie yanked the reins, and the horses lunged to the left—not a fraction too soon. The wheels spat gravel. Finally they were back on the roadway, her foot firmly on the brake.

"I'm so sorry, Elizabeth. I didn't mean to scare you."

"That's all right. Just for a second I thought we were going over." Ashen-faced, she glanced at Jessie.

"We're okay now." Her heart pounded against her breastbone. Don't think. Don't cry. Just drive the coach to Carson City.

Somehow Jessie made it down the grade. Don't think. Don't let yourself feel. Over and over she repeated Tonio's instructions about going around the curves to keep her mind occupied.

But more than once, the stab of truth came through the paralysis. Lyle was going to marry this girl beside her. He never intended to marry her. He had betrayed her.

"Are you all right, Jessie?"

"Yes."

"You're white as a sheet."

"We had a close call. I guess I'm realizing it now." But it wasn't their narrow miss. As they sped through the sagebrush with the thunder of hoofs and jingle of chains, she realized what it meant to have your heart broken. She felt physical pain and wanted to bend over in grief. But she couldn't let it show. No one must know.

"I can see some buildings ahead."

"That's Carson City. We'll soon be there."

By the time they pulled into their meeting place, the other convoy was there waiting. As soon as they came to a halt, Lyle rushed to Jessie's coach and climbed up to the seat.

He gathered Elizabeth in his arms. "You're here, darling. All safe and sound." He smothered her with kisses, then glanced at Jessie. "Thanks a lot for bringing her here."

They climbed down from the seat and stepped to one side, where they talked together in private.

Tonio walked over to Jessie's coach. He gazed at Lyle and Elizabeth and then up at her. "Here, let me help you down." He got up on the seat beside her.

She looked at him, her huge dark eyes stricken with grief. "Lyle's marrying her. He never intended to propose to me," she whispered.

"The son of a bitch! I'm so sorry, Jess."

She fought to control her trembling lip. "I had no idea. When she spoke of him she called him Bert. His first name is Albert."

"The minute I saw her in Sacramento, I had a hunch she was his bride-to-be."

Jessie steeled herself and fought for control.

Tonio made his hands into fists. "I'd like to bash his face in."

"No. Don't cause any trouble. Not a word. Promise me, Tonio. Elizabeth must never know."

Tonio nodded and took her arm. "You'd better get down."

Radiant and bubbling with happiness, Elizabeth joined them, pulling Lyle with her. "We are going to get married tonight in a church. It's all arranged—with flowers and an organist and everything." She turned to her groom and went on. "Jessie has promised to be made my maid of honor. She brought a dress with her. Isn't that wonderful? And Tonio, I want you to sing a solo before Jessie and I walk down the aisle. You will, won't you?"

"Of course." Tonio turned to Lyle. "If we can just step to one side, I'd like to explain why I'm here in Carl's place." The men walked away.

Elizabeth clapped her hands. "It's going to be a real wedding. Far more wonderful than I ever dreamed it would be. Now I must find all my boxes and bundles and take them to the hotel."

"Tonio'll help you get your gear together," Jessie said.

Later, when she was alone with Lyle, she said, "Was this your idea of a cruel joke?"

"What do you mean?"

"Having us bring her. Surely you must know how hard this is for me."

Lyle couldn't meet her eyes. "You and I weren't anything but friends."

"Surely you don't think I'd give myself to anyone I didn't care for?"

Lyle turned to her. "Please understand. Elizabeth and I have been sweethearts for a long time, and she's the one I expected to marry. I just met you a short time ago."

"I think you're a deceitful, despicable rat who betrayed me, Lyle Underwood." She glared at him until the color rose in his face.

"Those are pretty strong words."

"But I mean every one of them. You could have been honest and aboveboard right from the first, but you weren't. You even had us bring her to you with no word of warning."

"But I had to do something. She was all right coming out here because her parents arranged to have her on the same ship with a minister and his wife. I hired an older woman to accompany her on the riverboat from San Francisco to Sacramento. But I couldn't turn her loose to ride a regular stagecoach over the grade with all the rough miners. I knew she'd be safe with you."

"She was safe, all right. I hope you treat her well. You don't deserve a wonderful girl like Elizabeth. She's far too good for a man like you. She's looking for you right now, so you'd better leave." Jessie trembled with hurt and fury.

As soon as her coach was unloaded, she drove to the hotel and dropped off her suitcase, then took her rig to the livery stable for the night. On the way, she kept telling herself that she mustn't cry. Once she started, she'd never be able to stop. Instead she concentrated on the horses.

She slipped off the harnesses and hung them on pegs. She could pay a hostler to rub them down, but she wanted to take care of them herself. She had to keep too busy to think.

Carefully she wiped the light lather off the flanks of the red roans. She examined their hoofs to make sure there were no cuts and bruises. A dappled gray needed attention where he had a harness sore.

Finally she could spend no more time here. She had to get back to the hotel to bathe and dress for the wedding.

Ironically she knew she never looked lovelier in her green dress. Only the haunted look in her large eyes betrayed her inner feelings. If Papa were only here to comfort her. She could imagine what her father would have to say to Lyle for treating her so shabbily.

Tonio drove them to the church. Elizabeth wore a white bridal gown with a short veil over her red-gold hair. She carried a bouquet of pink and white roses. "Lyle bought them from a woman who grows them in her yard. She even decorated the church." She turned to Jessie. "This is the happiest day of my life."

"Of course it is," Jessie finally managed.

They waited in the foyer while Tonio tied up his rig and returned. They listened to his lovely voice sing out "I Love You with All My Heart." Finally, when the organist played the wedding march, Jessie led the way down the aisle, the bride coming right behind.

Lyle looked even more handsome in his dress uniform as he stood with his best man, a sergeant who was assisting him with the gold project.

While the minister began, "Dearly beloved: We have come together in the presence of God to witness and bless the joining together of this man and this woman in holy matrimony," Jessie fixed her gaze on Tonio, who stood by the organist. She tried to blot out the words by studying the shape of his head, the way his hair curled around his ears, the splendid width of his shoulders.

Mechanically she accepted the bride's bouquet when it came time to pledge their vows. She hardly heard the words. She kept her gaze on the kind expression on Tonio's face. He was suffering for her. She could tell by the way he clenched his fists.

Don't cry, she kept warning herself. Keep your heartache deep inside. Don't let it show. But it was a physical pain, almost more than she could bear. She wanted to cry out, Lyle, how could you do this to me? How could you be so deceitful? Surely you know how I felt about you.

Finally the service was over. Tonio picked up his guitar and began the lively folk song "Soldier, Soldier, Won't You Marry Me?"

Elizabeth kissed Jessie when she took back her bridal bouquet. "Everything was so lovely. Like a dream come true."

"I hope you'll be very happy," Jessie murmured. She ignored Lyle.

"We want all of you to come back to the hotel for a wedding supper," the groom announced.

"I'm not the least bit hungry," Jessie said. "I'd like to be—"

"Of course we'll come," Tonio interrupted, and slipped his arm around her waist. He whispered in her ear, "You've been a trooper so far. Just keep it up for a little while longer."

The minister and his wife joined them, and all the time they ate kept the conversation going, telling about all the characters they had met in Carson City.

Finally the ordeal was over. Tonio took her to one side. "Go up and change your clothes. We're going for a long walk."

She scurried up the stairs and got into her men's clothes and boots. She pulled on a heavy sweater and returned to Tonio, who was waiting in the deserted lobby. At least she had been spared seeing the newlyweds leave for their bridal chamber.

They stepped out to the wooden sidewalk, but Tonio led her away from the main street with its saloons and gambling halls.

They walked along the dark street. The black sky formed a backdrop to millions of twinkling stars that looked close enough to touch.

Tonio put his arm around her waist. "I know you hurt like hell. . . . And you won't believe me when I say that this is the best thing that ever happened to you."

She shook her head.

"Jessie, love, go ahead and cry. Let it all come out."

"I can't cry. I'm way beyond tears. Now I know what it means to have your heart broken. I feel like something was just torn away inside."

He stopped, held her against his chest, and caressed her back.

"A lot of this is just plain hurt feelings," he murmured in her ear. "No one likes to be rejected, to have his bubble burst. But you were building up a lot of false expectations . . . reading more into Soldier Boy's words than he intended."

"I know. I was an awful fool."

"You looked so pretty tonight in your green dress."

"I didn't feel pretty at all."

"Well, you were. You sure kept your courage up through it all. I know Elizabeth had no idea how you were feeling."

Tonio held her close, kissed the top of her head, and rubbed her back. Finally she felt better—but she stayed in his arms, needing his compassion and understanding.

After a while Tonio grinned. "You have to admit that it was damned ironic . . . you and I taking part in their wedding!"

Chapter 15

Amos Steinhuss tied the buggy to the hitching post in front of the boardinghouse and wearily climbed up the front stairs. When he found Widow White in her office, he took off his hat and entered.

"Ma'am, I did my best, but I didn't find Red McNalley."

She felt a pang of disappointment. "Sit down, Amos, and tell me exactly what you did."

"I didn't want to just wander around, so the first thing I did was to go to Nevada City, that's the county seat, and see if McNalley had filed a claim and where it was."

Kitty nodded. "You used your head, Amos."

"Thank you, ma'am. McNalley filed a claim, all right, along with his partner, Gene Rugani. It borders on Deer Creek, quite a piece out of the town of Rough and Ready. Anyway, once I had the location I went there—and I found this Rugani digging a shaft into the side of the hill. But so far, it wasn't showing much promise. Most of those claims don't amount to a hill of beans."

"But McNalley wasn't there?"

"No, ma'am. His partner said Red was heading south to do some prospecting. Seems he's got a horse and wagon and camping gear. I told Rugani that if McNalley showed up to send him down here to you."

"Good. You did all you could."

"All the way back I asked about him and showed that

drawing, but no one had seen him. Ain't likely to miss him with that red hair and handlebar mustache.''

"That's right. Now you go to the kitchen and the cook'll fix you something to eat. Then take the horse and buggy back to the livery stable. I'll have you start out again in a few days.''

"Yes, ma'am.'' Amos got up from his chair. "Seems to me you're going to an awful lot of trouble and expense for Mr. Henderson.''

Kitty's cheeks flushed. "We can't let him rot away in jail if we can help him in any way.''

After Amos left, she stared into space. Her handyman had no idea just how much trouble she had gone to for Carl Henderson. Every day she sent a hot meal to him, kept a cookie can filled for him, and saw to it that he had books and the newspaper. Besides that, she'd visited him often.

Right from that first day that Tonio had brought him to her boardinghouse, she had taken a shine to him. She liked his endearing smile, his pleasant manner, and his fine appearance. Of course he had his faults—his gambling and stubborness—but they were no worse than any other man's.

She had been a widow long enough. She'd had plenty of chances to get married again, but Carl was the first man to interest her. She was determined to make his stay in jail as pleasant as possible—and get him cleared of the charges against him. Surely a proposal would follow. She smiled to herself. A gold velvet dress trimmed with ecru lace and green braid would be lovely for a November wedding. She'd speak to her dressmaker.

There was no moon. Ross Eberson was grateful for that as he limped along the edge of the Sacramento River. Lights from the paddle wheel steamers shimmered on the black water that flowed swiftly toward the sea. He could hear it lap against the docks. Off in the distance a dog barked, the male crickets chirped, and a horse *clip-clopped* along Front Street.

But he made no noise. That's why he had come alone.

Another person would have whispered or stumbled, but in spite of his limp, he slipped soundlessly through the darkness. Finally he came to the side street where the livery stable was located.

He laughed to himself. How amusing it was that the army guarded the convoy so carefully when the coaches were filled with gold and quicksilver, but didn't give a diddley-dam about them otherwise. It didn't take but a minute to climb the closed gate and enter the stables. He could hear the horses whinny and scrape their hoofs.

But he wasn't interested in the animals. What he wanted to do was find the Concord coach with the words HENDERSON STAGE Co. painted on them. The storage area for the coaches was as dark as the inside of a closet. More than once he bumped his shin against a vehicle. Even now his game leg felt tender, and he winced with pain when he struck something.

By feeling the shape of the coaches, he could tell which were genuine Concord coaches. Their oval shape differed from the straighter sides of the mud wagons, celerity wagons, buggies, and other stagecoaches.

Finally he took a candle holder and a candle out of his pocket. When the candle was in place, he scratched a match on the bottom of his boot and lit it. He held it high. Yes, this was the Henderson coach, all right.

He let the candlelight play over the side of the coach until he found the brake. Carefully he tampered with it. He had to work skillfully and quickly. The trick was to keep it strong enough so it would hold under ordinary stress—and only give way coming down the steep Meyers Grade!

As soon as his task was completed, he extinguished his candle, slipped it and the holder in his pocket, and left the way he had come.

A little shudder of foreboding ran through Jessie as she drove the coach to the warehouse Monday afternoon. But what could go wrong? The weather was still clear. She was getting more and more skilled at driving up and down the grades. But deep inside was a niggling feeling of doubt. As if there was something amiss.

Sergeant Winter was waiting at the warehouse; he greeted her without enthusiasm.

"I guess you know that Lieutenant Underwood married Miss Foxworthy," she said as she started unhitching the team.

"Yes. He took me into his confidence when he brought me here from the presidio in San Francisco." He nodded his head curtly and stepped to one of the other coaches.

As Jessie led the horses to the adjoining stable for the night, she felt the wound in her heart rip open again. Lyle had confided in his sergeant weeks ago, but at the same time had courted her. Led her along. How could he have been so cruel when he knew that she cared for him?

When Tonio came in behind her with his team, she told him about it. She fought to control herself, but a tear escaped and ran down her cheek.

He listened to her, took a handkerchief out of his pocket, and wiped the tear away. He put his arm across her shoulders. "The day will come, dear friend, when you won't give a damn about this. Let's get our teams settled. If we hurry, we can go to the jail and see your father."

The visiting hours were almost at an end when they faced Carl across the barrier. He looked pale and haggard.

"Papa, do you get enough to eat?"

He nodded. "Fortunately Kitty White sends a hot meal over to me every day so I don't have to eat much of the chow here."

"She does? I'll have to pay her," Jessie put in.

"She won't take a cent. I talked to her about it, but she just wants to do it." He told them about all the things Kitty had done. "She even sends the newspaper."

"She's a gal in a million," Tonio put in. "You'd better marry her when you get out of here."

Carl shook his head. "She deserves better than an old jailbird like me."

"Papa! Don't talk like that. You've never been in trouble with the law before."

His eyes looked sad and discouraged. "There's something about being cooped up like an animal that makes you feel less than a person. If I ever get out of here, I think I'll go off in the woods and hide the rest of my life. I'm so ashamed."

"Papa, you make me feel terrible. Now you just straighten up and believe things will turn out all right. We're going to have a stage line and be successful. I'll help you."

"It'll have to be in the office, Jess. I don't want you dressed like a man and driving a team." He pointed to her clothes. "Every time I see you like that, I feel I'm letting your mother down. It would break her heart."

"All right, Papa. You just buck up and believe in yourself. Think of getting out of here. When you do, I'll run the office and keep house for you."

Tonio added, "I'll send all the business I can your way."

"That is if I'm not sent to prison for the rest of my life!" But when the guard came for him, he stood up straight and walked away with some of his old spirit back.

When they walked outside, Jessie said, "This certainly hasn't been one of the best times of my life."

Tonio patted her arm. "With your old man in jail, and your soldier boy married to someone else, I'd say you've hit bottom. So everything from now on has to be better. So buck up." He grinned at her. "At least you have me."

She looked at him and the expression on her face softened. "And you're a wonderful pal, Tonio. I know I can count on your help until Iris returns."

"We'll both be your friend."

Jessie didn't answer, but she knew that Iris wouldn't tolerate any closeness between them.

The convoy started out early the next day. She had their own horses—Prince, Star, Patches, and Baldy, as well as Pinto and Rufus. They trotted along with a pleasant jingle of the harnesses and the hum of the wheels.

The early morning air was fresh and cool. All was going well, so Jessie couldn't understand the uneasiness she felt. Perhaps it was because she'd be seeing Lyle and Elizabeth again.

Could she go through another masquerade—pretending all was well when she still felt so bitter and hurt? As she drove the team over the flat, dusty valley, she tried to analyze her feelings. How much of her despair was battered pride? Or the pain of rejection? Was part of it loss of faith in her own judgment? She was determined she would never be fool enough to fall in love again. Once Papa was free, she'd devote herself to helping him and getting a stage line started.

At the end of the day, they were at their stop above Placerville. They ate their dinner at picnic tables outside.

As soon as they were through eating, Tonio strummed his guitar. Soon they were singing folk songs with him: "Hey, Betty Martin," "Pop! Goes the Weasel," and "Old Dan Tucker."

But instead of feeling relaxed, she felt more apprehensive. Later, when she went to bed, she pounded her pillow so she could go to sleep. Finally she fell off, only to have worrisome dreams involving her father and all his troubles.

The next day, as the convoy made its careful descent down the Meyers Grade, she could smell her brake shoe. She kept the wheelers back in their collars to hold some of the load on their necks. Down, down they went. She had never been so aware of the brake getting hot and smelling like burned leather.

The coach swayed back and forth as the team rounded the turns. When she came to the steepest part, she pushed against the brake even harder and held the reins until her wrists throbbed. Suddenly she heard a loud pop, as if the brake had given way. She pushed down on the brake, but something was wrong. Then the truth hit her.

Her brake was gone!

Her heart leaped to her throat. Frantically she pushed against the brake again, but nothing happened. Its power was completely gone. She'd never felt so helpless in her life. The horses sprang forward to keep ahead of the coach. She could sense their terror. They raised their heads, shaking their manes and neighing in fright.

The big coach with its heavy load gained momentum and careened back and forth across the narrow road. She reined the horses in and turned them to the left. They swerved toward the bank, and the inside wheels climbed up on it. That cut down on some of the speed, but the coach nearly toppled over.

The driver in front of her turned to look. He waved and shouted, "Stay back! You're getting too close! Slow down!"

"I can't! My brake is gone!"

Cold sweat broke out on her forehead and rolled down her face. She shook with fear. Her throat was dry. The coach swerved back and forth. First dangerously to the edge of the grade, where she could see the long drop down to the canyon below. Then to the high bank on her left. The horses neighed and reared, nearly mad with fear.

What could she do? Her heart pounded. Were they going to crash into the coach in front of them? The wheels whirled and spinned, throwing gravel as the high body swung back and forth on the leather thoroughbraces. Panic struck clear through her. They were whirling down the grade.

The driver in front of her let loose of his brake so his team could lengthen the distance between them.

Around one hairpin turn and then another. Down, down they went. Foam spewed from the frantic horses. The harnesses creaked. The chains rattled. The wheels twisted and turned. Would they topple over the cliff? Jessie cried aloud, "Dear God, help me!"

As they whirled around a curve, she could see a wide turnout in the elbow of the next hairpin turn. Could they make it without capsizing? The coach teetered back and forth. They went reeling, swaying.

She yanked on the reins with all her might and turned her team into the wider space. The leaders seemed to sense what to do. They pulled as far ahead as possible and dropped down on their knees to hold the pole firm. The swingers spread out to avoid climbing over them.

The wheelers were knocked to the ground, their heads twisted sideways by the reins. The coach ran over them, wedging their rumps and flanks under the front axle of the coach.

At least they were stopped. Jessie sat in the box shaking with relief for a minute. She gasped for breath while her heart slowed down. Finally she climbed down. Her knees were too weak to hold her, so she grasped the strap on the boot for support.

Hank Willinski, the driver behind her, pulled up and stopped the coach. He jumped down from his seat. "What happened, Jessie? Hell, you were going like a house afire."

Ashen-faced, she turned to him. "My brake gave out."

"I'll be dammed."

"Let's see to the horses." She grabbed his arm. "I'm still shaking."

"Gosh, woman, that was enough to scare anyone."

Hank dropped to his knees beside the wheelers. "They're both dead. I guess it's for the best. Your coach about skinned them."

Jessie glanced at the bleeding horses and turned away to vomit. Was it her fault that these poor animals had been killed? Sick with remorse, she kept her eyes averted. When she felt better, she walked to the leaders and patted them. They were still quivering with fright, the foam dripping from their mouths. "Brave boys," she murmured. "We had a terrible scare, didn't we?" She turned to her swingers, two bays, and reassured them.

The soldier that had been riding rear guard pulled his horse up beside her. He dropped out of the saddle. "What can I do to help?"

Hank said, "Seems to me the first thing we should do is get the coach off these dead horses. Then maybe we can use the team to drag them to the edge of the cliff and push them over. We have to get them out of the way."

Sick at heart, Jessie asked herself, What else can go wrong? She'd have to pay for the horses, and that would take all the profit out of this run. "How can I get the coach down the rest of the grade?"

"Well, ma'am, I guess we'll have to fix some kind of drag for you," Hank answered. "Like a log or something." He nodded to the soldier. "Let's get busy."

As soon as the guard left the rear of the convoy, the driver of the light wagon following along behind cracked his whip to lessen the distance to the last coach.

Ross Eberson chortled with glee. It was all going just as he planned. He pulled his scarf up to cover his face and signaled to the two men sitting behind him to do the same. He turned to the driver. "Better cover your face."

Finally they were close to the last coach in the convoy, which was just creeping around an inside turn and was hidden from the others.

Eberson said, "This is it." He picked up his gun and climbed out of his seat. The others followed, and they surrounded the coach.

"Stop!" he called at the driver, and pointed his gun.

Before the driver could reach for his own gun, two men climbed up on the box to bind and gag him. They tied the reins to the seat brace.

Quickly they opened the door of the coach and yanked back the canvas covering. Just as they had practiced over and over, they formed a chain and passed the pouches of gold from one to the other and tossed them into the wagon. Since the road was still deserted, they even took some of the casks of quicksilver. Not a minute was lost. Not a word was spoken.

When Eberson signaled, they stopped. One covered the pouches with canvas and tied ropes across the load. The driver led his team while the others turned the wagon so they faced upgrade. As soon as they jumped back into their seats, the driver cracked his whip and they were on their way.

Eberson slapped his leg. "It went better than I expected. I was hoping that the guard would ride forward when the Henderson coach broke down and he did. That way we didn't have to tangle with him. I'd just as soon the army be left out of this.''

"Now I see why you made us practice so much," the driver spoke up. "We all knew exactly where we were to stand and what to do."

"And no time was wasted. Better yet, none of you guys shot off your mouths, so we left no clues."

With a real feeling of accomplishment, Eberson sat back in his seat and relaxed. They should get back to Sacramento in plenty of time to pack the boxes he had ready. Tomorrow morning he'd catch the river steamer to San Francisco and board the *Victorious Queen* for the East Coast. He'd chosen that ship because it stopped at Charleston, South Carolina. Eventually he'd have his bounty in the hands of those preparing for war.

Tears blurred her eyes as Jessie unbuckled the harnesses on the dead animals she had rented at the last station. She felt terrible to have caused their deaths. It was hard to imagine that at one time she had been so afraid of horses. Now she thought of them as friends and truly loved them.

Hank got the rest of the team free of the pole and led them around to the back of the coach. He hitched them to the back axle and pulled the vehicle off of the horses' bodies.

By now the driver from the coach in front of her had joined them. She didn't want to watch while they disposed of the dead animals, so she began walking down the grade to judge how she could drive the rest of the way with only four horses in the team and no brake.

When she walked around a bend, she saw Tonio had halted his coach. "What's going on?" he called to her.

"I had some trouble," she shouted.

He climbed out of his seat and hurried to meet her. She laughed wrily. "You said I'd hit bottom and everything from now on was up. Well, you were so wrong." She told him what had happened.

He put his arm across her shoulders. "Listen, Jessie. You let me take care of the situation. You drive my coach the rest of the way, and I'll take yours over. I can manage with four horses and a drag better than you can."

She struggled to answer, but she could only nod. She leaned her head against his shoulder and asked herself how she would ever manage without Tonio. He had to be the dearest man who ever lived.

He held her close and kissed her cheek. "Buck up, sweet Jess. . . . That's a gal. Now you just climb up on my coach and rest for a while. When you see us coming, start out."

By the time Tonio got back to the Henderson coach, the other men had things pretty well under control. They all looked relieved when he said he was going to drive.

The guard said, "I'd better get back to my post." He mounted his horse and rode back up the grade.

The other driver, Gus Steiner, spoke up. "A woman has no business driving a big rig like this. You ought to hire someone to take her place."

"I think so, too," Hank agreed. "She nearly ran me down. When she has a breakdown like this, it puts us all in danger."

Tonio bristled. "It wasn't her fault that the brake gave out."

"We men would have a better handle on things," Hank added.

"Let's look at the damn brake and see what happened to it," Tonio challenged. He walked over to it and made a careful examination. "Hey, fellows. Come look at this and see what you think."

Hank looked it over. "Goldurn, if I didn't know better I'd say it'd been monkeyed with."

Tonio turned to Gus. "What do you think? Take a look."

"Sure looks like it's been tampered with. But what would be the point?"

Just then the guard appeared at the bend. "Tonio!"

"Something must be wrong. You guys stay with your coaches. Better have your guns ready."

Tonio started climbing the grade. When he got around

the bend and saw the driver of the last coach bound and gagged, his heart plummeted.

The guard leaped up on the driver's seat. Tonio scrambled up there as well.

As soon as the gag was removed, the driver said, "They stripped the coach. Took all the gold."

The color drained from the young guard's face. "I'm in deep trouble now. Lieutenant Underwood'll have me court-martialed."

"Now wait a minute," Tonio put in. "You saw that the Henderson coach was out of control. The brake was gone. You rushed to help her. Isn't it your job to guard the whole convoy?"

"I suppose so."

"It's not like you fell asleep during your watch. I'll point that out to the lieutenant."

"Thank you, sir."

"He'll probably put the blame on me. I'm supposed to be in charge of the whole convoy."

The driver rubbed his arms when they were free. "I'm lucky they didn't shoot me."

"And Jessie's lucky she didn't get thrown over the edge, coach and all," Tonio added.

They all got out of the box and looked at the empty interior. Only a few casks of quicksilver remained.

Tonio thought for a moment, then spoke. "At least you've got brakes. So drive your coach around Gus's. We'll tie your team and coach to the back of the Henderson's so you'll act as a drag. Keep your brake on and hold your team back while I drive the Henderson rig the rest of the way to Carson City."

"It's going to be damn tricky to get around them curves with this long a setup," the driver put in.

"Start praying, fellow." Tonio gave him an encouraging pat on the back. He looked up at the young guard who had mounted his horse. "Underwood'll probably blow off steam, but he's got some common sense. So quit worrying."

When Tonio gathered the reins of the depleted team,

he muttered to himself, "I hate his guts, but I have to admit that he's fair."

Several hours later, when they pulled into Carson City and turned over the shipment, Tonio immediately sought out Lyle and told him the story.

The lieutenant's first reaction was anger. "Sergeant Winter should never have turned the convoy over to you in the first place. This is only your second trip—and you've already lost a fifth of the cargo!"

Tonio grabbed Lyle by the lapels. "You idiot. Listen to reason. This was a carefully planned attack on the convoy. It could have happened anytime, no matter who was in charge."

Lyle pushed Tonio away and straightened his jacket. "Looks to me like it was a group of highwaymen that took advantage of Jessie's brake failure."

"I think you've got it wrong, Lieutenant," Hank put in. "The Henderson brake was tampered with. It had to be done in Sacramento . . . before the coaches were loaded. They done it on purpose—so it'd give way going down the steepest part of the grade."

Gus added, "That's the way it was. I saw the brake myself. Once we had all that hullabaloo over the Henderson coach, we wouldn't be paying much mind to what went on behind us."

But the lieutenant had to have the last word. "The guard should never have left the end of the convoy. I'm going to have him reprimanded."

Jessie listened to all that was said. What a pompous man Lyle was, she thought. So full of himself and his authority. Finally she spoke up. "Don't forget that I was carrying a shipment in my coach, too. And two horses in my team were killed. If anyone needed help, I did."

She turned to the driver who had been tied and gagged. "Did you notice anything about the men who held you up? Their clothes, or the way they spoke?"

"No, ma'am. Their faces were covered with scarves. They didn't say a word. Except the guy with the gun. All he said was 'Stop.' "

"This is just wasting our time," Lyle said.

Jessie ignored him. "Did the man with the gun limp?"

"Yes. Now that you speak of it, I remember that he did."

"He's the same one who followed us in Sacramento. Who showed up at New Almaden. Mark my words, he's the man behind all of this."

Tonio said, "I'll bet it was that Southern activist who causes all the trouble in California."

"You could be right. I'll have Sergeant Winter look into it," Lyle said. "In that case, nobody in the convoy is to blame for what happened." He turned away to supervise the changing of the shipment to the new convoy.

As Jessie watched him, she realized that he hadn't expressed one word of concern about the ordeal she had just gone through.

Chapter 16

The storm, originating in the South China Sea, swept across the Pacific Ocean, stirring the water into gigantic waves and battering the coast of Nicaragua.

Ross Eberson, lying in his bunk aboard the *Victorious Queen*, clung white-knuckled to the side railing as he strained to keep from being tossed out. The vessel dropped down into a deep trough. It lurched wildly from side to side before it began its climb up again.

He could hear the waves pound over the bow, slither across the deck, and splash against the bridge. Every plank seemed to creak in protest as the high waves hammered the hull.

It was midafternoon, but Emerson didn't dare leave his bunk. He knew that with his crippled leg he couldn't move about in the tossing ship without falling. He certainly didn't need more broken bones, he told himself.

He could hear some of the other passengers vomiting from seasickness. At least he'd been spared that. They'd ride out this storm, he tried to reassure himself. By tomorrow the sea would be calm again and he could go out on deck.

But fear curled inside him like a reptile. To get his mind off the raging storm, he thought of the boxes of gold in the hold. He had no idea how much they were worth. There was no time to undo all of the pouches and

veigh the contents in Sacramento, but it had to be in the
thousands of dollars.

The long hours dragged by. Sleep was impossible.
Gradually the cabin he shared with five other men grew
dark. His stomach began to gnaw with hunger, so he let
go of one of the railings to reach for his hardtack and
jerky. That kept him occupied for a time. Then he thought
of his family at home. It would be good to see them. He
vowed he'd never leave Georgia again.

Suddenly a terrible crash shook the ship from bow to
stern. Eberson heard wood splinter.

"My God, I'll bet one of the masts broke off and went
through the deck!" one man cried out.

Another yelled, "We're doomed! We'll take on water!"

Ross could hear the waves pounding the decks, the
curses of the seamen, the shuddering of the vessel. Finally the captain shouted through his bullhorn, "Abandon ship! Man the lifeboats! Abandon ship! Man the
lifeboats!"

The other men in the cabin scrambled out of their
bunks, yanked on their jackets, and rushed out into the
passageway.

"Hurry! We're taking on water!" someone yelled.

But Eberson couldn't hurry. He struggled out of his
bunk and clung to it as he reached for his coat. When
the ship listed to one side, his bad leg collapsed under
him, and he fell to his knees.

Frantically he reached for the posts under the bunks
as he tried to pull himself along, but it was uphill. First
one hand, then the other. But it was slow going. He
gasped for breath with the effort. He pulled up a few
inches . . . only to fall back again.

Dimly, amid all the other noises, he heard the winches
creak as the seamen lowered the lifeboats from the sinking ship.

"Wait for me! Help! I need help!" Eberson called,
but no one came.

* * *

The storm changed course and headed north. It traveled along the coast of Honduras and Guatemala, only to go inland over Mexico and out to sea again, where it joined another jet stream heading for California.

All the way down the grade, Jessie felt the wind against the side of the stagecoach. The big vehicle rocked back and forth with each gust. It was October second, and the last trip for the convoy.

When they reached the desert floor at the foot of the grade, the wind blew the tumbleweeds over and over along the side of the road.

The horses' tails and manes swept forward with the force of the wind. They tossed their heads as if they couldn't wait to reach their destination.

When they pulled into Carson City and stopped to transfer their precious cargo, Jessie let out a long sigh of relief. Except for losing the one coachload of gold to the Southern activists, they had carried out their contract to the letter.

Tonio walked over to her and climbed up to the seat. "I'm afraid a storm is coming. If it snows, we don't want to be caught on this side of the Sierra."

"What should we do?"

"It's only midafternoon. I suggest that we change horses and head back as soon as possible."

She slumped wearily against the back of her seat. "I don't know if I'm up to it."

"Of course you are." He patted her arm. "Just as soon as we're unloaded, let's go to the livery stable. Fortunately these horses belong to them. We can pick up a team that's owned by the next station on our way."

"You mean no dinner, no rest?"

"That's right. If we move right along, we can get over this first grade before dark. Even if we have to drive around the shores of Lake Tahoe by lamplight, we could do it."

"If you say so, I'm game."

After Tonio spoke to the other drivers, he pitched in to help with the unloading so they could be on their way.

They bucked the wind head-on as they drove out of

Carson City. While they crossed the level land before the first grade began, Jessie felt dirt and sand sting her face. With the light load, the horses could move right along. However, it was all she could do to summon enough reserve strength to guide them back and forth around the hairpin turns again.

Fortunately they got to the summit before dark. They skirted around Lake Tahoe by lamplight. Jessie could barely see the way ahead. But the leaders were so familiar with the road, they were able to stay on it. The wind blew and the air was bitter cold. Jessie wrapped a blanket around her.

She could hear the tree branches swish and snap in the wind and feel the coach rock back and forth, but they plodded on their way.

They reached the station at the foot of Meyer's Grade at nine o'clock. Numb with fatigue and cold, they accepted the hot soup the stationmaster offered. He had cots where they could stretch out for the night.

"You'll be durn lucky if you get over the grade before it snows," he told them as he filled their coffee cups.

"It's an early storm, isn't it?" Jessie asked.

"It's not unusual to have snow this time of year. May not stay on the ground too long, but it sure plays havoc with the roads," the stationkeeper replied.

Still fully dressed, Jessie stretched out on her cot and dropped off to sleep. . . .

It didn't seem like much time before Tonio shook her. "Time to get up."

She groaned a little and pulled herself up. All of her clothes felt bunched around her knees and waist. There was no way she could brush her teeth or do much with her hair. So she straightened her clothes and was grateful for the hot coffee and oatmeal mush.

Just as they started up the long Meyer's Grade, a few flakes of snow drifted down. They wound their way back and forth through a light curtain of falling flakes. By the time they reached the summit, the snow was beginning to thicken. But they kept going.

Downgrade the road grew more slippery. Her heart

was in her mouth as she felt the coach slip and slide. Would they go over the edge of the road and fall into the American River Canyon below?

Even more worrisome, would it snow so hard that they would have to stop along the way at some stagecoach station and be stuck there for days?

When they stopped for a change of horses, she asked Tonio, "Should we go on?"

"This is our first storm of the season, so the road is still packed hard from the long, dry summer. And when we get to a lower elevation, this snow'll turn to rain. So let's keep going."

Tonio took the lead, so she followed close behind him. By keeping the team carefully bunched, she was able to stay in his tracks. In spite of the blanket around her shoulders, the cold wind chilled her clear through. Her gauntlet-covered hands lost all sense of feeling. The wind swirled the snowflakes around the coaches.

The snow had turned to a driving rain by the time they arrived at the station where they were to spend the night. The final fifty miles to Sacramento were to be covered the next day.

When they pulled in, the stationmaster came out to greet them. "I'm sorry, but we're filled chuck-a-block. You can put your coaches in the back—and we can take care of your horses—but I have no place for you folks inside. Everybody's coming out of the mountains for the winter."

"We can stay in our coaches," Jessie said. "It'll be cold, but at least we'll be out of the storm."

"Do you have something hot for us to eat?" Tonio asked.

"Beef stew with fresh bread just out of the oven."

They fought their way through the rain to get their stew and bread. There was no place to sit in the crowded station, so they brought their meal back to Jessie's coach on tin plates. A lantern hanging outside the stable gave them enough light by which to eat.

"The only blanket we've got is yours, and it's soaking wet!" Tonio said in disgust.

"Well, I needed it over the grade." Her teeth chattered with cold.

When they were finished eating, Tonio lowered the leather curtains and said, "The only way we can be warm is to stay together." He positioned himself against the back of the seat and held out his arms. "I'll hold you tight."

She shivered as she molded herself against him. He cradled her close; the heat from his body began to warm hers. Her head fit right into the hollow of his shoulder.

He kissed her forehead. "You're my pal, Jessie. The best friend a guy ever had."

She could feel his strong biceps against her arms and the rise and fall of his chest against her back. Never had she been so aware of his dynamic presence. His strength seemed to surround her until every taut nerve started to relax. The muscles in her neck lost their tension. Her bone-weariness began to drain away. Even the constant worry over her father seemed to ease. Her heartache over Lyle was a thing of the past.

Feeling safe and warm and cosseted, she closed her eyes. How nice it would be to have a husband like Tonio, she thought. One who would cherish and protect her. To whom she would be the most important person in the whole world. Her last thought before she fell off to sleep was how she envied Iris.

But Tonio couldn't sleep. There wasn't enough room to stretch out his long legs, and they began to feel cramped. But even more distracting was having Jessie in his arms, feeling her body against his. The rise and fall of her breast caressed his arm. A lock of her hair brushed his cheek.

As wave after wave of desire for her engulfed him, his blood quickened and he wanted to make love to her. It was all he could do to control himself. He suppressed a moan and lay his hot cheek against her cool one.

Finally he shifted position and scolded himself. He ought to be ashamed! Jessie was like a sister to him. His dear friend, his very own pal, but not a lover, for gosh sakes. And what about Iris? She was the one he was going to marry; he shouldn't be harboring these lustful thoughts about someone else.

He glanced down at Jessie. In the faint light he could see her long lashes against her cheeks. He thought of her beautiful eyes that revealed every mood, every sorrow, fear, and joy. As she lay sleeping, she seemed so vulnerable. She must never be hurt again. Damn that Lyle! And damn Carl! As he kissed her forehead, Tonio told himself that he'd do everything in his power to protect her. Now and always. Finally he dozed off.

The storm raged all night. The rain hammered on the roof of the coach. The wind howled in the trees. Sometimes during the night, Tonio would half-awaken and be aware of the way the coach rocked back and forth. At least they had been able to park near a building, which protected them from the worst of the wind.

The next morning, when they went into the station for breakfast, at least ten men approached them for rides into Sacramento.

Finally Tonio said, "You can go for half-fare if you're willing to get out and push when we get stuck in the mud."

And get stuck they did—more than once! A torrent of rain fell all the way to Sacramento, making a quagmire of parts of the road. They drove right into the stable and took care of Jessie's rig. Before Tonio settled his own coach and team, he drove her to the boardinghouse.

She ran a hot bath, soaked her chilled, weary body, and climbed into bed, too weary to dress and go down to the dining room. Kitty brought her some supper on a tray.

The widow pulled a chair alongside Jessie's bed. "Your father's in an awful state. He seems to have given up all hope of ever being free. I never saw a man so down-in-the-mouth."

"He's never been in trouble with the law before, so I think he's terribly ashamed of himself."

"I've tried telling him that this is California. Lots of our most prominent citizens served time in their own states before coming out here and becoming successful.

As soon as he's free, he must put it all behind him and get a fresh start.''

Jessie covered the widow's hand with her own. "You've been so kind to him.''

"I'll be honest with you: I've got plans for the two of us once he's free." Kitty's cheeks turned pink. "That is if he feels the same way I do.''

"Oh, I hope something works out for you two. I'd love to have you for a stepmother.''

"I've fixed myself up a real cozy apartment on the second floor. It's just below this room, so it has the same southeast exposure. It has a living room, bedroom, and bath, so Carl would have some privacy . . . and not have to be with the boarders all the time. And, of course, he'd be gone staging a lot.'' Her eyes sparkled in anticipation.

Jessie squeezed the widow's hand. "He'd have you to come home to at the end of his run. I know he'd love that. He's missed having a wife and companion.''

"Even if he's sent to prison for a while, I'll wait for him. Of course I'm praying that we'll find that Red McNalley. I have notices posted everywhere, up and down the river, and put ads in the papers here. So hold good thoughts that he'll show up in the next two weeks.'' She picked up Jessie's tray. "I almost forgot. Carl's lawyer left a letter here for you. I'll go get it.''

Later, when Jessie opened the letter, she found a note from Bob Grist.

(Enclosed you'll find a power of attorney, so you can take care of your father's affairs on his behalf.)

As she read it through, she realized it gave her complete authority to transact business for him. Her heart sank into a leaden ball. The lawyer must think that her father had no chance at all, that he was going to be shut up in prison for years. How had poor Papa felt when he'd signed it?

She found out the next day when she went to the jail and saw her father's haggard face on the other side of the screen. His shoulders slumped, and the expression in his eyes showed how discouraged he was.

"I haven't a chance in hell of going free," Carl said "Judge Lundstrom will be on the bench for my trial. You know what a tough bird he is."

"But we still have two weeks. Something might turn up."

"What, for example? Do you think that McNalley's going to come crawling out of the woodwork?" His lip curled in disbelief.

"Perhaps. I guess you know how hard Kitty has tried to find him."

"Yes, and I don't know why she's gone to all that trouble and expense."

"Because she admires you, Papa. She realizes what a fine man you are." How much did she dare say? "If you make plans for the future—and look forward to them— you won't be so despondent." She flattened her hands against the screen.

"If you're cooking up some kind of a scheme to make a match between Kitty and me, you can put it out of your mind right now. She's too fine a woman to be hitched to me. I wouldn't consider it for a minute." His chin set in a stubborn line.

"But you do think she's attractive and nice, don't you?"

"Of course I do. Now let's talk about affairs at hand. You did get that power of attorney, didn't you?"

"Yes. I looked it over last night."

"It was the hardest decision I ever made. To sign that paper, I mean. I'm no hand to turn my business over to someone else."

"But, Papa . . . I'm not just anybody. I'm your daughter and assistant, remember?"

He ran his fingers through his hair. "And I couldn't have a better one. But you're not to use that power of attorney unless it's absolutely necessary."

"Of course I won't. You can trust me."

"Now tell me about your trip over the grade."

She told him all about the storm. "I'm so thankful it

was our last trip and we got home safe. This could be an early winter."

"At least you and Tonio fulfilled the contract for me. Did Lyle have a check ready for you?"

"Yes. I'll deposit it on Monday. As soon as I post everything in the ledger, I'll bring it to show you."

He nodded. "So you have enough money to tide you through the winter? And pay Bob Grist?"

"Yes, Papa. You don't have to worry about me. I'll stay right at the boardinghouse with Kitty."

"Maybe you'd better sell the horses and the coach. Dadgummit, but it costs an arm and a leg to keep a team in a livery stable. It'll be years before I can drive again."

"Let's not do anything about that right away." But she vowed she wouldn't sell the rig. That would break his spirit.

Before she stepped outside into the cold air, she wrapped her cape close around her and tied her hood securely under her chin.

The wind blew in gusts as she hurried along the street, sending the fallen leaves skittering along the sidewalk. The clouds looked black and threatening, as if it would begin to rain again soon. She walked along one block, then turned up another.

A sign hanging out from a storefront banged back and forth. When Jessie glanced up at it, she read CAPITAL STAGE LINES—TRANSPORTATION TO THE NORTHERN MINES. Another sign in the window stated STAGES LEAVE MONDAY, WEDNESDAY, AND FRIDAY AT 8 A.M. MAIL AND PACKAGES CARRIED. A woman stood behind the counter receiving several boxes from a Chinese man and filling out receipts.

Jessie's heart pounded in excitement. Here was a woman doing exactly what she wanted to do. Not a male but a female! Why not go in and talk to her about it? She waited for the Chinese man to finish his transactions and come out.

When Jessie went inside, the woman asked, "May I help you?"

"Not really. I was just passing by and noticed you in

here. My name is Jessie Henderson. My father owns the Henderson Stage Company.''

"I've heard of you. You drive for him, don't you?'' She tucked a strand of light brown hair into her bun. She was in her thirties, but she looked worried and sad. "You've got more courage than I have. I'm scared to death of horses.''

"I used to be, but I got over it. Now I don't mind handling them at all.''

"My name is Ruth McWhorter, and I'm glad you stopped by. Come behind the counter and take a seat.''

When Jessie was settled, she said, "Our staging company just finished a contract with the army, so we'll be setting up an office, too. I'd like to be in charge of it— keep the books and sell tickets—but my father says a stage office is no place for a woman. Do you have any problems working here?'' Her cheeks flushed. "Like men getting too fresh with you?''

Ruth McWhorter smiled. "No, I haven't, but then I'm a lot older than you are. My husband was concerned about that, too, so he hired an old man for a pittance to be here with me most of the time. It gives Ed something to do. He runs errands and sweeps up. When we're loading and unloading the stagecoaches out in back, he helps with the packages—if they're not too heavy. His son has the barber shop next door.''

Jessie looked around. "You've got a nice setup here.'' The walls and floors had been painted and looked in good condition. Chairs lined the wall for the passengers waiting to board.

"It's a dream come true for us. We came out here from Kentucky five years ago, hoping to get ahead a little. My husband established the route going north, where more mines were opening up. He even got a mail contract, which keeps us going when times are slow in the winter. We have lots of passengers in the summer.''

"Well, that's wonderful,'' Jessie put in, thinking that something like this was just what her father should have.

Ruth shook her head. "The irony is that just as we became well established, started doing well, my husband found out that he has heart trouble. The doctor says he has to give up staging. It's too hard on him.''

"Oh, no! What are you going to do?"

"Sell this and buy a small hotel or rooming house. But this is the slow season for staging, so it's going to be hard to unload this.''

Jessie's interest perked up. This would be a perfect setup for Papa and her.

"Have you decided how much you are going to ask for this business? My father—''

"My husband says it's worth at least ten thousand dollars—since we have the U.S. Mail contract. Besides that, we have two coaches, fifteen horses, and all the harnesses. We have our own stable out at the edge of town . . . with a tack room and all.''

"Does your husband do all the driving?"

"No. We have an excellent driver who works for us. In the summer, we have to use both coaches because we have so many passengers. He wants to buy it awful bad, but he hasn't the money. We have to have cash on the barrel head so we can buy another business.''

Jessie stayed until a man came in with some merchandise to ship. She rose and said, "Thank you so much for talking to me. I'll tell my father and be in touch.''

When she returned to the boardinghouse, Kitty greeted her. "I'll make us a pot of tea. I want to hear what your father had to say today.''

Soon they were settled in Kitty's nice apartment with their tea and cookies. They talked about Carl for a while, and then Jessie said, "It's just tragic Papa is in jail. I found a perfect setup for him.'' She told the widow all about the McWhorter situation.

Kitty put her hand on Jessie's arm. "Let's investigate it together. If it's all Mrs. McWhorter says it is, then you buy it.''

"Buy it? I don't have the money."

"Well, I do."

Jessie's mouth fell open as she stared at Kitty. "You mean we should buy it together?"

"No. Goodness sakes, I don't want to own more busi-

nesses.'' She waved her hand. ''I have all the headaches
I want with this place. I'll loan you what you need.''

Jessie slumped back in her chair. ''But Papa would
never permit me to buy a business and go way into debt.
We might as well forget it.''

Kitty's chin stuck out. ''Oh, no, we won't! It sounds
like the ideal situation for Carl. Even if he goes to prison
for a while, he'll get out eventually—and this can be
waiting for him. You can run it in the meantime. You
manage the office—and hire another driver to assist the
one that's there.''

''Oh, Kitty, I'd love to do that! But Papa would never—''

The widow leaned forward. Her eyes sparkled with
mischief. ''Your father's in jail. He told me that you had
his power of attorney. There's nothing stopping you from
buying that stage line on your own.''

''But aren't there laws . . . ?''

''Yes, if you're a married woman. Then you have to
get your husband's permission for everything. But you're
a single woman, and you can act on your own. Just like
I, a widow, can own this boardinghouse. You could buy
that stage line in your own name if you wanted to.''

''Oh, no! I'd want Papa's name on it. The whole point
is to give him something to look forward to.'' She sat up
straight, her shoulders back. ''But my name would have
to be on it, too.''

''Of course it would.''

''I want to be a full partner—and have my say. I'll run
the business end of it. I think I've earned it.''

Kitty patted her arm. ''You sure have, my dear. I wonder if your father realizes what a jewel he has in you.''

''And in you, Kitty.'' Would her pigheaded, stubborn
father ever return this lovely widow's affection?

On Monday morning, the two women walked to the
office of the Capital Stage Line. Mr. McWhorter was
there with his wife. His drawn, gray face showed that he
was not well.

After the introductions, Jessie said, ''We came to get
more information about your stage line.''

"Mr. Henderson is not available today," Kitty added.
"But—"

"Of course he's not available!" McWhorter put in.
"He's in jail for murder, isn't he?"

Jessie's face flamed. "Well, I'm afraid so."

"When my wife told me about your conversation, I
said, 'Oh, we don't want any truck with them.'"

Kitty spoke up. "Just a minute, Mr. McWhorter. You
don't know the circumstances. Isn't it true that here in
America a person is presumed innocent unless a jury
finds him guilty?"

McWhorter looked away. "I guess I spoke out of
turn."

"If the Hendersons should be interested," Kitty went
on, "it will be a cash deal. So you don't need to concern
yourself about anything."

Jessie asked, "First, do you own or rent this space?"

"We lease it," Mrs. McWhorter answered.

"I understand you do own a stable and several horses
and two coaches," Kitty said.

Mr. McWhorter seemed anxious to get back in their
good graces. "Say, I've got a horse and buggy out back.
Why don't we just run out there and look things over?"

Later, when they saw the whitewashed fences, the
painted buildings, the horses grazing in the field in back,
the orderly tack room, Jessie knew that she had to have
this stage line. But what would her father say?

Chapter 17

When Kitty and Jessie left the office of the Capital Stage Line, they were filled with enthusiasm.

"I think it's an excellent setup," Jessie said. "But we'd better get Tonio's advice."

Kitty nodded. "I want to talk to my lawyer, of course, and have the company thoroughly investigated—to be sure there are no debts you'd be assuming. I'd want their books audited so we know they are doing as well as they say they are. But don't you say one word to your father. He'll say no right off."

"I'm afraid so. If we decide we want to go ahead with it, we can deal with him. But it's so exciting." Jessie gave Kitty's arm a little squeeze. "Right now I have to go to the bank, then on home to bring my ledger up to date. I want to take it to him this afternoon."

"I think I'll drop in on my lawyer right now so things can get started."

Later that afternoon, when she visited her father, it was all she could do to contain herself and not burst out with the good news. He needed something to lift his spirits. She explained all the entries in her ledger and was pleased when he nodded his approval.

As she walked down the steps of the jail, she saw Tonio tying his team to the hitching post down the block. She hurried toward him. "Hi. Are you coming to see my father?"

He grinned. "That's right. How many friends do you think I have in there?"

"I'm anxious to talk to you about something. Would you have time after you see Papa?"

"Sure. Just wait in the coach for me. I won't be long."

When he joined her later, Jessie said, "I want your advice about something." She told him about the Capital Stage Line being for sale.

Tonio groaned. "I'd give my right arm for that company. They have that route straight north, up the valley, established. Then when they get to the Yuba River, they turn east to take in the mining camps. In fact, when I went to Chicago to get a line of credit, I had it in mind to ask them to merge with us. And then we could extend the route clear to Oregon. McWhorter told me a long time ago that he had heart trouble."

"Have you seen their stables? You'd be impressed."

"No, I haven't. Let's take a run out there right now and look them over."

When Tonio had thoroughly looked the buildings over and noted the clean stalls and orderly tack room, he shook his head. "I could wring Gianni's neck. Damn him, anyhow, for bucking all my ideas of expanding. I don't know what's gotten into him. He hasn't been the same since I've gotten home from Chicago."

"What do you think of the horses? They're part of the package."

He walked around the pasture inspecting each horse. When he was through, he said, "They're in fine shape. There's a couple you could unload eventually. That roan and that bay." He almost ached inside with longing. He wanted to own the company himself. "This would be perfect for Carl. It's a one-day run and back the next. And the valley's as flat as a pancake. No damn grades to creep up and down. There are some hills as you get up to the mines, but they aren't too steep."

"So if Kitty's lawyer approves, you think I should go ahead?"

"Grab it, Jess. I think it's a steal for what you're getting."

"Of course I'll have to do it behind Papa's back. And that scares me to death."

"But once you prove yourself, he'll be okay." He put his arm across her shoulders. "I'll back you up—tell him that I looked everything over first."

She smiled at him. "Do that. Papa has a lot of respect for your opinion."

When they got back to the coach, she went on. "What if someone else comes along and buys the company while we're thinking about it?"

"You can always put a refundable deposit on it and keep it off the market for a while."

"Come with me and let's do it right now . . . before I get cold feet."

As the days went by, she longed to tell her father what she had done, but she didn't have the courage. The date of the trial was getting closer, and Carl was beside himself with worry, which made him irritable and impatient when she went to visit him. It was no time to bring up some radical idea.

October twentieth finally came. Kitty, looking lovely in a becoming green suit, walked with her to the courthouse. The widow sighed and said sadly, "I kept hoping and hoping that we'd find Red McNalley by this time. But I haven't heard a word about him."

In the paneled courtroom, they found a seat in the front row on the left side, just in back of the defendant's table. Bob Grist turned around and spoke to them.

Soon the officers led Carl in. Jessie felt grief-stricken at his haggard appearance. He was thinner than ever, and he looked as if he had aged ten years. The humiliation and shame of being in jail had taken a terrible toll.

They were told to rise. Judge Lundstrom strode in, looking very serious and stern, and stepped up on the bench.

During all the proceedings, Jessie ached to lean forward and reassure her father. She wanted to let him know how much she and Kitty supported him. But, of course, she restrained herself. She didn't want to be evicted from the courtroom.

While they selected a jury, Jessie was surprised at the men Bob Grist excused. It seemed to her that he rejected all the professional and businessmen and concentrated on the working class.

Even Kitty noticed it, as well. During the noon recess, as they walked down the corridor together, she said, "Bob, it seems to me you want an entirely different kind of person to serve on the jury than the prosecutor."

"You're absolutely right. I want men who are likely to gamble themselves—and who are apt to carry a gun."

"I can understand that," Kitty agreed.

The lawyer went on. "I want jurors who can understand the anger a man feels when he's the victim of a card shark. A man who might act without thinking in a fit of rage. That type of juror would be much more sympathetic to Carl's case."

"And the prosecutor wants a more analytical type. One who is in control of himself," Kitty added.

"Of course he does."

It took two days to select a jury. Jessie got so nervous over what lay ahead, she could hardly sleep at night.

Chills went down her spine when the prosecutor declared, "I will prove without a doubt that this man, Carl Henderson, deliberately took out his gun and shot Mr. Oberheimer during a poker game."

In his opening argument, Bob Grist said, "Carl Henderson acted in self-defense. The gambler known as Fats Oberheimer pulled out his gun first. Every effort to find the third player, a man by the name of McNalley, has been made. He was a witness to the shooting. Unfortunately we have not reached him."

Later, it was time for the witnesses to testify. When Mr. Dumont, owner of the saloon, was on the stand, the judge asked, "Did you call the police?"

"No, I didn't. The wound seemed so superficial."

"But it was assault with a deadly weapon. If the police had been called, they would have brought Mr. McNalley to headquarters and questioned him. I'm going to order that your license be suspended for a month for this negligence. If you have trouble in your saloon again—and fail to call the police—your license will be suspended permanently.'' He banged his gavel for emphasis.

Dumont shrank back in the witness chair, looking completely chastised.

The bartender testified and, finally, the doctor, looking bleary-eyed and disreputable, described how he had treated the wound.

The next day Bob Grist argued: ''Gentlemen of the jury, you heard the doctor state that the wound that my client inflicted was superficial. I am going to call the coroner to the witness stand; he will testify as to the exact cause of death.''

Jessie's spirits rose when the coroner took the stand and was sworn in.

''What is your official position?''

''I am coroner for Sacramento County.''

''Where did you first see the remains of Mr. Oberheimer?''

''In the J Street Hotel, after the chambermaid found him dead in bed.''

''What did you do then?''

''I had the remains sent to the morgue and an autopsy performed. I have the report here.''

''What was the cause of death?''

''An infection from a gunshot wound in the abdomen.''

''How extensive was the wound?''

The coroner held up a drawing to show the entrance and exit of the bullet, then discussed the caliber of the bullet.

''Did the bullet strike any vital organs?''

''No, it didn't. The wound was confined to the fatty area of the abdomen.''

''You could characterize it as a superficial wound?''

''Yes.''

''So the cause of death was from an infection in the wound . . . and not from the bullet striking a vital organ?''

''That is correct.''

Jessie turned to Kitty and nodded. The widow patted her hand and smiled.

But during the cross-examination, the prosecutor made the point that Oberheimer would never have had the infection if he hadn't been shot by the accused in the first place, so the defendant was still responsible for the death.

By the end of the afternoon, all of the witnesses had been called.

The two lawyers gave their closing arguments the following morning. The judge instructed the jury before they were sent into seclusion to make their decision.

Kitty and Jessie waited all day for the jury to return. Finally they were told that the members had been sent home for the night.

"Bob Grist is doing a good job," Jessie said as they walked toward home. "But I'm afraid Papa's going to have to serve some time in prison." Her heart sank in despair.

"It may not be too long."

When they arrived at the boardinghouse, they found a bearded man waiting for them in the parlor. He was holding one of the drawings that Kitty had made.

"Ma'am, I'm sure I saw this man at Phillip's Crossing, down the Sacramento River about fifteen miles."

"Yes, I know where that is."

"I swear it's the same man. He was working there, pulling that barge ferry across the river. You know, the one with all the ropes overhead. Well, when I came on into Sacramento and saw this notice in Al's Saloon, I told myself to come right over and tell you."

"I'm grateful you did. If it is the man we want, we need him as a witness at a trial."

The man tapped the notice. "It says here there's a reward."

Kitty opened her purse and took out a ten-dollar gold piece. "I don't know if it's the man we want, but I thank you for your trouble."

After she let him out the front door, she turned to Jessie. "I'll send Amos to the livery stable for a horse and buggy. It's too late to go to Phillip's Crossing now, but we can start out at daybreak.''

''I can go with you, Kitty.''

''No, you go to the trial. Tell Bob Grist what we're doing. If the jury returns with a verdict, he can ask for a delay.''

Jessie clapped her hands. ''I just know it's Red Mc-Nalley. He'll come and testify that Papa shot Oberheimer in self-defense and they'll free him.'' She hugged Kitty. ''You were such a darling to try so hard to find this man.''

''No one wants Carl out of jail more than I do.''

The next morning, as soon as it was light enough to see, Kitty and Amos were on the road that ran along the river. Heron and crane grazed in the fields, their long spindly legs deep in the spongy ground. Overhead a flock of geese, flapping their wings and honking, formed a V, heading south for the winter. A few sea gulls swooped and squawked at them.

Kitty figured it would take two hours to get to Phillip's Crossing. If the man *did* turn out to be McNalley, perhaps they could persuade him to come back with them right away. The court wouldn't reconvene until ten o'clock. Surely Bob Grist could delay the proceedings for a little while.

They pulled up at Phillip's Crossing by eight o'clock. There were two houses by the side of the road and the high posts that held the ropes for the flat barge that served as a ferry.

A man in a heavy jacket, with a fringe of red hair coming out of the bottom of his knitted cap and a big handlebar mustache, came out of one of the dwellings.

''Howdy, folks. You fixing to cross the river? It's fifty cents.''

Kitty spoke up. ''We don't want a ferry ride. We came to talk to you. Are you Red McNalley?''

''Yes, ma'am. What can I do for you?'' He grasped the edge of the buggy.

Kitty slumped back in her seat with relief. ''I've been hunting for you for weeks. We need you to come to Sac-

ramento with us to be a witness at a trial.'' She introduced herself and explained the circumstances.

''Well, ma'am . . . It all happened so fast I'm not sure
what I did see. I know that Fats Oberheimer was dealing
from the bottom of the deck. And I reckon he did pull
his gun first.''

''Mr. McNalley, I'm not going to tell you what to testify to if you'll just come. I'll pay you for your time—
and put you up—until we can bring you back.''

''I've heard that a witness can be subpoenaed, so I
reckon I'd better come. I'll make arrangements with my
boss and change my clothes.''

The jury was just ready to return to the courtroom with
their verdict when Kitty arrived with Red. When she
opened the door and saw Bob Grist, she nodded her head.

He rose and addressed the bench. ''Your Honor, the
missing witness, Red McNalley, has been found. On behalf of my client, I request that the jury be recalled and
the trial be reopened.''

The judge banged his gavel. ''Request granted. We
will have a thirty-minute recess. The court will reconvene at eleven o'clock.''

Bob Grist hustled McNalley to a conference room. The
bailiff led Carl away.

Jessie gave Kitty a hug. ''You did it! You really found
him!'' Everything was going to be all right now. Papa
would soon be free. Their worries were over.

While they waited, Kitty told Jessie about the trip, and
about how easy it was to get McNalley to come with
them.

''He seems like such a nice man,'' she went on. ''He
came down from the mountains—where he'd been prospecting—and wanted to hole up for the winter. He happened to stop at Phillip's Crossing and got that job. He
had no idea that we were looking for him.''

When the judge opened the court session again, the
jury was back in its box, and Carl was seated next to his
attorney.

The judge looked at Bob Grist. ''You may call your
witness.''

After Red McNalley was sworn in, Bob Grist said, "Tell the court exactly what happened during the card game where Mr. Oberheimer was shot."

"The defendant, Fats Oberheimer, and I were watching a poker game at one of the tables for some time," McNalley began. "We all wanted to get into the game, but there wasn't much chance of getting a place. I guess no one wanted to leave. Well, this Oberheimer suggested that we start our own game, and we went to a table in the corner."

"Did you ask anyone else to join you?" Grist asked.

"No, we didn't. We set up the rules first, so we all understood how we were playing. For the first hour the game went well. We all took turns dealing, and the cards fell fair to each of us. Then I began to notice that every time Fats Oberheimer dealt, he got the best cards. A full house. A flush. A straight. I watched his hands, and I was sure he was dealing from the bottom of the deck. But he dealt as fast as lightning. You couldn't really tell exactly."

"Then what happened?"

"All of a sudden, Henderson yells out, 'Damn you! You're cheating.' Things happened awful fast then. Oberheimer pulled a gun out, and Henderson did, too. A shot rang out, and Fats slumped over. Blood began to ooze out. Everyone in the room began milling around and shouting. Finally a big man who seemed to be the boss came and they took Oberheimer to the back room. I was about out of money, so I went to my rooming house and went to bed."

Jessie leaned back in relief. This Red McNalley had given a straightforward account. Surely the jury would decide in her father's favor right away.

"Your witness," Bob Grist said to the other attorney.

The prosecutor came forward. "I'm willing to concede that the deceased probably was a regular card shark dealing from the bottom of the deck, although you said you couldn't tell exactly. No doubt both you and the defendant had every reason to be angry with him."

Jessie sat up straight, alarmed. Every instinct told her

that this lawyer was setting Red McNalley up for the kill. Getting him off-guard.

"Now show us exactly where Oberheimer's hand was when he pulled out the gun."

McNalley put his hand on his hip.

"Did he pull it out of a holster?"

"I don't think so." He began to hesitate and act uncertain.

"Did the deceased wear a coat?"

"Yes."

"What color was it?"

"It was dark blue or black. I noticed he had a plaid vest with a watch chain across it."

"Let's go back to the coat. Did it have a side pocket in it?"

Red hesitated. "Yes, I guess so."

"If Oberheimer didn't wear a holster, he must have carried the gun in his pocket."

Bob Grist called out, "I object. That's leading the witness."

The judge said, "Sustained."

"Please describe the gun for us."

"It was small."

"What brand? Derringer? Colt?"

"I don't know. It happened so fast."

"It happened so fast that you don't know who drew their gun first, do you?"

Grist was on his feet. "Your Honor, I object."

"Sustained."

"Remember, you're under oath." The prosecutor walked up and down in front of the bench. Suddenly he turned and pointed his finger. "Can you swear that, without a doubt, Oberheimer drew his gun first?"

McNalley didn't answer.

The prosecutor shrugged. "No more questions."

The judge said, "You may step down." He gave his instructions to the jury again, and they filed out.

Jessie slumped back in her seat, too disappointed to speak. She was so sure that everything was going to be all right now. All they needed was Red McNalley's testimony.

She turned to Kitty, who looked as dispirited as she felt. "And you tried so hard."

The widow nodded. "I'd hoped McNalley would be more positive. Especially after Bob Grist talked to him. But you can't put words in a witness's mouth."

The jury filed back to their seats an hour later. The judge asked, "Have you reached a verdict?"

"Yes, Your Honor," the foreman replied.

"Will the defendant please stand."

Carl and Bob Grist got to their feet.

The foreman stood. "We find the defendant guilty of manslaughter."

Guilty! The word seemed to bounce from the walls. Jessie tried to take it in, tried to realize all of the implications that went with it. Her father stood with his head bowed and his shoulders slumped.

The judge thanked the members of the jury and said the sentence would be pronounced on Wednesday of the following week. The bailiff led Carl away.

Both Jesse and Kitty were so close to tears they couldn't speak. They walked outside and found Red McNalley jamming a hat on his head.

"I'm sorry, ma'am. I should of lied."

Kitty shook her head. "No, Mr. McNalley. You were under oath. You had to tell the truth. Did you want to stay in town, or shall I have Amos drive you home?"

"I'd rather go back. I just started that job and I don't want to lose it."

Kitty paid him for his time and told Amos, who was waiting with the horse and buggy, to take him back to Phillip's Crossing.

As they walked back to the boardinghouse, Jessie said, "I feel strung as tight as a top. I'm so nervous I don't know what to do with myself for the rest of the day."

"Me, too. When I'm jittery like this, I like to bake cookies. Let's go home, change our clothes, and get busy."

Late that afternoon, Kitty's lawyer stopped in. "We've

completed our investigations, and as far as we can tell, the Capital Stage Line is in fine condition. The audit verifies that the company is doing well. Here's a written report.''

After he left, Kitty took the papers up to Jessie's room. ''I'm ready to loan you the money if you want to go ahead with the deal.''

Jessie looked at the report. ''I'll study this over, but I'm sure I want to buy the company. I have to earn a living now that Papa's—'' Her voice choked.

''Your father won't be in jail forever. It's not murder in the first degree. It's manslaughter, so he will get out eventually. This company will give him something wonderful to look forward to. As you pointed out, it isn't too hard a run, and he'd be home on Tuesday, Thursday, and Saturday nights, as well as all day Sunday. He'd have a chance to rest and have some home life.''

''One reason I want it, is because I'd like to try my wings at something. Staging fascinates me. I'm sure I could make a success of it. I could manage the office and let the present driver handle the run. When the busy season comes, we'll just have to find someone else to take care of the overflow. Goodness knows we have plenty of horses and coaches.''

''You always have Tonio to turn to for advice,'' Kitty put in. ''The time may come when you might want to merge the two companies.''

''Absolutely not! Once he and Iris got married, I know very well that I'd be out. She wouldn't stand for me being in it.''

Kitty nodded. ''I think you're right. She's a possessive kind of girl. And spoiled rotten. She's not going to share Tonio—even in a business arrangement!''

Jessie went to Kitty's lawyer the next morning. After some discussion about the Capital Stage Line, she said, ''I want you to do the legal work for the loan and for the sale.''

''Well, I'd better go to the jail and talk this over with your father.''

"No. I'll discuss it with him later. He's too upset to make decisions now."

"But I don't think we can go ahead—"

"Oh, yes we can. I have a power of attorney to act in his behalf. I know he's been looking for a stage line, and this will suit his needs perfectly. But when you write up the papers, there's one thing I want you to remember. I want to be a full partner in the company. I'm to be consulted on all major decisions."

The lawyer shook his head. "You and Kitty White sure are two peas in a pod. I don't know what this world is coming to with you females running things!"

Jessie smiled. "You'll have to admit Widow White has made a real success of her business."

"Indeed she has."

"I intend to be just as successful with my stage line."

The next few days flew by, but the closer they came to the day the judge would pronounce the sentence, the more worried Jessie became.

Finally they were back in the courtroom. The judge said, "Carl Henderson, you were found guilty of manslaughter. I sentence you to one year in the county jail."

Chapter 18

Jessie sat in her seat in the courtroom for a long time, too stunned and heartsick to move. Poor Papa—being locked up for a whole year! The thought of it made her ill. How terrible he must feel. He would never be the same. If she could only be with him and comfort him.

Finally she realized they were getting ready for another trial, so she rose and walked outside.

Kitty was sitting on a bench waiting for her. She reached up and grasped Jessie's hand. "I know what a blow this is to you. But keep your chin up. This nightmare will be over someday."

"But a whole year in jail!"

"It won't be that long. Bob Grist just told me that the time Carl has already spent in jail will count toward the year. So that gets it down to less than ten months. And he will get time off for good behavior. Bob's going to confer with the judge and see what can be worked out."

As they walked home, Kitty went on. "Now that your father's been sentenced, we can't go to see him so often. In fact, we can only visit him on Sundays between two and four. But I can send food to him."

"That will help. But I insist on paying you for the meals. I won't hear of anything else."

"If you'd feel better about it, all right." They walked along in silence for a while, then Kitty went on. "You must get your mind on other things, Jessie. Take over the stage line as soon as possible."

"Yes, I will. I can hardly wait to begin."

Late that afternoon, Tonio came over, looking very handsome in dark trousers, a tan coat, and fresh linen. When Jessie told him about the sentence, he held her close. "I can imagine how awful you feel, but I'm not going to have you sit around and mope. Get your best duds on; I'm taking you out to dinner. There's a very funny play on at the Riverside Theater, and we're going to see it."

"Tonio, thank you. But—"

"No excuses. Go get dressed up pretty. I'm sure Kitty will give me a cup of coffee while I wait for you."

There was no use arguing with Tonio, so she went upstairs. She sponged herself off and put on a brown suit trimmed with ecru braid that highlighted her brown eyes and hair. Gold earrings and a locket that belonged to her mother, as well as a small brown velvet hat with an iridescent bird wing on the side, completed the outfit.

Tonio tucked her hand under his arm. As they left Kitty's, he said, "You look lovely."

They sat in a restaurant overlooking the river. Lights from a dock across the way sent a shimmering path over the dark water.

The candlelight from a centerpiece flickered on Tonio's face as he leaned across the table and took her hands in his. He smiled. "If it weren't for Iris, I'd propose to you right now. You look so beautiful."

A strange sensation ran through her as she bantered back, "If it weren't for Iris, I'd accept. You're a darling to take me out tonight and cheer me up." She hated to think of him marrying that spoiled, selfish girl—who would make his life miserable. Tonio was a man in a million. Aloud she asked, "Have you heard from her recently?"

"Yes. She's having a wonderful time attending all the tea parties and balls. But she says there's sort of an air of desperation back there. All the Democrats in office are afraid that Lincoln'll be elected next month. Of course, they'll be out when he's inaugurated in March.''

"Did she say anything about feelings running high between the North and South?''

"Yes, the tension is tremendous. If war breaks out after Lincoln is president, they're sailing for home. Besides, the climate doesn't agree with Mrs. Cunningham. She's suffered from asthma all her life and is lots worse back there.''

The show was delightful. In spite of her heartache over her father, she thoroughly enjoyed it. As they walked home in the star-studded night, Tonio put his arm around her waist. She matched her step to his. How nice it felt to be so protected and cherished, to have such a delightful companion. Why did they both have to fall in love with the wrong people when they were probably meant for each other? . . .

Because of Mr. McWhorter's health, the arrangements for the sale of the stage line moved along rapidly, and Jessie took possession of it on November fifteenth. Chuck Douglas, the other driver, agreed to stay on.

"You must realize business is slow in the winter,'' Mr. McWhorter warned her. "Not much money coming in. If it rains hard, the coaches can't go at all. The wheels sink down to the hub in the mud.''

Jessie nodded. "I know all about that. I was caught in that early storm.''

"Besides that, men don't hanker to go upcountry during the winter. Of course, as soon as the rainy season stops, you'll have plenty of customers.''

"I'm prepared to carry the expenses during this off-season.''

"You have to pay rent and utilities.''

"I realize that.''

"Then there's salaries for Chuck, as well as for the stable boy and the old gentleman, Ed Petroni, who hangs around here.''

"Yes, I know.'' Jessie smiled. "I imagine that feed for the horses is the biggest expense. My father had a stage line in Missouri, and I kept his books.''

"Then you're aware that there's always something that puts a monkey wrench in your plans."

They shook hands. Mr. McWhorter turned the keys over to her. "You realize that if the roads are at all passable, you have to get the mail through?"

"Yes, that's in the sales contract."

"Seems like you're awfully young to take on a venture like this." He seemed reluctant to turn the business over to her.

"I have a friend, Tonio Maquire, who'll help me."

"A fine young man. I never cottoned to his cousin Gianni, though."

When she was finally alone, she walked around the office and relished the fact that it was her very own project. She'd make a success of it, have everything ready for Papa to be her partner. She touched her desk, ran her fingertips over the counter, took the roll of tickets out of a drawer just for the thrill of handling them.

As the days went by, she realized she would have some time on her hands, so she bought a used pedal sewing machine and put it behind the partition that closed off a storage area. She had Ed install a bell on the front door so she could tell if she had customers.

She loved to sew, so she bought some plaid wool to make Tonio a shirt for Christmas. As soon as it was ready, she planned to make Kitty a pretty pink dressing gown. Her heart felt heavy as she thought of the coming holidays. It would the first time with neither of her parents around. And what could be worse than spending the holidays in a dreary jail cell? Just thinking about her poor father there brought a lump to her throat.

Every day she bought a copy of a newspaper and saved it to take to her father on Sunday. The final count was coming in, and it looked as if Lincoln had definitely been elected.

Late one afternoon, Tonio stopped by the office. He held up a beautiful salmon. "One of my passengers gave this to me. He'd just caught it. You know the rivers are full of salmon. They're coming up from the ocean to spawn."

"You'll have a feast tonight."

"I was planning on you helping Gianni and me eat it. I already stopped at Kitty's and told her you wouldn't be home for dinner."

"Tonio Maquire, you're always telling me what to do." Jessie laughed, however. "Since you canceled my dinner at Kitty's, I'd better come or I'll go hungry. Will it be all right with Gianni?"

"Sure. I've been gone for three days, so I don't know what the flat looks like. We might have to clean the kitchen before we can cook in it."

"Just wait until I get my coat and I'll be right with you. I have to lock up, too."

Jessie took one last look around before she turned off the lights and locked the door. It gave her such a wonderful feeling to think she was a partner in this stage line.

They walked rapidly along the wooden sidewalks to Tonio's office building with the flat above.

"Strange . . . It's all dark," Tonio said. "I wonder where Gianni is."

After he unlocked the door, he reached for a lantern on a shelf and lighted their way up the stairs, which were in a hallway adjacent to the office. When he reached the flat, he opened the door and walked around lighting the kerosene lamps.

He pulled down the overhead fixture in the kitchen and got it lit. Dirty dishes filled the sink. A frying pan on the range was filled with congealed bacon grease.

Tonio looked around in disgust. "What a mess. Gianni's a slob." He put the big salmon in the icebox. "I hate it when he leaves everything like this."

"Never mind, Tonio. I'll get some water heating and start washing the dishes. I don't mind at all. I haven't washed dishes since I've been living at Kitty's." She picked up the teakettle and started filling it.

"He might be taking a nap. I'll look in his room."

Jessie found a dishtowel and tied it around her dress. Just as she started stacking the dishes, she heard a shout. She ran down the hall.

Tonio stood in the middle of the bedroom, looking

completely dumfounded. "He's skipped out!" He yanked open a closet door. "All his clothes are gone." He pulled out the dresser drawers. "Look at 'em. They're all empty."

"Maybe he left a note for you in the office."

"Come on. Let's see."

He grabbed the lantern, and they hurried down the stairs. After he unlocked the door and got the lamps lighted, they looked around.

"The safe! He left the door open." Tonio rushed to it. "He's cleaned everything out."

"There's a passbook on the floor." Jessie hurried over to it and picked it up.

When Tonio opened it, the color drained from his face. "He's withdrawn all our savings."

Jessie looked at it. "The withdrawal is dated three days ago."

Tonio leaned against the desk in shock. "I can't believe this!"

"Let's see if we can find a checkbook. He probably took out all the money from the checking account, too." She opened a drawer and found a big checkbook. "See? Here you had a balance of three thousand, six hundred and seventy-eight dollars and forty-five cents. Then on the next page, there's a stub showing a check had been written for that amount. The balance is zero."

Tonio slumped down into the chair in front of the desk. "Damn him! He's cleaned me out. Every cent." He pounded his fist on the desk.

"Look at the back of this stub, Tonio. Your cousin drew a figure thumbing his nose."

"The dirty bastard! I feel like I've been rammed by a bull. I'm stunned. It's unreal." He pounded his fist and swore some more.

Jessie sat on the edge of the desk. "I'll bet he's been embezzling from your stage company for months. Ever since you left to go to Chicago last April."

"I wouldn't doubt it. I was so dumb. I let him keep all the books."

"I couldn't figure out his method of bookkeeping, remember? It was awfully strange." She patted his shoulder. "Tonio, I'm so sorry."

He looked at her with stricken eyes. "I know you are, Jess."

She snapped her fingers. "I just thought of something! That explains why he wouldn't take Papa in as a partner. He knew he couldn't face an audit."

"Of course." He leaned his elbows on the desk and cupped his face with his hands. "Good God, what am I going to do? I'm flat broke."

"We'll think of something."

"I can't even pay my livery stable bills."

"You can bring your horses out to my place. There are some empty stalls—and you could build some more—as well as a lean-to to cover your coaches for the winter. That would save you a lot of money. There's plenty of pasture."

He sat up. "Jessie, you're a real pal. I'll do that. I've got a little cash from that trip I just made. That will keep me going for a few days. But what about your feed bill for all those horses?"

"The McWhorters left a big supply of oats and grain. We can get by for a while." She looked around. "What about this place?"

"Thank God, it's free and clear. We paid cash for it when we first came. I know the property taxes and business taxes are all paid. I did that myself the first of the month."

"If you have no outstanding bills, you can get along until you have some more passengers."

"But we're going into the slow season. It's tough for a staging company during the winter."

Neither spoke for a few minutes as they tried to adjust to what had happened. Finally Jessie said, "Gianni sure timed his departure just right. He's probably been planning this a long time. You left for Chicago, so he had a free hand to rob the till. He stayed on the job and got the benefit of the busy season. You got back and made all those runs to Carson City with the convoy, plus all the

other trips you've made. In other words, he waited until
your bank accounts were full.''

Tonio picked up the summation. ''And I was gone for
three days, so he had plenty of time to clean out the
accounts and pack his clothes. He probably got passage
on a ship to the East Coast and is long gone. Well, to
hell with him!''

Jessie stood up. ''I might as well go upstairs and wash
dishes. Shall I put the salmon in the oven and bake it?''
Tonio nodded, so she added, ''Can I find some potatoes
to cook with it as well?''

''They should be up there in a bin.'' He laughed bit-
terly. ''That is if Gianni didn't take 'em with him!''

She found potatoes and a piece of Hubbard squash.
While dinner baked, she washed the dishes and scrubbed
the drain boards. The oilcloth tablecloth needed cleaning, also. She set the table, and, by the time Tonio came
upstairs, the food was ready to eat.

In spite of the shock of finding Gianni and the funds
gone, they were both hungry and able to enjoy the delicious food, especially the fresh salmon.

''Thank God you were here with me, Jess. What a
comfort to have someone to talk to about this.''

''I can't tell you how sorry I am this happened. I'm
just sick about it. But you do have this building—and
your coaches and horses. So you'll get back on your
feet.''

''What worries me is Iris. If they do come back next
spring, I won't have anything to offer her.''

''Except your wonderful self, Tonio.'' She leaned
across the table and grasped his hand. ''Any girl would
be so lucky to get you.''

''Remember what Mr. Cunningham said—fine horses,
a maid, and a big income. That'll take years to achieve.
Especially after this setback.''

''Surely they'll understand. Probably Iris would be
glad to fix up a more modest home at first. Think what
she could do with *this* place.''

Tonio looked around. ''This place? I couldn't possibly
expect her to live here.''

"Why not?"

"It looks so awful. Especially after what she's been used to."

"You'd be surprised what the two of you could do with some paint and slipcovers and pretty curtains."

Every Sunday afternoon, she and Kitty went to visit her father. She knew she should tell him about the stage line, but the jail was always so crowded, there was no privacy. There was just a long bench on one side of the screen barrier, where the visitors had to crowd together to talk to the inmates on the other side. Before Carl was sentenced and she could go any day, there were times when she was alone with him. That would have been the opportunity to explain about her purchase, but she had let it slide by because he was already under such stress worrying about the trial.

As she and Kitty walked home from the jail, Jessie said, "I should let Papa know about our stage company, but it's so hard to talk in that visitors' room."

"Oh, it's impossible! The babies crying, and all that confusion. Why don't you write him a letter?"

"Do you suppose the mail is censored? It would be like publishing all your private business in the newspaper."

"The next time I see Bob Grist, I'll ask him."

On Thanksgiving Day, Kitty invited Tonio to dinner and asked him to bring his guitar and sing. She made every effort to make it a memorable holiday for her boarders, with a sumptuous turkey feast served about two o'clock in the afternoon. But all the while Jessie was eating, she kept thinking about her father and how depressing a holiday it must be for him.

She and Tonio took a walk after dinner to help digest all the food they had eaten. They walked toward the river and found a path along the edge. They could see water flowing swiftly along. The sky looked threatening overhead, but it was good to be out in the fresh air.

"You know, I was thinking," Tonio said as they walked. "Now that Gianni is out of the picture, there is no reason that our two stage companies couldn't merge. It would be advantageous for both of us. Your father planned to be my partner right from the first. As soon as you break the news to him about purchasing the company, I'll talk to him about it.''

"Aren't you forgetting something, Tonio?'' A flare of anger rose in her.

"What?''

"Me!''

"What about you?''

She stopped walking and glared at him. "I am a full partner in the Capital Stage Line. I am the one who bought it, the one who's running it. Yet you didn't say one word about consulting me.''

"You don't need to get so steamed up. I took it for granted you'd want to. So now I'm asking. Would you be interested in merging the two companies?''

"No!''

"Why the hell not? You're going to have more business than you can handle with one driver this spring.''

"I know that.''

"I've got the experience and know-how. Some excellent coaches and horses. I've built up a good reputation for reliability and honesty.''

"I grant you all that. And I have fine stables and a tack room and pasture. Not to mention my coaches and horses.'' She put her face close to his. "To say nothing of a mail contract, which you'd love to have as part of the operation.''

By now his face was flushed in annoyance. "Jess, get off your high horse. Of course we should form a partnership. Give me one good reason why we shouldn't.'' He tapped his chest.

"All right. You want one good reason so I'll tell you. It's Iris.''

His mouth fell open in surprise. "Dammit, what does Iris have to do with it?''

"You know very well she wouldn't put up with having me associated with you for one minute. And I am a full partner in my company. I had the lawyer write that all out. If our companies merged, she wouldn't stand for it. I'd be pushed out in the cold.''

"That's the craziest idea I've ever heard. You females are so illogical. That's why you aren't good business people. You get too emotional over a cut-and-dried proposition.''

Now Jessie was really angry. She shook her finger at him. "Mark my words, there'd be nothing cut and dried about Iris's reaction if she came home and found out that we were partners. She wouldn't marry you until you got rid of me. And Papa'd support her, too, because he'd want you for a partner—and he'd want me home keeping house!''

"Let's turn around and go back. You're talking a lot of nonsense.''

"Am I?''

Neither spoke as they walked along. But Tonio asked himself: *Would* Iris refuse to marry him if Jessie was part of the operation? He had to admit that she might. He recalled how she had treated Jessie at the farewell party. As if she were jealous. How ridiculous. She was beautiful and enchanting, but she'd been badly pampered and spoiled by her parents, especially her father. When they got married, she'd have to grow up and realize that she couldn't always have her own way. He longed for her. He could hardly wait for her return. But he glanced at Jessie walking beside him. How could he give up their friendship?

Iris wasn't the only one who resented Jessie, she found out one morning when she came to the office and discovered her door had been splattered with eggs. Why would anyone do that? She got soap and water and cleaned up the mess.

Another day she found a crudely printed note on the door that read, "Stay home where you belong." A shiver of fear ran along her spine. Who would harass her this way?

When Mr. Petroni arrived, she showed it to him. "Stay with me all day, Ed. I don't want to be alone here.''

"Could be some kids trying to make mischief. We have some boys full of devilment in this neighborhood."

But when she showed it to Kitty that night, the widow said, "If anything else happens, send for the policeman on the beat. If there are boys around there that cause trouble, he'll be sure to know about them. He can put a stop to it."

Nothing happened for the next few days. Then, when she went to work, she found that a brick had been thrown through her window. Shards of glass were scattered all over the floor. She ran next door and got Ed's son, the barber.

He looked over the damage. "I'll lock my shop and go find a cop. Don't clean up anything."

Soon he returned with a friendly looking policeman. "I'm Officer O'Malley. What can I do for you, ma'am?"

Jessie showed him the brick and broken glass. She went to her desk and got out the note. "Someone seems to have it in for me. I just took over this place, so I don't know why."

"It could be some neighborhood boys. I'll see what I can find out." He took out a notebook and jotted several things down. When he was finished he asked her her name and address.

"I appreciate your help."

"Are you here by yourself?" the officer asked.

The barber spoke up. "My father's usually here. I see him coming now."

"It's not a good idea for you to be here alone. Not an attractive young lady like you. Are you running this stage line yourself?"

"My father and I own it."

"I suppose he's out with his coach most of the time."

"Yes, he is." Thank goodness the officer didn't recognize the name.

"I'll go down to the station and see if I can find any records of malicious mischief like this around here. Usually an older boy is a ringleader of a gang that stirs up trouble. Or it could be another stagecoach driver who's hurting for business and resents competition."

After telling her he'd be back soon, the policeman left.

Mr. Petroni asked, "Shall I sweep it up, ma'am? Don't look so good if a customer should come in."

"Yes, I should think so." It was worrisome having this happen. It took the pleasure out of owning the stage company.

Before the morning was over, Officer O'Malley was back, a man in civilian clothes with him. Was he a detective? The officer mumbled an introduction.

The new man asked her name and address. He questioned her about the other harassments. Finally he said, "I thought a Mr. McWhorter owned this stage line."

"My father and I bought it from him recently."

"Where did you come from?"

"St. Louis, Missouri. My father had a stage line there." She wondered why that information was relevant to the present problem.

"Aren't you the young lady stagecoach driver? It seems to me I've heard about you before this."

"Yes." Why did he need to know that?

"Weren't you in that convoy for the army? The one that got held up by the highwaymen?"

She nodded, and he wrote furiously on some folded paper.

He asked question after question. Most of them had nothing to do with the matter at hand.

She wondered why he was asking them. Perhaps they were getting information about new businessmen in Sacramento. Finally she asked, "Are you a detective with the police department?"

"No, ma'am. I'm a reporter for the *Sacramento Union*. I work out of the police headquarters."

Her heart sank. "You mean you're going to put this in the paper?"

"Yes, of course."

Frantically she grabbed his arm. "But you can't."

"Yes, I can, ma'am. You sent for the police. The report is a public record. Anyone can read it."

"Please don't."

He picked up his hat and put it on. "Sorry." He walked out of the door.

That night she told Kitty, then asked, "What am I going to do?"

"Nothing."

"But Papa will read all about it."

"Now don't you fret. We just won't take him the issue it appears in. He'll never see it."

But would he?

Chapter 19

The newspaper story about Jessie came out the next morning in the *Sacramento Union*. Fortunately it was not on the front page, but it was in the local news section. All the information she had given the reporter was included. She cringed at the very thought of her father reading it. Everything she wanted to tell him, in the most tactful way, about the two of them owning the stage line was blabbed right out for the whole town to see.

On Sunday she told Kitty, "I think I'd better go alone to see Papa today—just in case he's read the write-up."

"All right, dear. But the chances of his seeing it are very remote. My goodness, he can't go out and buy a paper. He depends on us to bring the copies to him. You can pretend you forgot to bring the one with the story in it."

"In any case, I'm going to tell him today. I don't dare put if off any longer."

She took the week's supply of papers and the usual lard can of cookies. It was fifteen minutes before the visiting hour of two o'clock when she arrived. As she handed the guard the papers and cookies, she managed to slip him a dollar bill.

"I have something I must discuss in private with my father. Would it be possible for him to come now . . . before the crowd gets here?"

The guard glanced down at the money before he put it in his pocket. "I guess he could, just this once."

When her father came to the screen and she saw the expression on his beet-red face, she knew he had read the piece. His eyes sparked with fury. His mouth clamped shut in a grim line. His hands made white-knuckled fists.

He put his face close to the screen. "Daughter, you betrayed me!"

The blood seemed to freeze in her veins. "Papa, let me explain—"

"You used that power of attorney and acted behind my back. You never said one damn word to me first."

She had never seen her father in such a terrible rage. Fear paralyzed her throat. She could hardly speak. "Father, listen. It all happened just before the trial and when you were waiting to be sentenced."

His voice screeched, "My God, that was nearly seven weeks ago! And you never told me!"

"Father, please listen—"

"Where did you get the money?"

"From Kitty . . ."

"Kitty? You borrowed money from Kitty without asking my permission? How much?"

Tears flooded her eyes. Her chin quivered, but she held her head high. "The stage line cost ten thousand dollars. I used two thousand dollars of the money from the army contract, and Kitty put up the rest."

Her father sputtered with anger. He couldn't get any words out.

"I paid off Bob Grist with your money," Jessie went on. "So I don't owe anything. Except to Kitty, of course."

"I suppose she put the idea in your head."

"In a way . . ."

"All right. Listen to every word I have to say. I don't want to see you again. Don't write to me. I'm through with you. Understand? And the same goes for Kitty White. I don't want her food. I don't want her damn cookies. And she's not to come here, either." He turned and stalked away.

Jessie slumped against the back of the chair, too shocked to feel anything. She closed her eyes; her arms hung limp at her side.

"Are you all right, young lady?"

She looked up into the guard's concerned face and nodded.

"Your old man's in a rage. Has been ever since he read that story about you in the paper."

"Who showed it to him?"

"One of the other guards. Thought your father'd be right pleased, but I can tell you that weren't the case." He rolled his eyes up.

"I was going to tell him all about it today."

"You should have done it sooner, miss."

"I know." Jessie pulled herself out of the chair and left as the other visitors crowded into the room.

She found Kitty in her sitting room, so she sat down and told her all about the terrible confrontation. A chill ran through her, and her chin trembled.

"Jessie, don't be so upset. He'll get over it."

"You don't know my father. He meant every word he said. He doesn't want anything more to do with me. Or you, either."

"Time heals, dear."

"It won't heal him. He's the most stubborn person you could ever know. He'll hold this grudge against me the rest of his life."

"You're white as a sheet, Jessie. You'd better go upstairs and lie down for a while."

"I think I will. I feel completely drained."

After Jessie left the room, Kitty went to her desk and wrote a note. Then she took it to the basement to Amos.

"Please take this note to Tonio Maguire. If he's not in his office or upstairs flat, he'd likely be in the Riverfront Saloon."

An hour later, Tonio arrived at the boardinghouse.

"Have you had any dinner?"

"No, I've been working on one of my coaches at the livery stable. Amos found me there. Had to change a wheel. What's up? You said in your note you wanted to see me.''

"It's quite a story. I'll warm you up some victuals from our dinner and tell you all about it. You can eat it in here.''

It wasn't long before she returned with a tray full of food. While he ate, she told him the whole incident.

"That's what I get for sticking my nose in someone else's business,'' she concluded.

Tonio finished the last of his pumpkin pie. "Guess I'm guilty, too. I encouraged her. And I should have gone with her to break the news.''

"Do you think there'll be a permanent rift between them?''

Tonio shook his head. "I don't know. He's a wonderful man. Straight as an arrow. Usually just as even-going as they come. But he can be mean and stubborn as all get out when he gets riled up over something.''

A long sigh shuddered through Kitty. "We've got a heartbroken girl upstairs. You're the only one who can help her.''

Tonio pulled his tall frame out of the chair. "I'll see what I can do.''

He took the stairs two at a time. When he got to Jessie's door, he opened it and walked right in. She was stretched out on the bed, her face buried in the pillow. First he untied his shoes and took them off, then he lay down beside her and gathered her in his arms.

"Oh, Tonio, thank you for coming,'' she whispered, and pressed her face in the hollow of his shoulder.

"Cry if you can.''

"I can't.''

"Do you want to talk about it?''

"Not now.''

So he began to sing, low and soothing, in his beautiful tenor voice . . . while he caressed her back and held her close.

Early the next morning, a man approached the front door of the Capital Stage Line office with a bucket of black paint and a brush. Just as he started to paint a streak across it, Officer O'Malley stepped out of the adjoining doorway and grabbed him.

"Ah-ha, Frizbach, so you're the mischief maker."

Later that morning, as Jessie worked at her desk, Officer O'Malley stopped by to see her. "I caught the man who's been causing you trouble. Ever since your window got broken, I've kept a special eye out for him. I figured he'd strike again just after daybreak, before folks began to open up their businesses."

"Thank you. That's wonderful. Who was it? Why did he pick on me?"

"A radical named Wendell Frizbach. He was with that gang of Southern sympathizers who raised such a ruckus when California went into the Union as a free state instead of a slave one."

"But that was ten years ago."

"They all came crawling out of the woodwork again with all this talk about war coming. I guess he had it in for you because you were in the army convoy."

"You'd better question him about the robbery of one of the stagecoaches in the convoy. He was probably in on that."

"I did ask him about his leader, Ross Eberson. Seems he was on a ship on his way back to the East Coast. The ship sank, and he was lost at sea."

With all the gold, no doubt, Jessie thought to herself.

"Well, miss. I'll be on my way. I don't think you'll have any more trouble with vandalism. But I'll keep an eye on your place."

When he was gone, Jessie got down to work again. She still had some sewing to do on the shirt for Tonio. She could hardly wait to have Christmas over . . . then New Year's—and a fresh start. Somehow she would have to adjust to the fact that with her mother dead—and her father disowning her—she had no one of her own. And she would lose Tonio as soon as Iris returned.

Kitty held a big Christmas Eve party for her boarders and neighbors. Tonio sang and played his guitar. There

were games, along with plenty of food and drink. Jessie
was determined that she wouldn't spoil the party by acting despondent. Instead she helped organize the charades
and kept things as lively as possible.

Tonio came back for breakfast the next morning. When
it was over, Kitty invited him and Jessie into her sitting
room to exchange presents. Kitty gave her a silk nightgown trimmed with exquisite handmade lace. She had a
leather wallet for Tonio.

He pulled out his old one and showed her how worn it
was. "All I need is to earn some money to put in it."
He had made a nicknack shelf for each of them.

"I know just where I'm going to put mine," Kitty
said. "And I'll put a trailing plant on it."

"I'll probably do the same," Jessie added. She caressed the polished wood. I'll always have this to remember him by, she thought. Once Iris returns, it will all be
over. "It's so beautiful. Thank you. I'll put the lovely
Indian basket you gave me on it, too. And I have some
other things."

"I'm too broke to buy gifts, so I had to make you
one."

"Well, I made you something, too." She handed him
the shirt.

When he opened the package and found the shirt, he
held it up. "You made this? It doesn't seem possible."
He took off his coat and shirt and tried it on. The soft,
maroon-colored wool blended with his tanned skin. "It
fits just right. It's so comfortable. Thank you, Jess. I'm
tickled to pieces."

He came over and kissed her on the mouth. An excited
thrill ran through her. The color rose in her cheeks.
"Now you're blushing," he said, and trailed his fingers
over her skin.

Kitty was just as pleased with her dressing gown. "It's
lovely, Jessie. I didn't realize you were such a skilled
seamstress."

"She's going to make some guy a wonderful wife one
of these days."

"If you had a grain of sense, Tonio Maguire, you'd marry her yourself!" Kitty retorted.

"Hush, both of you. I'm not going to marry anyone," Jessie said.

During the week, Tonio dropped in at her office wearing his new shirt. He patted the front. "Doesn't it look great?"

"I'll admit it's very becoming."

"I just got a letter from Iris. The Cunninghams are coming back to Sacramento later in the spring. They're staying in Washington for Lincoln's inauguration March fourth, and then are going to New York for a month. They have reservations on a clipper ship, so they should be here about the tenth of June."

"I know you're anxious to see her."

"I was thinking that now that it's the slow season—and I have a lot of time on my hands—I ought to fix up my flat and office. Paint it and slick it up, so it isn't such a dump. If it looked better, I could entertain Iris and her folks and make a better impression."

"That's an excellent idea. The whole place is in pretty bad condition. But it has real potential, Tonio."

"Would you help me, Jess? I can wield a paintbrush, but I'm no good at fixing all the frills and doodads."

"I'll close now and walk back to your place with you. We can look things over and see what needs to be done."

First they looked around the shabby office area. Then they walked up the stairs and went through the flat. There was a good-sized living room on the corner, with the front window facing east and a side window on the south. The stairwell landing made the room near the kitchen larger, so it could be used as a dining area. The kitchen was adequate and had a window on the south side.

From there Jessie stepped into a hallway, which had an alcove containing washtubs and an icebox. A corner bedroom, a bathroom, and a smaller bedroom led off the hall.

"The building is only about fifteen years old," Tonio said. "And, of course, Gianni and I didn't do anything with it. We just used the furniture that was left here."

"It seems to be a well-built structure. But whoever put it up didn't spend any money finishing it nice. They used the cheapest of floor coverings, which are all worn out now. The curtains are in shreds."

"I suppose they ran out of money. There was a little grocery store downstairs when we bought it. Likely they had to stock the shelves, and that takes a lot of cash."

Jessie slowly walked through the flat again before she sat down in the living room. "I have some ideas, but it's going to take some money. But if we go to all the trouble of fixing it up, it ought to be done right."

Tonio shook his head. "I don't want to borrow money. I've got to get on my feet again from Gianni's embezzlement. The only thing I can do is sell a couple of horses."

"Why don't you give me two of yours? We can sell them."

"All right. Now what are your ideas?"

"First thing, I'd make this front east window larger. Make it a bay window. Do the same thing in the office below. That would add some interest to the rooms. Up here I could made a pad for the seat in the window that would match the curtains. After the woodwork is painted, I'd paper the walls and have some nice carpet laid. Then some paint in the kitchen and bath would help. Also we'd have to tackle the furniture. It all needs refinishing or slipcovers."

"Of course I'd have to paint the office downstairs," Tonio added.

"And change the floor covering. If you made a bay window down there, we could hang drapes on each side. We should also get rid of those chairs and buy some new ones. We could use plants and put some pictures on the wall. Varnish the desks. Give the office some class."

Tonio whistled. "I may be selling *three* horses!"

"Starting tomorrow, you can begin washing the woodwork—and contact a carpenter about the windows if you decide to do that. And you'll have to be thinking about your colors for the paint and wallpaper."

"I'll furnish the brawn, Jessie—and you furnish the

brains. You plan it just the way you would like it for yourself.''

''Shouldn't you wait and consult Iris after she gets here?''

''No. I want it fixed up nice before she gets here.''

''Then let's get started right away. We want to be all done before the Cunninghams arrive. And don't say anything in your letters to Iris about me helping you. She won't like it.''

''For gosh sakes, Jess, get that bee out of your bonnet.''

But when he reread his letter from Iris that night, he noticed a postscript that read, ''I hope you're not having anything to do with that queer stagecoach woman,'' and a sinking feeling came over him.

When it wasn't raining, a gloomy fog enshrouded the whole interior valley during all of January and early February. They didn't see the sun for weeks. But Jessie was so busy with her stage line and working with Tonio, she didn't mind it at all.

Only her heartache over her father dampened her spirits, but she tried to push that worry to the back of her mind and concentrate on the project that was beginning to take shape.

The bay windows were soon finished, and it was surprising what a difference they made. Jessie suggested, ''Let's finish up the office first—so it will be attractive for your passengers when business picks up again.''

They redesigned the office so the passengers could walk directly from the waiting room to the loading area in the back. The walls were painted a soft buff color. Brown draperies hung on each side of the bay window. New chairs lined the sides. With hanging plants and a picture of a stagecoach on one wall, and a colorful map of northern California on the other, the place looked so attractive.

The patterned floor covering in green, buff, and brown showed footprints the least. Also important were the newly installed lavatories for the convenience of the passengers. Other businessmen came in to see the improvements. Passersby dropped in to comment on how nice it looked. Officer O'Malley brought the police chief to look it over.

"Wow, I had no idea it would cause such a sensation," Tonio said to Jessie one evening, his eyes glowing with pride.

"You'll get your investment back many times over," she answered. "The legislators will especially want to use your stage line with this setup."

But Jessie's heart was in the flat upstairs. She chose paint colors, wallpaper, materials for the window treatments, and slipcovers. After looking at a dozen samples for carpets, she finally made her choice. Whenever she tried to consult Tonio, he said, "You decide, Jess. You know a hell of a lot more about it than I do." But his enthusiasm over each improvement touched her heart.

One evening, as she pulled a slipcover in a beautiful floral pattern over a worn overstuffed chair, she realized with a shock that she wanted to live here with Tonio. She gasped and leaned her head against the arm of the chair.

She loved him with all her heart. She wanted to marry him. While tears flooded her eyes, she pounded the chair with her fist. Drat him, anyway. First Lyle . . . and now Tonio. Why did she always care for men who wanted to marry someone else?

But this feeling for Tonio ran far deeper than what she had felt for Lyle. It had been more of an infatuation with the soldier's handsome appearance, his bearing, his uniform, and his air of authority—a hot flame that flared up and consumed itself.

But Tonio . . . Drat him! He teased her. He laughed at her. He knew all her faults and foibles. He drove her crazy. But he had rescued her from danger more than once. His strong arms had drawn her close to comfort her when her heart had been broken. His gentle fingers had wiped away her tears. Drat him! Now she loved him.

The weeks flew by and, finally, the redecorating was finished. They invited Kitty for dinner to celebrate. Jessie let Tonio show their guest around.

"It's like a miracle, Kitty. You saw it once when Gianni was here. What a dump! Look at it now. Jessie picked out everything. Worked her fingers to the bone to sew the curtains and slipcovers and bedspreads. She even did some of the painting. But wow! It turned into a palace.''

The muted pattern of the living room wallpaper served as a background for the deep rose carpet and the floral prints in the slipcovers on the armchairs. The soft beige love seat was enhanced with pillows of the same floral print. Crisp tieback curtains on the bay window hung above the rose velvet pad on the window seat.

As Kitty looked over the freshly painted kitchen, the attractive bedrooms, and listened as Tonio enthusiastically pointed out every detail, she wanted to give him a good hard shake. Didn't the fool realize that Jessie was the girl for him? Not that silly Iris. And as she noted the expression in Jessie's lovely eyes while gazing at Tonio, she knew what was in the wind. Why did life have to be so complicated?

Finally the rainy season ended, the sun shone again, and the roads dried out. Everyone was on the move, and both Jessie and Tonio were rushed with business.

Early in April, just before Easter, Bob Grist dropped by the boardinghouse. He told Kitty, ''I've arranged for an early release for Carl Henderson. He gets out on parole on May first.''

''Wonderful! How does he look? I haven't seen him in months.''

''He's thinner than ever. And very bitter.''

''I can imagine.'' She told him about the rift. ''Of course, this is confidential, but it might help you deal with him.''

''I guessed something like that had happened. He wants to rescind the power of attorney he signed. . . . Also change the title to the stage line to get rid of his daughter as a partner.''

''Can he do that?''

''He's determined to go to court if he has to.''

Kitty shrugged. ''What a foolish man.''

After the lawyer left, she made some plans. They might backfire, but she was going to try. But she didn't take anyone into her confidence. Not even Jessie when she told her about her father's coming release and what Bob Grist had said about the title to the staging company.

"I'm so glad he's getting out. And he doesn't have to take me to court. I'll give up the stage line and move away."

We'll see about that, Kitty told herself. Aloud she said, "He'll have to come here and get his things. I have them stored in the basement."

Fortunately Carl's old room was vacated a few days before the end of the month. Kitty and the maid cleaned it thoroughly. Then she reserved a horse and buggy for May first.

When that day arrived, she dressed in her most becoming spring outfit. Just as she'd anticipated, Carl came to the door. They greeted each other curtly. But when she looked at his ashen, haggard face, she wanted to take him in her arms.

He said, "I've come for my things. I suppose you have them stored. Maybe Amos will help me carry them away."

"Where are you going to live?"

"In the Riverview Hotel."

"That flea-ridden dive!"

"It's better than where I've been staying."

"I have a horse and buggy in the alley. I needed it today, so I'll take you there."

"I'll be much obliged, Widow White."

"We'll go down to the basement and get your things."

She had ordered a large buggy, so there was plenty of room for Carl's possessions on the backseat. They started out.

"Do you mind if I run an errand on the way?" Kitty asked.

"No. I'm not doing anything."

Kitty drove downtown and went by the Capital Stage Line office very slowly. She could see a crowd in front of the counter buying tickets from Jessie. She didn't say a word, but out of the corner of her eye, she could see Carl looking in there, too.

Next she drove out to the stables that his company owned. She stopped in front. After she climbed out, she tied the reins to the hitching post. "Would you please come in with me? I have some business in here and I'm nervous about going in alone."

"All right."

They walked around. She made sure that Carl saw all the stalls. They even went through the tack room. She waved to the stable man out in the pasture. She hoped that all of Carl's horses were being driven today.

One horse came to the fence and, as Carl rubbed his muzzle, his expression softened.

Finally she said, "Well, I'll have to come another time. The man I wanted to see isn't here."

She untied the reins and climbed back in the buggy. But she didn't start the horse. Instead she turned to Carl and said, "Carl Henderson, you're a damned stubborn, pigheaded fool! Do you realize you own this place?"

He stared at her in astonishment. "Own this place?"

"Yes. Indeed you do. And you have a thriving business that your daughter has been killing herself to have ready for you. You saw her in *your* office, selling tickets for *your* company. She has already paid me five hundred dollars of the money I loaned her. By the end of this summer, she'll probably have half the amount paid back. She's a jewel. Far better than you deserve."

He stared at her, too astonished to speak.

Kitty stuck her face close to his. "Granted she acted without your permission. You know damn well you would have said no. She had a marvelous opportunity and took it. But not too hastily. Oh, no. I had my attorney go over everything. The books were audited. Tonio checked all the equipment and this stable. Looked at all the horses. I loaned her the money so she could buy it. She's making a success of it, and all you have to do is step in there and drive your coach up and down the valley."

Carl started to answer.

Kitty held up her hand. "Wait. I'm not through yet.

What thanks did we all get? You disowned your daughter. Now you're going to rescind her power of attorney. Going to get rid of Jessie as your partner. And what about me? In spite of every courtesy I could possibly show you, I got slapped in the face. You were through with me. Well, who needs you, you ungrateful wretch! You brought all your trouble on yourself. Yet the rest of us have had to suffer for it!''

"I think you'd better take me to the hotel."

She slapped the horse with the reins, and they started out. After her outburst, the reaction set in. Tears gathered in her eyes and ran down her cheeks. Soon she was sobbing. She covered her face with her hands. Her shoulders heaved.

Carl never could stand to see a woman cry. "Oh, Kitty, please don't." He reached over and pulled the reins; the horse moved to the side of the country road and halted. "Don't cry."

But she sobbed harder than ever. He didn't know what to do. Here was Kitty, usually so lively and cheerful, crying as if her heart were broken. He tried to stare out at the field, but he kept looking back at her.

Finally he couldn't take any more. He put his arms around her. "Dearest, don't cry."

Gradually her sobs subsided. A long sigh shivered through her. Carl held her close. "I apologize for the way I acted."

"I had such great plans for us, Carl." She sighed again.

He took out his handkerchief and wiped her eyes. "Tell me about them."

"I'd hoped that we could be married and spend the rest of our lives together. I have my own apartment there in my boardinghouse where you could have some privacy. Oh, Carl, now that's all spoiled." She started to cry again.

"Is it? If you can forgive me—and are willing to marry me in spite of everything—I'd be the luckiest man in the world."

"I'll marry you if you'll make up with Jessie. If you'll let her be your partner. God knows she deserves it."

"I spoke out of anger that day at the jail. I've been grieving for her all these months. And for you, too."

"You'll go see her?"

"Of course I will. I hope she'll forgive me. If she wants to be a partner in the business, I'll go along with that." He kissed her. "Oh, Kitty, I'm crazy about you. I can't wait to marry you."

She looked at him and smiled, her eyes glowing, her face radiant.

"Let's go see Jessie." She gave the horses a triumphant slap with the reins.

Chapter 20

When they pulled up to the loading area in back of the Capital Stage Line, Kitty said, "I'll send Jessie out."

She climbed out of the buggy and tied the reins to the hitching post. When she went inside the office, she found Jessie working on her ledger. "There's someone out back who's awfully anxious to see you."

"My father? He was to be paroled today." As she rose, a kaleidoscope of emotions raced through her. Anxiety. Dread. Happiness. Fear. "Is he . . . all right?"

"Go find out for yourself. I'll stay in here."

Jessie raced out to the loading area and saw her father standing by the buggy. He held out his arms.

"Oh, Papa!" She ran to him. Neither could speak. For a long time they stood together in an embrace.

Finally Carl whispered, "Can you forgive me, Jessie?"

She nodded, fighting back the tears and swallowing the big lump in her throat.

"Kitty called me a pigheaded, stubborn old fool, and I guess she's right."

Jessie looked up at his pale, haggard face and hugged him again. "I'm so glad to see you, Papa. I've missed you terribly. I hope we'll never be separated again."

"We'll make up for lost time, honey." Carl cleared

the huskiness out of his throat. "Now that we're partners, we'll be seeing a lot of each other."

Her face was radiant as she looked up at him. "We have a wonderful stage line. I'll take you through the office, but you ought to see the stables we have."

"Kitty took me out there. She wanted to see someone, but he wasn't there. We went all through the place. I never dreamed we owned a setup like that."

Jessie smiled to herself. Good for Kitty. She must have stage-managed something.

"Papa, we have more business than the two drivers working for us can handle. I hope you can take a coach on the route."

"I can start tomorrow. Dadgummit, but it'll be good to be holding the reins again. I sat in that cell day after day just thinking about the horses trotting along, the coach a-swaying back and forth, and the wheels a-humming."

She ached with pity for him. How hard it must have been on him. "The horses will be glad to see you. Prince and Webster and Beauty . . . Well, all of them. And we have more you'll have to check out."

"I will. From now on that's what I'm going to do. Just devote myself to staging. I learned a mighty bitter lesson—so no more gambling."

Jessie gave him another hug. "Come in now and see the office."

When they went inside, Kitty put her arm through Carl's. "Did you have a chance to tell your daughter our good news?"

"Not yet." He smiled down at her. "This lovely lady has consented to be my wife."

Jessie hugged and kissed them both. "This is one of the happiest days of my whole life. First, you're out of jail, and then this wonderful news. When will the wedding take place?"

Kitty's eyes sparkled. "We haven't had a chance to decide yet. But it'll be soon, I imagine." She looked up at Carl. "I have to go on home now. Don't you want to stay here with Jessie? She must have a lot of business to discuss with you.''

Carl nodded. ''That's a good idea.''

''I'll have Amos put your things up in your old room. I got it ready for you.''

After she left, Carl scratched his head. ''Dadgummit, how did she know I'd be going back there?''

Jessie stood in the narthex of the small Episcopal church wearing a white dotted swiss dress over a rose-colored lining, which she had made. A wide rose ribbon around her waist formed a bow in back. She pinned a corsage of white roses on her shoulder.

Kitty had announced much earlier, ''Carl and I are going to walk down the aisle together. After all, this is a second marriage.''

Tonio, who was to be the best man, smiled at Jessie. ''You look pretty enough to be the bride.''

Her heart gave a lurch. How she wished she were marrying him. ''You look mighty fetching yourself.'' And he did, in his dark suit with a white carnation boutonniere in his buttonhole.

Kitty joined them. She was wearing a cream lace dress with a small flowered hat. She carried a bible and a single rose. ''You two go first. When you get to the altar, Tonio's to step to the right and you, Jess, to the left. Then when we come, we'll stand between you.''

Carl came out of an anteroom wearing a new dark suit and looking like a different man. He had gained a few pounds over the last five weeks and his gaunt, haggard look was gone. Instead, his face beamed with happiness. Kitty pinned a boutonniere in his lapel buttonhole and gave him a quick kiss on the cheek.

The change in the organ music was their signal, so Tonio put out his arm and Jessie took it. They walked down the aisle. Soon Carl and Kitty came. She smiled at the small group of her special friends, as well as the boarders who sat in the pews, but his eyes were only on her.

All during the traditional ceremony, Jessie kept think-

ng how right this marriage was. Kitty wanted a husband and companion to share her life. Her father would
njoy his wife's lively personality and having someone
o come home to at the end of his trips. He liked being
round people, so the life at the boardinghouse would
uit him.

After the wedding, the bridal party and guests walked
back to Kitty's for a reception. Then the newlyweds
boarded a river steamer to make the overnight trip to San
Francisco for the weekend.

On Sunday Jessie felt let down and lonely after the
excitement. She could hardly wait for Tonio to come to
ake her to dinner. But when they went to an Italian res-
aurant, all he could talk about was Iris.

"Only four more days and her ship will arrive in San
Francisco!" His face came alive with anticipation.
'I'm going to take a riverboat down to meet her and
her folks. We'll have a leisurely trip back . . . to get
all caught up again." He talked and talked about his
future plans with Iris as if he couldn't say her name
often enough.

All the time Jessie listened to him, she felt an ache in
her heart, a thrust of envy. If only those plans involved
her instead of Iris!

Finally, to change the subject, Jessie said, "I have to
get up early tomorrow morning. I must catch the first
trolley so I can go to the stables. I'm bringing the coach
into the office for Papa. He's going to get right off the
river steamer, change his clothes, and start out on his
route."

"I'll be at the stables getting my own coach, so I'll
help you harness your team," Tonio offered.

"Thank you. I'd appreciate that."

As they walked back to the boardinghouse in the balmy
evening, he said, "You're acting kind of sad, Jess. Didn't
you want your father to marry Kitty?"

"Of course I did. I'm delighted. She'll make him a
wonderful wife. I guess I'm sort of down because this
will be the last evening we'll be together. You'll be

gone with your passengers. . . . and then Iris will come
first.''

"We'll go on being friends. Iris, too.''

Jessie didn't answer. She knew that wouldn't happen. . . .

She worked with Tonio the next morning and they soon
had both the coaches ready to leave the stable. Jessie
drove out first. From her perch high up on the box, she
felt the strong wind sweeping through the valley. It
swayed the coach and whipped the horses' manes and
tails. Even so, it felt good to be driving the team again.

They trotted briskly along the road, the morning sun
glistening off the harnesses and the animals' glossy coats.
A farm wagon came toward her carrying a load of hay
covered by a canvas tarp. It flapped and billowed in the
wind.

Just as the two teams started to pass, the piece of
canvas blew off the farm wagon, tumbled in the air,
and slapped Jessie's leaders across their heads, blinding them.

They reared up, neighed in terror, and started to run.
The canvas blew into the field as the frightened team
galloped as fast as it could down the road.

Jessie screamed, "Whoa! Whoa!'' She pushed
against the brake and yanked on the reins. But nothing
stopped them. On and on they flew, with the coach
rocking precariously back and forth above the squeal-
ing wheels.

"Whoa! Whoa!''

It was a runaway!

"Whoa! Stop!''

She braced herself against the footboard and pulled
the reins toward her. But nothing stopped the horses.
She could hear them heaving for breath, and their hoofs
pounding on the hard ground, sounding like thunder.
The terrified horses unleashed all their reserve power
to get away from danger. Foam flew from their mouths.
As the coach lurched first one way and then another,
Jessie slid back and forth across the seat.

Her heart thrashed against her throat. Her arms quivered as she tried to hold the reins. Her throat felt dry with fright. Ahead there was a bend in the road. Would they make it without toppling over?

They approached the curve. Frantically she climbed the reins on the leaders to make the left turn. But instead of changing direction, they plunged straight ahead. The coach left the road, slid down into a shallow ditch, and almost capsized. It swayed back and forth. Finally it went up the opposite side and over a big rock with a terrible jerk. Jessie flew up in the air . . . and then landed on the hard ground with a bone-crushing thud.

From the moment Tonio had seen Jessie's coach take off in a runaway, he had tried frantically to catch up with it. He'd seen the canvas tarp fly through the air and guessed what had happened. But her horses were running as if demons were after them.

He swatted the backs of his horses with the reins and cracked the whip above their heads to get them to go faster. His heart leaped to his throat when he saw her coach lurch violently from one side of the road to the other. The spinning wheels sent a trail of dust behind them.

Ahead he could see the bend in the road. Could she make the turn? But instead, her horses kept going straight. The next thing he knew, he saw her body fly through the air and land on the ground.

"Whoa! Whoa!" he yelled. He yanked on the reins and stepped on the brake. Fortunately he was able to bring his team to a halt.

"Jessie!" He scrambled down from his seat and ran toward her. She looked still, her face alabaster white. He dropped beside her. "Jessie!" Was she alive?

He knelt down, his heart in his throat. His hands shook as he felt for her pulse. At first he thought there was none. Frantically he put his fingertips on her wrist again and sensed a faint thump. "Thank God!" he cried aloud. But she was unconscious.

Gently he picked her up and carried her to his coach

and laid her out on the rear seat. He'd have to get her to a doctor as soon as possible.

Her horses had come to a stop in the field and stood sweat-drenched and quivering. They needed calming and reassurance, so he ran across the dry weeds and grabbed the bridle of one of the leaders. "You're all right, fellows. So just come along with me."

Tonio led them back to the road and tied them to the back of his own coach. As far as he could tell, none of the animals had been injured in their wild dash. Now to get Jessie to a doctor. How seriously was she hurt? Worry gathered inside of him. He wanted to hurry to get help for her, but the only way he could manage the two rigs was to take it slow.

Eventually they came to the edge of town and were soon outside a doctor's office, which had a small hospital wing. When Tonio rang the bell at the hospital, a nurse came to the door, and he explained what had happened.

"I'll get a stretcher and help you. She shouldn't be handled any more than necessary," the nurse said.

"Can you send for the doctor?"

"Yes, he lives next door. I'll go get him as soon as we get her inside."

Impatiently Tonio waited while the nurse summoned the physician. Finally he came.

"I'm Doctor Williamson. What happened?"

While the doctor lifted Jessie's eyelids and examined her eyes, Tonio told him. Dr. Williamson felt her neck and throat. "No doubt she's had a concussion. Probably other injuries, too, so we'll have to keep her here until we find out what's wrong."

"Her father's arriving on the river steamer a little later, so I'll meet it and bring him back here."

The doctor nodded. "Yes, you'd better."

Tonio left and drove the rigs down to the loading area of the Capital Stage Line. The other two drivers were there with their coaches, so he told them about the accident.

"We'll load the mail and as many passengers as we

an on your two coaches. I know Mr. Henderson will
want to stay with his daughter today and won't be driv-
ng. If there's anyone left over, they'll have to wait until
Wednesday.''

By this time, the waiting room was filled with passengers. By having them sit on top of the coaches and with
he driver, as well as inside, the travelers all got on, and
the vehicles took off.

Immediately Tonio locked up the office and drove to
he dock, where Kitty and Carl were waiting.

"We were ready to start walking—" Carl began, and
then stopped when he noted the serious expression on
Tonio's face. "Is something wrong?"

"I'm afraid so." He told them about the runaway and
Jessie's injury. "Climb in. I'll take you to the hospi-
al."

The doctor seemed very concerned when he discussed
he injuries with Carl and Kitty. "Her breath is shallow
and her heartbeat irregular. I'd call it feathery."

Tonio gazed at Jessie. "Has she gained consciousness
at all?"

"No. That's nature's way of conserving her strength.
We'll just have to see what the day brings. We've made
her as comfortable as possible and are doing everything
we can. We've put sandbags around her head to hold it
still. That'll give the blood around the concussion a
chance to absorb."

Kitty patted Carl's arm. "Jessie's young—and in excellent health—which will help."

Carl nodded, too stricken to speak.

The doctor said, "Now if you'll go out to the waiting
room, the nurse will call you if there's any change."

When they were settled in the waiting room, Carl
turned to Kitty. "I know you're anxious to get home. So
why don't you go, check up on things, and come back
later?"

"I'll drive you there," Tonio offered.

After he took her home and carried the luggage into
the boardinghouse, he said, "I'll come back and get you
whenever you say."

"Thank you. But I'll have Amos get us a horse and buggy from the livery stable so we can go back and forth."

Tonio returned both rigs to the stable and came back to the hospital on the trolley. There was no change in Jessie's condition. The nurse let him and Carl take turns sitting by her bedside.

When Tonio sat by Jessie, he gazed at her ashen face and prayed, "Dear God, please help her." He thought of the many adventure-filled times they had spent together. Her indomitable spirit, her courage, and her spunk. His throat thickened as he thought of the times she'd been heartbroken, and he smiled at all the fun they had shared. She had been such a vital part of his life for the past year. His own pal. She had to recover. He clenched his fists. She had to get well.

On Tuesday he took a party of mining men to a gold mine in the foothills, but he rushed right back and spent the evening by Jessie's bedside. There was no change. If anything, she seemed more fragile than ever.

The next day he had to go to San Francisco to meet Iris's ship when it arrived. But he hated to leave Jessie's bedside. What if anything happened to her while he was gone? He'd never forgive himself.

On Thursday afternoon, he was at the pier waiting for the sailing ship. He saw the pilot launch leave to meet the vessel outside the Golden Gate, the two points of land that formed the entrance to San Francisco Bay.

Finally it sailed in, looking majestic and beautiful. Tugs maneuvered it into place alongside the pier. He could see Iris waving at him from the deck.

But even as he waited for her to come down the gangplank, his mind was on Jessie. How was she doing? Was she still holding her own? He could hardly wait to get back to Sacramento to be with her.

Finally Iris came down the gangplank with her hands outstretched. Radiant and beautiful, dressed in an outfit he had never seen before, she looked lovelier than ever. He kissed her and greeted her parents.

Iris squeezed his arm. "It's so good to see you again."

Her father chuckled. "The minute we hit the California coast, she was as jittery as all get out. Couldn't wait to get here." He led them to seats. "We've got to wait for our luggage to be unloaded. We have three trunks besides our suitcases. I foolishly took these women to New York for a while."

"We had a wonderful time shopping, didn't we, Mama?" Iris chattered on about some of the outfits she had purchased, but Tonio hardly listened. His mind was on Jessie. Was she all right?

After a while, their luggage was brought by porters and then carried to a wagon outside, where it was to be transported to the river steamer. They followed in a hack.

While they rode along the streets paved with cobblestones, Mrs. Cunningham asked, "How have you been, Tonio?"

"Very busy." He told them about some of his trips. "And my flat has all been refurbished. I'm looking forward to having you folks see it. I'll invite you for dinner sometime this summer."

Mrs. Cunningham answered, "We'd love to come."

"Choose a night when it's not too hot," Iris put in. "I imagine your flat gets terribly warm and stuffy."

They finally boarded the riverboat and got settled in their staterooms. It was delightful crossing the bay and watching the sunset.

Tonio returned to his stateroom to put on a fresh shirt and cravat for dinner. He listened to the throb of the engines and the paddle wheel churning through the water, grateful that he was heading back to Jessie.

All during dinner, Mr. Cunningham discussed the outbreak of the Civil War. "We left the East Coast just in the nick of time. We sailed out of New York April seventh, and the Confederate forces bombarded Fort Sumter just five days later."

"I'll be so glad to get home all safe and sound," Mrs. Cunningham said.

Iris spoke up. "I suppose that handsome Lieutenant

Underwood will be promoted and put in command of some Union soldiers."

"He got married. As a matter of fact, I sang at his wedding," Tonio put in.

Out on deck, when he and Iris were huddled together in deck chairs in the dark, Tonio put his arm around her, but he felt detached. With only half his attention, he listened to her tell about all the parties she had attended in Washington and New York and her shopping sprees. He kept thinking about Jessie fighting for her life.

"You seem so different, Tonio. I thought you'd be a lot more excited about my return."

"I'm thrilled to pieces, dearest. I guess it seems to be too good to be true." He held her close and kissed her, but he had no desire to talk bout their future plans. He had to wait until Jessie was better to think ahead.

"Papa says I'm not to rush into anything. I'm still young—and should have fun for a while before I settle down. I should meet lots of the young men who come to the state capital on business first."

Before now, Tonio would have felt jealous of anyone intruding on his territory, but instead he had the queerest sensation that he wasn't really here on this river steamer with Iris. Finally he said, "I'm not in any position to offer you anything right now, Iris. I wrote and told you how my cousin embezzled all the money from our company. I'm still trying to get on my feet again. He left me flat broke."

"Then how could you refurbish your flat? That takes a lot of money."

"I sold a couple of horses and did a lot of the work myself." He didn't dare tell her about the part Jessie played. "I wanted to fix up everything before you returned, so your father would have a better impression of me."

"How sweet, Tonio. I think that's adorable of you." She snuggled closer to him. "But don't expect me to live there." She shuddered. "I couldn't stand having all your passengers coming and going and your stage-coaches pulling in right there behind your place. I'd be so embarrassed if any of my friends came calling.''

"Don't worry. You won't live there," he answered drily. Besides, he didn't want Iris finding fault with his flat after all the hard work that went into it.

"There'll be lots of garden parties when we get home, and I want you to come as my escort," Iris went on. "You know how lovely the balmy evenings are in Sacramento in the summer."

"I'll come when I can, but you know that the summertime is busy in the staging business. I have to make most of my money then for the whole year."

"I wish you were in some other kind of business."

"Well, I won't be. Not in the foreseeable future."

From then on they didn't have much to say to each other. Finally Iris said, "I'd better go in. I'm sharing a cabin with my folks. Papa'll be cross if I'm up too late."

Tonio took her to her cabin and kissed her good night. When he climbed into his own bunk, he lay in the darkness and thought about Jessie.

A big crowd was on the dock to meet the river steamer the next morning—especially Mr. Cunningham's associates from the state government. Just as they landed, Iris said, "Come to see me soon."

"I will. Right now I have to take care of something."

He dashed through the crowd and grabbed a hack to go to the hospital. Panic made him want to urge the horses to go faster. Was Jessie still alive? He could hardly wait to get there.

When the hack pulled up in front of the hospital, he paid his fare and ran inside, where he tiptoed into Jessie's room and slipped into a chair beside her bed as quietly as possible.

But she opened her eyes and smiled. "Hi, Tonio."

"Oh, my darling." He twined her fingers in his. "You're awake." A flood of relief surged through him.

"Yes. I'm going to be all right. I have to take it easy for a while. I'm in a cast—for a broken shoulder." She pulled back the sheet and showed him how her arm was encased.

He caressed her forehead and her hair. The morning sun poured into her room. He gazed at her brown eyes so filled with love for him.

"I was so afraid you wouldn't make it," he whispered, his voice husky. She was part of his very soul. The other half of him. He couldn't imagine life without her. "I love you, Jessie. We belong together. Will you marry me?"

"Yes."

He leaned over and kissed her. "You're the loveliest girl in the world. I want you with me always."

"What about Iris? Isn't she coming home soon?"

"She's already here." He told about going to San Francisco to meet the Cunninghams and coming back on the river steamer. "It was the funniest sensation, Jessie. I knew I was there with her . . . and yet it was as if I was here with you."

"So the magic was gone?"

"Every bit of it. The only woman I want is you. When you're able, I want to get married. Just as soon as possible."

She smiled at him. "At least we have our flat all ready. And just the way I wanted it, too."

"I'll be the happiest man in the world living there with you, my darling."

"That's what I've wanted for a long time." Jessie smiled at him. "Now that Iris is out of the way, let's merge our staging companies. That is, if I can be a full partner."

"Of course you can. I want to share everything with you."

"We could move Capital Stage Line over to your place and be one big outfit. It'll be so convenient with the flat right above. Wait till Papa hears all this."

"Hears what?" her father said from the doorway.

''Tonio and I are going to be married.'' Her heart echoed the words over and over. She was never so happy in her life.

ABOUT THE AUTHOR

Stagecoach Woman was inspired by one of the finest drivers in the Old West, Charlie Parkhurst. Charlie drove stage for twenty years in the gold country of California in spite of hold-ups by highwaymen, blizzards and floods, and rough passengers. When Charlie died, it was discovered that this famous whip was a woman.

This historical novel is the seventh in Dorothy Dowdell's series on the entrepreneurs who developed the West. Her first was *Glory Land*, about the building of the transcontinental railroad over the Sierra. *A Woman's Empire* portrayed the timber industry in the Northwest. *Golden Flame* on mining was followed by *Wildcatter Woman*, which was set in the oil fields of California. *Seafaring Woman* dealt with early shipping out of San Francisco. *Highflying Woman*, with the setting in southern California, told of the beginnings of the aircraft industry.

Dorothy Dowdell was born in Reno, Nevada, but has spent most of her time in California. She was graduated from the University of California in Berkeley with a major in English and history. In addition to her historical novels, she has written suspense, gothic, and romance novels as well as eight nonfiction books for young people in collaboration with her late husband, a college science instructor. She lives in Los Gatos, near San Jose, California.

''Tonio and I are going to be married.'' Her heart echoed the words over and over. She was never so happy in her life.